# THE GUARDIAN DUKE

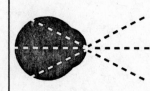

This Large Print Book carries the
Seal of Approval of N.A.V.H.

# THE GUARDIAN DUKE

## JAMIE CARIE

**THORNDIKE PRESS**

*A part of Gale, Cengage Learning*

GALE
CENGAGE Learning·

Detroit • New York • San Francisco • New Haven, Conn • Waterville, Maine • London

## GALE
### CENGAGE Learning®

Copyright © 2012 by Jamie Carie Masopust.
Scripture quotations are taken from the King James Version.
Thorndike Press, a part of Gale, Cengage Learning.

**LIBRARY OF CONGRESS CATALOGING-IN-PUBLICATION DATA**

Carie, Jamie.
    The guardian duke / by Jamie Carie.
        pages ; cm. — (Thorndike Press large print Christian
    historical fiction) (A forgotten castles novel)
    ISBN-13: 978-1-4104-4796-8 (hardcover)
    ISBN-10: 1-4104-4796-0 (hardcover)
    1. Guardian and ward—Fiction. 2. Parents—Death—Fiction. 3.
Nobility—England—Fiction. 4. Large type books. I. Title.
    PS3603.A7465G83 2012b
    813'.6—dc23                                           2012015453

Published in 2012 by arrangement with Broadman & Holman
Publishers.

Printed in Mexico
1 2 3 4 5 6 7 16 15 14 13 12

# DEDICATION

To my son Seth,

This story is yours. You dreamed up the scenes and the characters with me. We spent hours talking about what these people were like and where they would go and all they would see and do. . . . It was our best adventure together, something I will cherish forever.

I love you so much! Your potential is vast, your heart is guarded in a wise way, and your spiritual being is splendor personified. You are a gift to the world and a son of God who will fulfill His purpose for all eternity. I am blessed to call you my son.

# ACKNOWLEDGMENTS

A special thank you to Clive Scoular of Killyleagh, County Down in Northern Ireland.

Your willingness to share your knowledge of Hans Sloane, Killyleagh Castle, and the picturesque village of Killyleagh made this story richer in authenticity and more vibrantly Irish.

I dream of seeing the Land of Ever Young myself one day, but for now I feel as if I have had the best virtual tour possible. I thank you, kind sir!

# CHAPTER ONE

*King's Theatre, London — August 1818*

Heaven could be found in music.

Gabriel Ravenwood, the Duke of St. Easton, closed his eyes and leaned his head onto the velvet cushion at his back. A small smile played across his lips as he felt each and every muscle in his face relax. Little by little he gave way, an internal shifting, a giving over to something greater than himself. Waves of baritone and mezzo-soprano wafted over him and around him and through him until the world — a dark and gray place before he stepped inside these doors — gave way to the sustaining notes of life in full color.

He drifted . . . complete.

A deep breath and then utter peace. It wafted over him and through him. It undid him in a way that every other pursuit fell short. Music never fell short. Blessed resonance of relief. It was always thus, and why he'd spent every afternoon here for the past few years.

The opera.

Thank God for it. Thank God there was still something.

He lifted his fingers to the bridge of his nose and squeezed.

"Your Grace. Please, Your Grace."

Gabriel lifted his arm in a slight, relaxed motion, as if a fly would dare intrude on this time. *Go away. Everyone, just go away.*

"Your Grace. I do apologize, but there is a matter —"

Gabriel turned his face away, still consumed by the aria, but he frowned. His piece of heaven was being pulled at, snagged, and punctured like a great air balloon. A roil of unease eked through his bubble of serenity.

" 'Tis of the utmost importance, Your Grace. I've been trying to reach you."

Gabriel's eyes shot open. He reared up to find his secretary, Mr. Meade. *Unbelievable.*

The slight man who was his personal secretary paled white as the walls around them and took a step backward. He was holding a letter. It shook like a wind was blowing at it, though there was no wind. He held it out.

Gabriel took a deep breath and jerked his

head toward the door to his private box. He might be disrupted, but he would not ruin the opera for the other twenty or so people in the audience.

Once in the long, red-carpeted hall, Gabriel took the letter and flipped it over.

The royal seal.

A chill settled over him. Now it was a different matter altogether.

What could the prince regent want with him now? He glanced up at his secretary, who only shrugged with a nervous pinch to his mouth, and then carefully pried up the rose-colored wax.

A dull roar started in his ears as he unfolded the thick paper. He shook his head, trying to rid the sensation of water filling his ears, then looked back down at the rich vellum. Words shot out at him and then glanced away. *Lady Alexandria Featherstone . . . Holy Island . . . Northumberland . . . his ward . . . the Duke of St. Easton . . . relation . . .*

He looked up, nonplussed. Featherstone? Must be a very distant relative indeed. He closed his eyes for a brief moment and shook his head as if he could shake the clogged feeling from his ears. He rubbed his hand over his eyes and looked back at the letter. *Missing parents . . . presumed dead . . . guardian . . . only heir . . . Alex-andria . . .* A flash of bright light exploded inside his head.

*Alexandria . . .*

The strange dizziness closed around him. He felt the paper, so fine and thick, crumple in his fist. He shook his head and looked over at his secretary.

"Meade? Speak up. Can't . . . hear you . . ." He wasn't sure if he'd said the words aloud.

His man leapt forward as he stumbled. Gabriel leaned to one side and covered his ears with his hands, trying to block the sudden screeching in his head.

*God! Oh, God. What is happening to me?*

He felt himself flail and fall. *Alex . . . an . . . dria . . .* He crashed to the floor, dizzy, the impact on his shoulder registering in waves of pain that reverberated from shoulder to head and back again. People rushed forward to crowd around him, looking at him with faces in varying degrees of shock and concern.

"Get back!" he barked, rising with an outstretched arm. At least he hoped he had said something; he really couldn't hear the words.

Abrupt dizziness forestalled his attempt to stand. He reached out for Meade's shoulder,

12

right beside him, but couldn't focus on it long enough to grasp hold. "Meade, hold still, man."

Mr. Meade's lips moved but the roar in Gabriel's ears made it impossible to make out what he was saying. His knees buckled again and he went down, sprawled on the red runner. Fear swept through him in waves of agony from head to toe. Something was not right. He closed his eyes and took deep breaths, blocking everyone from his mind.

*Alexandria Featherstone* — felt familiar somehow, and yet he'd never heard the name before, had he? Who the devil was she? *Alex* . . . It was his last coherent thought before the darkness swallowed him up.

Gabriel woke in his state bedchamber with his head resting comfortably on several fluffy feather pillows. He blinked, noticing the strange quiet in the place. Unease filled his throat as he lifted his head and turned it this way and that, trying to hear the usual bustling sounds of London outside his town house at number 31 St. James Square. Nothing. Complete silence.

"Meade?" His voice must be raspy, as he couldn't hear it. He cleared his throat and sat up, a slow action as though moving through water. "Meade," he pressed the word harder through his throat and from his lungs. Nothing. A chill started at the base of his skull and crept down his back. Swinging his legs over the side of the bed, he stood, threw back his head, and bellowed.

"MEADE!"

The door swung open and three men, one his pale-faced secretary, rushed toward him. Gabriel clenched his teeth and clung to the coverlet like a flapping rope. He glanced from face to face. Their mouths were moving in an irritating fashion. *Too fast. Slow down.* He barked out a word, *stop,* but they didn't stop. God help him, their mouths were moving but no sound came forth.

"Water." He stretched out his hand as one of the men, his doctor he now realized as Bentley's whiskered face came into focus, took him by the shoulder and motioned for him to get back into bed. He didn't want to go to bed. He didn't need to sleep. He wanted the panic that was constricting his throat to cease. He wanted to start the day over. To sit in the opera house and drown his ennui in the throes of a musical score. He wanted his brand of normal back, for heaven's sake — even if it was a shadow's life.

The doctor said something and patted the bed like he was speaking to a three-year-old refusing nap time instead of a thirty-two-year-old duke. Gabriel shook his head, much like a recalcitrant toddler. He wanted to ask what was wrong with him, but he couldn't let them know of such a weakness. And they certainly could never know this fear that was gripping him like a demon's crushing embrace.

Clearing his throat again and trying to see past the fog in his brain, he pulled himself together and stated in what he hoped was a normal tone. "A glass of water, Doctor. That's all I need."

The request was thrust into his hand by the third man, Lord Bartrom, his good friend and boyhood cohort for as long as he could remember. "Thanks, old boy." He nodded toward his blond pal with all the normalcy he could manage, then quickly looked away before his friend had a chance to speak and threw back the drink.

The doctor tapped him on one shoulder. He had such a look of pleading on his face and questioning, with those bushy gray eyebrows halfway up his forehead.

Gabriel blew out a harsh breath, narrowed

his eyes, and stared at his lips. If he concentrated hard enough, he might be able to make out what he was saying.

Something about bed and exam, maybe? And then the old man pointed to his mouth and mouthed the words. "Can you hear me? Your Grace, can you hear what I'm saying?" He gestured words coming from his mouth.

The fear squeezed at him again, forcing him to sit down.

They knew.

They all knew.

The Duke of St. Easton had suddenly, inexplicably, gone stone-cold deaf.

He blocked the new wave of fear with fierce determination. Dr. Bentley took a firm hold on Gabriel's chin and leaned toward his right ear. With his other hand he pulled out a fluted piece of metal and inserted it into his ear. Cold, foreign, uncomfortable. Gabriel closed his eyes and let out a breath of air as the instrument moved around inside his ear.

The doctor stepped to his other side, causing Gabriel to open his eyes. Without the use of sound, he found himself lost . . . drifting . . . terror-filled to be so unanchored. He glanced askance at the old doctor, a man he'd known since his first fever. Gabriel was the third son born to the Duke and Duchess of St. Easton. His two elder brothers, Robert and William, had died before their second birthdays, so if Gabriel so much as sneezed . . .

Well. He'd known this face peering into his face for a very long time. And it felt the same now, even though he'd reached the grand old age of thirty-two and had acquired the dukedom on his father's death not yet two years ago. Now he was the head of the family. Three sisters had followed him and survived, so his parents had finally settled down a bit and relaxed their tenuous hold on his exploits and boyish adventures. Gabriel looked sideways at the wiry hair of his protector as he maneuvered the earpiece and candle and remembered a particular time he'd escaped all their clutches with his sailboat, *Nap.* Short for Napoleon, of course.

It had been a perfect replica of a navy brigantine. And it had sailed. Oh, how it had sailed across the choppy waters of the streams near his childhood home, Bradley House, in the lush hills of Wiltshire's countryside. He almost felt as if he were back there, remembering with a stark clarity that rarely came to him. For a moment he almost felt normal.

Then he looked at Albert Bartrom. The concern in his friend's eyes was unmistakable and rare indeed. Lord Bartrom was a year older and prone to schemes of adventure that would rival a tactical genius. When Gabriel had lacked courage or fortitude or strength, Albert had lent an easy and understanding hand. Always there. Always knowing and filling in the gap. Ribbing him when he'd become a duke and insisting on calling him all manner of titles instead of the expected, "Your Grace." No, Albert let him know when he was mulish and insensitive, prideful and overbearing, and any number of other aspersions that spoke of true, long-standing friendship and all the rewards of such a cost.

Now, when he looked at Albert's stricken face, his throat tightened. These men, men he'd known and loved his whole life, they were afraid for him. Afraid for the new world in which they all might live.

No! He wouldn't let something bad happen to him or any of them. He was strong. He could still feel the strength he'd always had in such abundance rippling through his body. He could stand. He could fight. *Dear God . . .*

The doctor took the cold metal from his ear. Gabriel turned toward him, knowing his face was harsh, feeling his breath rush in and out of his chest, but no longer hearing its rasping sound. That scared him a degree more. His heart was racing now, wasn't it? He pressed his hand to his chest and felt the *thud, thud, thud,* but there was nothing of a pulse in his ears, in his mind.

He shook his head as if shaking off the panic. He could speak. He could still talk like a duke.

He turned toward the doctor and demanded answers. "What has happened to me?"

Bentley reached behind him for stationery. After a long moment, a gut-wrenching moment of waiting, they'd procured ink and quill. Gabriel gritted his teeth while the doctor wrote in more lengthy silence. He watched the scratching, knowing he should be able to hear it but not hearing it. *Scratch, scratch, scratch.* He imagined hearing it. He closed his eyes and prayed to hear it.

The edge of the paper touched his hand. His eyelids fluttered open. He grasped it and turned it right side up.

I don't know what's happened, Your Grace. Your ears need to be examined by someone at Moorfields. They specialize in the eye and ear. I shall make an appointment with Dr. Saunders or another man I've recently heard of: John

Curtis. With your permission of course, Your Grace. We shall get to the bottom of this.

Gabriel looked up into the watery blue eyes, tense jaw, and compressed lips of a man he knew as well as his father. His gaze passed over at Bartrom and then his secretary.

They were afraid for him.

They were all afraid.

He wanted to ask questions, a million questions, but he knew he had to be strong . . . for them. He had to show them that everything would be all right. Everything was under control. Everything must go on as normal.

"I find I am famished, gentlemen." He cracked a smile, a smile he knew was familiar to each of them. A smile that said he was alive and fine. Of course he was fine. "Have we missed breakfast, do you think?"

# CHAPTER TWO

*Holy Island, Northumberland, England —
September 1818*

Clunk.

*Clink. Clunk.*

The wind blew a misting sea spray into
Alexandria's face as she picked her way
across the rocky shore of her home on Holy
Island. She paused, listening for the location of the sound against the gentle patter
of the rain.

*Clink. Clunk.*

The sound roused her already keen sense
of curiosity, knowing that it was new,
something different that didn't belong on
her beach. She veered to the right and
climbed over a large boulder, thankful for
the light of a full yellow moon. Her mind
swam with possibilities and her heart sped
up with the beginnings of a new adventure.
What if the object making that sound was
an old bottle with a letter inside? Mayhap

the author of such a letter had decided to end his poor life, and she would be the one person who discovered why. Or even better, a bobbing treasure box from the wreckage of a pirate's ship. Her generous lips curved into a smile as she imagined opening the brine-encrusted lid to reveal golden coins, no — glittering jewels — a jade emerald the size of a nightingale's egg.

Lifting the hem of her thin nightdress to better gauge her footing, she picked her way toward the rocky incline. Much of the beach was flat with small, dull-hued rocks and a little sand, but the sound was coming from a low outcropping of stone. She hurried toward the jagged precipice, eased herself onto her stomach, and peered over the edge into the dark sea below.

Alex sucked in her breath as she saw the cause of the noise. Rolling white. Turning with the slapping waves. She reached down, not bothering to stop and consider what she was doing, and stretched out her hand. There. Her eyes squeezed shut as her fingertips brushed the smooth surface. She stretched farther, her toes curling into the sand as a drifting anchor, and then it was in her hand. She scrambled to her feet and lifted the pale, glowing object toward the moonlight, almost dropping it in her shock.

It was a skull. A broken skull. The face intact, like a mask, but the back of its head was missing.

Alex turned it back and forth, a hundred new questions forming in her mind. Was it a child? A young woman? From what far-away place had it come?

"The poor dear," she muttered as she lifted the skull toward her face and peered — eye to eye — through the blank sockets. Alex blinked . . . and then blinked again through the ancient spyglasses as her gaze swept the hazy, mist-shrouded horizon. She stopped. It couldn't be. She slowly lowered the skull and gasped.

A ship.

Alex watched it grow closer and then ran up the steep incline of the rocky hill toward the castle that was her home. Much of the castle was uninhabitable, but the family had salvaged and repaired the great hall and several smaller rooms for bedchambers. Centuries ago the castle had been a first line of defense for Northern England against the Scots, but it was eventually attacked and overrun by Vikings — nasty pirates who had destroyed the monastery.

In those days ships were common on Holy Island's shores, but it had been decades since anything other than local fishing boats bobbed on the North Sea, and Alex could not ever remember a visitor gracing their small village that had not come from the land route. That is until now. With the ship growing bigger and bigger before her eyes, she knew someone was indeed coming and they would be asking for the lord and lady of the castle.

That thought had her running in earnest through the old great hall and then up the stone steps to her bedchamber. She still clutched the skull and paused on the threshold of her room to look down at it. What if the ship had something to do with this? Perhaps they were murderers come back to kill them all!

She shoved the skull underneath her pillow at the same time reaching for the ancient sword propped against the wall beside her bed. She brandished it in front of her, or rather tried to. The thing was so heavy she only managed one swipe through the air before it fell with a thud onto her bed. Oh well. Little good one sword would do against a ship full of murdering pirates. If only the castle's cannon still worked.

Turning from that thought she pulled her nightdress over her head, rushed toward the armoire, and flung the doors wide. She stood, baffled, at her simple dresses. There wasn't anything of elegance or refinement here. If she showed up to greet them in any of this garb, they would hardly believe she was the lady of the castle. Then again, maybe she should pose as a servant or the chatelaine perhaps, and give over the castle willingly to protect the villagers.

No, she shook her head. She was a Featherstone and a Featherstone would never take the coward's way out.

Another idea stopped her short. Her breath caught at the thought. Dare she? With a small smile she turned from the armoire and rushed from the room.

The door to her mother and father's bedchamber was closed. A sudden stab of sadness shot through her heart. They had been gone so long this time. And no letter in months. She took a deep breath and pulled up her chin. No time to feel sorry now.

She turned the knob. The creaking hinges groaned against the silence. Moonlight spilled into the room from a long, narrow window. She glanced at the bed, the coverings thick with dust. Why had no one kept the room clean? It wasn't like Ann, the housekeeper, to shirk her duties. Unless of course the rumors were true. That her parents were never coming back. That they had met with some misfortune and were —

No. She wouldn't believe a village sooth-sayer and a bunch of foreboding gossips. She would continue to pray and believe in God's power to save. And anyway, she would know, deep in her heart; if something had happened to them, she would have a feeling of it, and she did not have that feeling.

Turning from the thoughts, she ran, near blind, over to her mother's large armoire and opened the doors. Her hand shook a little and she bit down on her lower lip as she reached into the back and drew out a faded blue satin gown. It was old, older than she at twenty, but still lovely. It had been her mother's wedding gown. Alex held the garment up to her chest and took a deep breath. It should fit perfectly.

After donning the dress, she sat at her mother's low dressing table. A mostly empty jewelry box sat on one corner. Alex dragged it toward her and opened the lid. Inside was a small set of combs with paste jewels look-ing like tiny emeralds and blue sapphires along the edge. With practiced ease she twisted her long, dark hair into a knot that was slightly askew and secured it with the combs.

She leaned forward and studied her reflec-tion, hoping she looked older and authoritative. Arched, dark brows over large, pale blue eyes. An oval face of classic lines with a small, straight nose and full lips. She pinched some color into her pale cheeks and then shrugged at herself in the mirror. She always had looked younger than her years. She would just have to brazen it out.

Now to awaken Ann and Henry, the servants who were now so old Alex did most of the work around the castle. She had to be sly about it, of course, or risk hurting their pride. Ann and Henry were more like grandparents than servants to her. Heaven only knew the shock her appearance would give them this night! A laugh escaped her throat as she pictured their faces. And where had Latimere trotted off to? Her giant, white Great Pyrenees was usually at her heels. He would put the fear of God into the scoundrels. She would send Henry out to search for him with one of those large bones from supper if time permitted.

The thought of time running out had her scurrying back toward the great hall and then deeper into the castle where the servants' quarters were next to the kitchen.

"Ann! Henry!" She called out as soon as she was near. "Wake up! A ship is coming."

She banged on Henry's door hoping he would hear her. It wasn't long before Ann stuck her head out of her bedchamber, cap askew, worry in her eyes. "Lady Alex, it's the middle of the night. What are you doing up and about? You should be in bed, child."

Ann came out into the hall just as Henry opened his door and gaped at them like a beached fish. "What's happened to cause all this racket?" His expression turned awestruck as he peered through his spectacles at Alex's unprecedented attention to her appearance.

Alex hurriedly explained. "There is a ship in the harbor. A real ship. And it's coming this way."

"A ship? Who could it be? Whatever could they want with our little island?" Ann looked down at Alex's bare feet and frowned.

"I don't know but we're soon to find out. Hurry and dress. Henry, I want you to find Latimere and meet me in the great hall. Ann" — Alex shrugged, her brow wrinkling in thought — "mayhap you should make some refreshments. Just in case they are not here to murder us and take the castle."

Ann's eyes grew huge with fright. "You must hide, child. Just look at you dressed like that."

Alex wasn't sure if Ann was complimenting or insulting her. She huffed out a breath of frustration. "This is our home and I will not let anyone take it from us. Now hurry — both of you." She turned to go, a parting command shouted over her shoulder. "I found one gun. Bring any other weapons you can find!"

Hoisting up the heavy satin skirts, Alex groaned to see her dirty bare feet. She was turning to fetch her only pair of satin slippers when a heavy pounding sounded on the castle's front door.

Bare feet or not, it was time to meet her future.

With a pounding heart and the rusty pistol she'd found in the deep recesses of the kitchen pantry hidden in the folds of her skirt, Alex opened the massive door. It groaned on its old hinges and the wind blew strong and salty in her face as she looked up at the smartly dressed man standing with two soldiers on either side.

The man cast a quick head-to-toe glance at her and then bowed low over a turned-out leg. Swinging his hat round to his chest, he gripped it and stared at her, seemingly dumbstruck.

Harmless looking enough. Alex gulped down a chuckle at the sight.

"I have come to see Lady Alexandria Featherstone," the man said in a thin, nasal

29

voice that sounded like he was more afraid of her than she was of him.

Oh, bother. He would never believe her the lady of the castle now. She should have had Henry answer the door like any proper noblewoman would have thought to do. Instead she curtsied out of confusion and lifted her arm toward the great hall without even asking his name or business. She was seriously botching this.

"Wait." She stopped his progress into the castle with her flat palm thrust toward his chest. "What is your business with Lady Featherstone?"

He bowed again, the two men on either side of him standing like statues with ominous expressions frozen on their faces. "I have news for her ladyship. News of great import."

He could be lying. Even if he didn't look it, he could be dangerous. The thought brought to mind her gun. She lifted it, hoping he couldn't see the rust in the dim moonlight, and pointed it at his chest. It would have been so much more fortuitous to have found some bullets to go with it. The soldiers eased back . . . assessing and reaching . . .

"Don't even consider it!" Alex flashed her best squint-eyed look of disdain at the soldiers, pointing the weapon at each of them by turn. If nothing else she did have experience brazening her way out of dire situations. Why there was the time she was caught red-handed camping out in the Yardley's barn searching for the ghost they swore was knocking about keeping them awake each night. And then the time . . . oh, wait. Now was not the time to be thinking of her debacles. *Task at hand, Lady Featherstone,* as if anyone around here ever called her that! She almost snorted.

"No need to fear, sir, so you may call off your hounds, though I am an excellent shot. It's just that I realized I don't even know your name. Can you prove your story of news?"

They stared at her for a long, slack-jawed moment, and then the smaller man in the middle reached into his pocket and pulled out a heavy packet of papers. He motioned toward them with his head. "My name is Michael Meade, secretary to the Duke of St. Easton."

Alexandria's heart sped up at the sight of the papers. The Duke of St. Easton? She shook her head, spiraling down, down, down. Something was wrong. This man hadn't come to rape and pillage in the usual way. No. Some dark feeling hovered and then wrapped around her shoulders, sending spikes of fear exploding through her head and down her back.

This man had come with another kind of destruction.

"My lady?" The man, Mr. Meade, took a step toward her, his arm outstretched toward the gun. "Are you Alexandria Featherstone?"

"What do you want, sir?" It took all the control she had to ask the question without a quiver in her voice.

"I regret to inform you that your parents, the Lord and Lady Featherstone of Holy Island, Northumberland, England, are, um, presumed dead. The Crown has awarded your guardianship to his grace, the Duke of St. Easton."

Dead? Alex gripped the gun tighter in a hand gone cold. It shook from the rusted tip, up her arm, all the way to her shoulder. Her breath came in little puffs. She shook her head.

"I would have known. I would have felt it." She shook her head again. "It's not true." The gun was so heavy. Fingers, arms, chest — everything went numb. She couldn't hold the gun any longer. She dropped it to the floor, where it promptly exploded with a massive sound and spun in a circle. Mr. Meade screamed.

With wide, unblinking eyes they stared in shock at each other.

Great heavens. There must have been bullets in it after all.

# CHAPTER THREE

The silence was shattering.

Music. God help him, he missed it. His bits of heaven every afternoon had turned to a dark hole that sucked him further toward the edge. The days dragged on in hellish silence and in the most inner parts of him, he wondered if he would ever hear it again. What that life would be, he couldn't bear to fathom, didn't want to fathom.

It had been weeks since Gabriel had finished his breakfast as fast as may be, sent the doctor off to find the specialist of the ear, and then closeted himself in his library. He'd been a whirl of motion at first, gathering the men he trusted to look after his affairs, while putting about rumors that the Duke of St. Easton was preparing for a long journey. It wouldn't do to let his fellow investors and speculators discover a problem, especially an illness. No, that wouldn't do at all. So he closeted himself in his town house and tried to go about his day as best he could, as normal as he could, but he wasn't fooling those close to him. He could see it in their eyes — the pity. More alarming was the bleak despair of life without sound.

There had been moments, a few precious moments, when he'd thought he heard something. It was coming back. It would come back. Then he'd seen the special ear doctors — Saunders and Curtis — both blooming idiots as far as he was concerned. They'd poked and prodded, experimented with their metal contraptions and torturous devices, and then handed him a ghastly looking ear trumpet made of tortoiseshell.

"Only the best for a duke," Saunders assured him.

He looked at the man, not much older than he was, and curled his lip. He hated it. Hated putting it to his ear and leaning toward the person speaking. He'd even once been tempted to say *eh?* He bit off the word and nearly his tongue in the process instead. It made him feel old, even though when he looked into the mirror — short black hair, black brows over what some claimed were startling green eyes, a straight nose, a little too thin in his opinion, and two days' growth of beard on his face — well, he looked like the same confident man in his prime that he'd always been. The ridiculous-looking contraption hadn't worked anyway.

The best the doctors could do was to stare at him with their pinched lips and scribble out driveling sentiment. "So sorry, Your Grace. We don't know what to make of it. There appears to be nothing wrong with your ears." He'd sent them packing with sharp words much as if he'd been shooting bullets at their heels.

Nothing wrong with his ears! Gabriel slammed the book he was reading down on his desk. If there was nothing wrong with his ears, then why couldn't he *hear anything!* His mind screamed the question, but he really didn't know if he'd said it aloud or not. And he really didn't care. Let the servants pity him. It was why he stayed locked in this room, refusing to see anyone, even his cloying, meddling sisters and mother. The thought of his reportedly distraught mother brought a pang of regret to his chest, but he just couldn't bear it. He could not endure her grief — the wringing hands, the weeping, the feeling that all was lost for the family.

He felt the vibration of his throat as he growled like the panther he'd sometimes been compared to with his short black hair and green eyes. He was about to rise to pace again when he saw something white on the floor. He bent and picked it up. A letter, the letter from the prince regent. He flipped it open and reread it. *One hundred thousand pounds annual.* The Featherstone estate was well provisioned, it would seem. Who knew such wealth could be found in the northern climes of Northumberland, on a craggy island in fact. There must be investments. Coal? Shipping ventures? He would have to find out if the estate was to be administered by him until the girl married. His Majesty had not mentioned her age or situation, typical of the prince regent, but without knowing any details and unable to go himself, he'd been forced to send Meade after the chit. She could be a babe for all he knew, and what he would do with a baby or a child was more than he could fathom. Mayhap he could foist her off on one of his sisters.

Charlotte was the eldest sister, married and already tied down with four youngsters, but when he thought of the way they'd been as children, she always bossing him and looking at him with that stern-eyed, tight-lipped glare whenever he did something annoying, he shivered with the memory of it.

Then there was Mary, a sweet thing, shy

and becoming. She was married but he'd always wondered if it had turned out a happy union. She seemed smaller, somehow, when Lord Wingate was about. She rarely spoke or smiled. It was something he should inquire about. He hadn't given it enough attention, and as head of the family it was his duty to see that his sisters fared well. Yes, he would give Roger a summons and have a little chat, put some of the panther's steady gaze on the younger man and watch him sweat.

The fact that he could not have that chat drove into him like a fist in the stomach. Oh, yes. He was *deaf* and *could not hear anything anyone said!* He growled again, tears pricking, balling into his throat until he could hardly breathe. He'd never known such frustration: stifling, choking, enraging . . . heart wrenching — he hung his head. He buried his face into his hands, holding on to his sanity with little more than a thread of reason.

*Alexandria.*

Alexandria Featherstone. The name comforted him somehow, brought to mind a fairy creature from a world too brightly colored to ever be sad. He would concentrate on her and distract himself until his hearing returned. Stay focused on the task

38

at hand.

She was most likely a child. Behind his closed eyes he imagined a pretty little girl, bright blonde hair and blue eyes with a laughing smile. She wouldn't know he couldn't hear her. She would smile at him and laugh at his attempts at humor and make his heart feel light enough to take another breath. He would not give her to Charlotte or Mary or even his youngest sister, Jane. Jane would be perfect for her as she'd only been married just above a year and was pining for a child from all accounts. But no, he would raise her himself. He would double her estate with careful investments, making her one of the wealthiest women in the world, and then he would find her a perfect match . . . and she would love him for it. She would love him just as he was.

*Oh, God help me.*

He had truly lost his mind with such thoughts. He wanted to lie on the floor and sob, but he couldn't do that again. He'd already shamed himself beyond the pale by lying in his great bed and very quietly crying into his feather pillows. Enough was enough.

He rubbed his face with his hands and sat back up. Maybe he would try fencing this afternoon. It was a face-to-face sport and might not be dependent on sound. The thought of a quick succession of parries and then the elegant thrust of attack with a turned-out wrist and forward hip thrust caused a rush of anticipation to course through him. Physical activity — that's what he needed.

He turned in his chair to see that the door was cracked open and his secretary had poked his head in. As soon as Gabriel made eye contact, Meade waved and motioned that he come in with raised brows. His secretary had proven skilled at making up signs Gabriel could understand, which should have made him happy, but it only made him more surly and embarrassed.

"Meade, you're back from the wilderness. Do come in."

The door opened a little further and to Gabriel's astonishment, his secretary made a slow hobble into the room with a wooden crutch.

"What the devil has happened to you?" Gabriel eyed the wide swath of white bandage on his man's left leg, just below the knee.

Meade grinned and sat down, reaching for the ever-handy "speaking book," as the special doctors of the ear had informed him it was called. After an interminable wait while he scratched away with the quill, Meade spun the page around for Gabriel to see.

*I was shot, Your Grace.* He grinned again as if imparting happy news.

"Shot?" Gabriel knew his voice was thunderingly loud. The doctors had warned him about the habit of shouting that many deaf people developed, but he couldn't seem to help it. "Who would dare shoot you?"

The grin grew wider and Gabriel wondered if he was dreaming.

After some more scratching he leaned over to read the identity of the scoundrel who had the audacity to shoot the best man in his employ.

*Alexandria Featherstone, sir. She has quite an arm, if I may say so.*

The image of his golden-haired angel-child popped with a mental bang. "Alexandria Featherstone *shot* you?" Gabriel gestured toward the book. "Tell me everything."

Mr. Meade nodded, seeming eager to comply as he dipped the quill. After a short amount of time, he turned the paper around and pushed it in front of Gabriel. *I have something for you to read while I'm writing down the tale.*

41

He reached into a satchel and pulled out a cream-colored paper, handing it over the desk. Gabriel grasped hold of it and flipped it over. A seal. An unfamiliar seal pressed into the wax with a lion's head opposite an eagle's head, roaring and screeching, two crosses on either side with a banner overhead that read something he couldn't quite make out from the faded Latin text. The Featherstone seal? In all of England's heraldry, he'd never seen anything like it. They were an odd, old family indeed. He pulled out the paper and opened the note. The handwriting flowed with long, elegant slashes of black ink. Feminine. Dainty, yet resolute somehow. Pointed then rounded, dotted and crossed at just the right angle.

He exhaled as the beauty of the script hit his gut and then he flushed, his face filling with heat. A sweat broke out on his temples and he pressed the bridge of his nose with his fingers. *Stop being foolish.* But he couldn't deny that something within him loosened at the sight of it, the same kind of response he had to . . . music.

He took a steadying breath and began to read:

Dear Mr. Duke,

Had she really just called him *Mr.* Duke? Gabriel shook his head and continued on.

First of all, I do apologize for shooting your secretary. We have visitors so rarely here, you see, and well, I'm a bit discomfited to admit it, but I thought he might be a pirate out to "rape and pillage" — that sort of thing. Yes, I know, very addle brained of me. After getting to know him, a more kind and considerate man does not exist, I am sure (and it was an accident!), so please accept my heartfelt apology. He has assured me he is already on the mend and holds no ill will against me, for which I am eternally grateful.

Second, as to the news. I do not for an instant believe my parents are dead. I daresay HRH shall feel the veriest fool when they show up here on Holy Island, good as new and having solved their latest puzzle. They are socialites who travel the world with a flair for mysteries and are rarely to be found at home. Years (and I mean years) would have to go by before I believed them so ill fated.

Gabriel had to pause here and wipe the shock from his face before Meade saw it. Hoping he hadn't made a sound to give away his astonishment, and from the looks of Meade's scribbling quill he hadn't, Gabriel continued reading.

Thirdly, I beg you, most esteemed Duke, to leave me be! I will not be ripped away from my home like chattel by the likes of you! That is, I have been perfectly fine here for my entire life

Hmmm, how old was she?

under the care of our dear servants and the village folk who are like family to me. I would absolutely, positively wilt to DEATH should you demand my presence in London. Of course, I will still need my monthly allowance to sustain us as my parents always left me ~~one~~ two hundred pounds a month for upkeep, food, and miscellaneous expenses.

Gabriel nearly choked. It was an outrageous sum. What was a woman in the backwaters of Northumberland doing with that kind of money?

In closing, I do pledge with all my heart to pray for you, sir. Your health, your well-being, your gout? I've heard most dukes do suffer from the gout. Be assured your name has been added to my bedtime prayers. I count it a blessing that the great Almighty has made me one of those in which sleep eludes them.

Your servant. (Botheration, how does one sign off to a duke? I have a bad feeling about that word servant. Let's pretend that's not there.) Oh dear, perhaps I should start this letter over. Paper is so rare here that we shall just have to pretend all the crossed-out words aren't there. Eh?

With ~~much, great,~~ enormous regard,
Alexandria Featherstone, Holy Island

Gabriel leaned back in his chair, a state of shocked numbness making his limbs feel leaden. Was this some kind of joke? Who was this creature and how had she existed on her own for so long? *Unfathomable.* Before he had time to voice his doubts, his gleeful — why was he so gleeful? — secretary slid the speaking book across to him. There were several pages in his neat, compact hand.

"This is the account of your shooting?"

Meade nodded.

Gabriel frowned. "How old is she?"

Meade shrugged and then flashed both hands twice.

"Around twenty?"

He turned one hand back and forth.

"Give or take." Gabriel pressed his finger-tips together and puffed out a breath. Old enough to find her a suitor already. "What does she look like?"

Meade's eyes grew round. He shrugged again, a bigger, bolder move as if to say he hadn't paid much attention to that.

"Come now. Is she above average? Plain? Face like a horse?"

Meade pressed his lips together and then shrugged again. He pointed to his own brown hair. A medium, nondescript brown.

"She has brown hair?"

Meade nodded and then motioned for Gabriel to stand and follow him. Grumbling inside but curious, the duke followed him out of the library, down a long hall with vaulted ceilings and gilded woodwork, then into the blue salon, the color of the sky on a perfect day. It had been his grandmother's salon and was the most lavish room in the house. Every detail had been painstakingly purchased for it. It was a room fit for a queen. Meade walked over to the light-blue painted wall and pointed and then pointed to his eye.

"She has blue eyes?"

Meade nodded as though they had solved

a great puzzle.

Wonderful. The best description his secretary could come up with was a twenty-or-so-year-old woman with dull brown hair and pale blue eyes. "Never mind." Gabriel turned and marched back to the library to read what was sure to become the most notorious account of Meade's shooting.

# CHAPTER FOUR

"Well, you couldn't have messed that up any more if you had tried, Lady Alex. We're in a fine kettle of fish now," Ann muttered then threw her hands into the air for the third time.

"I know!" Alex wailed as she threw herself back onto the hard wooden bench that faced the enormous fireplace in the great hall. "I still can't believe I shot the duke's secretary! Do you think he'll ever forgive me? He must think me a complete addle brain."

"You should be on your knees giving thanks that the young man was so forgiving. I shudder to think what a man of another ilk would have done to you, to us, dragged us all off to London to face the duke, I daresay. You may thank your lucky stars —"

"Yes, yes, I have and am! Please stop haranguing me. I've pled forgiveness from Mr. Meade, the duke, and God. What more can I do?"

Ann opened her mouth to answer that and Alex threw a hand up. "No, no, I've heard enough on the subject. What we should be discussing is what's to be done next. I've sent the duke that letter, and as soon as the funds arrive I will start my search."

Ann's face transformed into the very picture of disapproving doom, but Alex hurried on before another lecture could commence.

"The last letter I received from my parents was from Ireland. The man who hired them said they would find the first clue there. But there is still the question of just where to start my search. I've no idea where to begin looking."

"How do you even know that much, I'd like to be knowin'? Your folks never let on where they were going, especially to you after that time you tried to follow them." Ann sat on the only chair in the cavernous room, shaking her gray head and tapering off into a mutter, ". . . treasure hunters and adventurers, saints a mercy. Just look where that's got them, the poor dears . . . poor us, I say! Leaving you alone much of the time, child. What were they thinking going off to the hindquarters of the earth —"

"Ann, you know they never meant to have

children. I was an accident."

Alex looked away, remembering how her mother had assured her that they were quite happy to have her. She said it to reassure Alex, she knew, but it had somehow sounded more like her mother was trying to convince herself, a fact Alex never let herself dwell on. She was determined to believe the best in them, that they loved her despite living most of their lives without her. It was her fault if she was sometimes lonely, pining for their love and attention. She was blessed to have such daring and adventurous parents, blessed that God let "accidents" like her happen.

"I overheard them talking before they left, as you well know," Alex reminded Ann as she continued her planning. "They were going to take a ferry from Whitehaven. That's where I will go first and see if I can find out anything about where they went in Ireland. But I can't leave without that traveling money! I do hope the duke hurries with his response. Time is of the essence." A stab of very real fear threatened when Alex thought of her parents in trouble and needing her. If they weren't dead, and certainly they weren't, then something must be very wrong that the prince regent had appointed her a guardian.

"The old duke could have all manner of reactions, my lady. Why, he might think it's time you married. That would get you off his hands."

Alex sucked in a sudden breath. "He wouldn't dare."

"And why not, I ask you? It's past time you married, not that you'll find anyone around here. I've been harping on your mother for years that you need a London season, but she never got around to it."

It was an unspoken fact that her mother's mind was rarely concerned with her daughter or her future. Besides, Alex didn't want a London season, and she certainly didn't want to get married. She frowned. Ann's reminder of the duke's sudden power over her made her stomach flip over. "I don't need a husband. I intend to follow in my parents' footsteps and take on cases, just as soon as I can convince someone to give me one. I am twenty, for goodness' sake, and not a child."

"Just as I was sayin'." Ann nodded. "You may think the world runs different out here on Holy Island, and maybe it does, but that duke will have London ways on his mind, you mark my words."

"Oh, bother, do you always have to be so

glum?" Alex turned her face away and sighed.

"Just speaking the truth, my lady."

Alex had heard quite enough of the truth for one afternoon and stood up to flee. "I believe I will go and check on Thomas William's knee. I do feel a mite responsible for his tumble from that tree."

Ann snickered. "He was spying on you again, was he?"

Heat filled her face. He and another boy had been trying to catch her swimming again. She'd only been wearing a shift, and it was wet and sticking to her . . . and well, she'd best find something that covered better or her swimming days just might be over.

Alex started to walk away but shot over her shoulder, brows raised, "Don't you have supper to start?"

Ann rubbed her knees and nodded. "Aye, that I do, mistress. You'll be home before dark to eat it, won't you?"

"Of course." It was the typical push and pull of their relationship. Alex threw back her shoulders and marched from the room. Why was it that Ann always harped at her about every little thing?

The crisp fall air cooled her cheeks as Alex walked down the steep hill called Beblowe where the castle seemed to grow right from the flat-topped outcropping of whinstone. She followed the dirt path that ran beside the shore of the North Sea toward the village. The path was rock and weed choked, but Alex knew every curve and obstacle, more familiar than her face in her bedchamber mirror. She kept her chin up as her gaze scanned the seemingly endless blue horizon that surrounded her from every angle. It was like being inside a dome, she thought with a whimsical smile. Her home. And for this time in its history — her island.

She thought back on its long and sometimes bloody history. Holy Island was a small plot of land on the eastern edge of Northumberland and near the Scottish border. In the seventh century the Irish monk St. Aidan founded the Benedictine monastery of Lindisfarne. It became the Christian base for centuries, allowing traveling monks to come and go as they spread the gospel to Northern England. Now the monastery was in ruins, but there was still a grand air about the place, as if it were holy ground, the way the sound of her voice echoed among the huge arches and towering columns of crumbling stones. She had played there countless hours, among the eerie tombstones, some tall Celtic crosses, imagining the monks going about their business.

Then there were the Lindisfarne Gospels, the famed manuscript she longed to see one day. An illustrated book of the first four Gospels of the New Testament and one of England's most treasured antiquities, it was said that the manuscript had been created right here at the monastery. Her parents had even seen it once, in the British Museum in London.

Scant centuries later the tale told that the Vikings raided one day. There had been signs, omens of evil tidings where the winds grew dark and swirling over the island, but none had been prepared for the heathens as they called them then. Wild men who raided up and down the coasts of England and here, where they murdered the monks who weren't fast or able enough to escape, where they burned down the old wooden parts of the priory and destroyed what they could of the stone.

Alex paused as the path skirted what had once been the monastery gardens, her gaze lingering on the broken-down walls to the gravestones beyond. She took a deep inhale and looked up at the piercing blue sky, thinking of God and heaven, shivering and wrapping her cloak more closely around her. When would her life begin so she could do something great for God? One thing she knew for certain — she would never accomplish what God had created her for if she lived in London as a married woman of the nobility. She belonged here on this wild and windswept isle. She could not let some duke change her life.

Hurrying now, Alex came into the island village. She was headed toward Thomas's house to check on the lad when a horse came pounding up the road. Mr. Winbleton! He would have the mail if there was any. Their village only received mail once a week and usually, in her haste to see if her parents had written, Alex would travel across the causeway, a path that was revealed only twice a day when the tide let out, to Beal, the closest mainland village of any size, to check for mail more often. What with Mr. Meade, the duke's secretary, only gone from them a little above two weeks, she had little hope there was a reply to her letter, but if Mr. Winbleton was here three days early! It just might be due to an important letter from London.

Alex picked up her dark green skirts and hurried across the street toward the town market. There were only two taverns that doubled as inns if the need arose, the church, an apothecary-doctor-dentist-undertaker's office, and the village shop, which sold everything from cloth to dry goods to fresh produce when the farmers supplied it. It was also the place to get news of life on and off the island. There was even a weekly newspaper brought in from London that made its rounds around the island. As lady of the castle, Alex was always offered the first chance to read it, an offer she usually resisted, waiting until it was well worn and the ink a little smeared, but when her parents had gone missing, everyone, including Alex, had gladly insisted she have the first news of any kind. "What would become of the little mistress without her parents?" she'd overheard them wonder more than once. Well, they'd not find out because she was going after them.

With that thought and a nod of her head, she entered the shop to the familiar sound of tinkling bells.

"What's to do, then?" someone was saying as she stepped inside, taking in the homey smells of fresh-baked bread and various spices for sale. It was Mrs. Peale, the shopkeeper's wife.

They all looked up and clamped their mouths together upon seeing her.

"Lady Alex! We were just wondering what

to do with this letter for you. It's straight from London and a duke!"

Alex's heart sped up a notch and seemed to catch in her throat. Her steps rang too loud against the hollow wooden floor in her hurry. She reached out her hand and smiled at Mrs. Peale. "How fortuitous! I suppose you should give it to me, don't you think?"

Mrs. Peale nodded her head, brown curls bobbing. She wasn't much older than Alex, but her parents had given over their shop to her and her new husband when they married, and she enjoyed an elevated status around town, one that seemed very much to her liking. "Yes, of course, I was just saying that to Roman."

Her husband looked askance at his wife but remained quiet. The domestic tiff restored Alex's sense of normalcy and sent a calming wave through her spine, allowing her legs to work properly again. She gave them a tight smile, reached out again, and wiggled her fingers. "My letter, if you please."

Roman passed the thick vellum into her hands.

"The paper is so fine," Mrs. Peale murmured with wide eyes and batting lashes. She leaned toward Alex as if to read it with her, but Alex just waved it toward them and backed away.

"It's nothing to get excited about, I'm sure. An old — very old — relation, the duke. He's probably heard of my parents' recent adventure and is inquiring as to their success." Alex gave them a vapid smile and turned toward the door, saying over her shoulder, "Nothing to be concerned about, you know." She waved and then turned and fled into the bright sunshine of the autumn day.

She didn't think, only hurried at a near run until she reached the edge of the village. There was a small, circular grassy spot where someone had placed a bench in front of the town well. It had become a wishing well over the years, mostly attended by the children of Holy Island. Alex had tossed in her share of coins over the years but hadn't visited recently. It somehow seemed the perfect place to read the duke's first letter.

With shaking hands and a racing heart, she flipped it over and studied the turquoise-colored wax with the Duke of St. Easton's seal. A unicorn on one side and a bull on the other. In the middle was the shield with a great crown above it. Unicorn . . . the symbol brought images of purity, dreams, and a magical quality to mind. The bull was strong, full of wealth and male protective strength. She ran her finger gently over the wax impression. What a unique mix of gifts. It sounded powerful and a bit intimidating.

With a deep breath she pried up the wax with her fingernail. She slipped the seal into the pocket of her dress, wishing to save it to study later, and opened the thick writing paper the color of cream. She smoothed out the folds of the best stationery she'd ever seen and lifted the page to read.

10 September 1818
From the office of the Duke of St. Easton, His Grace,
Gabriel Ravenwood

Alex sucked in and held a breath at the address. How someone such as he could have anything to do with *her* was beyond reasoning!

Madam,
I deeply regret the cause of our recent introduction and am as surprised as you must be at our ancestral tie. Upon the prince regent's order, I have spent considerable time investigating the claim of your parents' deaths and their current estate. (Do not ever put in writing again what you wrote about our most honored

monarch, do you understand me?) I have been astounded on both accounts. Firstly, your parents have had no contact with anyone known to us in nearly a year. Does this not surprise you? You mention your lack of faith that they are deceased and I am sure it is difficult news to accept, but a year is a very long time to have someone's relatives come up missing. Please advise if there is something you know that I do not. In the meantime, I think it wise to continue as the prince regent deems appropriate with my taking charge of your estate and well-being.

This brings me to the other surprise of my investigation into the Featherstone affairs. It would appear that your parents have been hiding, hoarding perhaps, a very large fortune. I tell you this only in the vein of protecting you from fortune hunters should the news come out. You, my dear Lady Featherstone, are the sole heir to lands and moneys that I must confess nearly equal my own. And my dear, I am among the wealthiest of Englishmen at this time. Do be careful.

As to your allowance. I am currently preoccupied with some important matters or I should call you to London. For now, stay put and do as you have been doing, taking care of that island and your herds of sheep (yes, I've inquired as to your activities). I have included some of the money you requested for your management of the estate. Should you need more, write to me, of course, but I must say, any good manager could do very well, even increase profits, on what I've sent you. Let's see what you can do with it, shall we?

Your servant,<br>St. Easton

Alex's hands shook and her eyes blurred as she read the cold words again and again, the bank notes falling from her lap to the ground.

He hadn't said those things!

Her parents dead and he the sole guardian to her fortune? A very great fortune? Why hadn't she known? She looked down at her dress, more a servant's garb than something a grand lady would wear. Why hadn't *they* told her?

Oh! She looked up toward heaven and shook her head. There was only one thing she was certain of after this day: She despised the all-knowing, seemingly almighty Duke of St. Easton.

She rushed home to write him back.

Dear Mr. Duke,

Thank you so much for the kind words and monetary addition to our larders. I am so sorry you are currently too pre-occupied with what must be a horror of social events and business dealings of your own that you cannot extend me more than a mere letter of instruction and a few pounds to a lone woman suddenly bereft of her family. I shall do my best to stretch my allowance to cover the costs of the estate. Be assured, I am trying to comprehend it all and keep you in my prayers. Your care of me has been most considerate. I confess a lack of knowledge as to a guardian's responsibilities, but I'm sure your attention to my needs has been sufficient. The prince regent himself would likely agree should he hear of it. I thank God for you, Your Grace, as I have no one left to me. And I do continue to pray for you. As my family now, I must love you with all that is patient and kind.

Your ward,<br>Alexandria Featherstone

Alex's lips curled in a satisfied smile as

she folded the letter, dribbled wax from her bedside candle onto the fold, and pressed her own seal, the Featherstone seal, onto the wax.

He might be a duke.

But he had no idea who he was dealing with now.

# CHAPTER FIVE

"Uncle Gabriel! Uncle Gabriel, come see!"

His niece, a five-year-old with blonde hair like dandelion fluff, turned and looked up at him with a cherub's face.

He paused, turned toward her as if in slow motion. But it wasn't Felicity he saw, it was his father. He looked different, bright and peaceful. He smiled at Gabriel, a kind smile, one he'd never seen on his father's face while alive. The moment caught in his throat and left him bereft, unmoored, filled with confused sadness.

The desolate feeling woke him in a cold sweat. He reared up, his gaze swinging around the room. Was his father here? Could it be possible? Of course not. He looked down with a heavy sigh. There was no one in the room but him. It was a dream, just a dream.

With a great sigh he fell back onto his pillows, raking his hand through his short black hair. What a strange dream. His niece here and talking to him. That feeling of family. And his father at peace, at rest like that? Was he in heaven? It seemed unfathomable that his father could be that man in the dream. Hugh Ravenwood, the sixth Duke of St. Easton, had always been a dispassionate man, stoic, somber, but always dependable, always there for them. There had been comfort in that. A wave of grief washed over Gabriel, surprising him. He hadn't consciously missed his father in a long time. Must be the weakness, the new vulnerability he felt with his current "condition."

He rose with a sigh, walked over to the water basin, and plunged his hands into the cool water left by his servant. He splashed a little onto his face to awaken, then ran his fingers over his stubbly chin. A shadow from the far side of the room flickered against the wall. Must be his valet stirring against the early morning sound. He turned his back to the approaching figure.

He didn't need help.

And he certainly didn't want company.

Shrugging away from the man and his morning toilet, he took up his riding costume and slipped into the clothes. Feeling like a child escaping his parents, he fled the room, boots in hand, his stocking feet not making the least sound to wake the servants ever abroad. At least he hoped he was quiet.

When he reached the outside, he smirked, slipped into his boots, and breathed deeply of the cool morning air. A carriage clattered by. He watched it pass, not hearing it but feeling the vibration from the cobblestones run from the heels of his boots up the bones of his body. He knew what it should sound like and made the mental connections so he felt he heard it. He was almost able to convince himself of it . . . but then the voice of reason, or the voice of despair, he didn't know which, mocked him.

*You didn't hear anything.* It was true. He only saw the flash of black wooden lacquer, only remembered how it should sound.

A moment of bleak despair streaked through him. *You'll never be the same. Just face it. This is your life now. You are changed . . . broken . . . different.*

He had to fight it. He couldn't surrender to these thoughts of weakness. He had to find a new normal he could live with. "No!" he muttered.

Gabriel Ravenwood, one of the most powerful men in England, looked around in anxious fear as to who might have heard him. He gripped the railing of the steps with one hand, slapped on his new-styled hat

66

that was more stovepipe than tricorn, and commanded his legs to walk. It didn't matter that he couldn't hear anything, no it did not matter . . . it couldn't matter . . .

He hurried down the street toward his usual haunt on Tuesday mornings — the famed fencing yards of Roberé Alfieri. They had a weekly appointment and Gabriel didn't want to stir up gossip with more absences. He opened the gate, not hearing the click-clack of the latch. Not hearing the thud of the gate shutting behind him. Hearing nothing but sensing a rhythm in his feet as he walked up to the door. It was strange, not hearing his footsteps ring out against the cobblestone walk, but he shook it off.

Those in his household that knew of his affliction had advised he not venture out alone. He had assured them that he could and would. Now he was faced with the reality of it. Deep breath . . . stop. Deep breath. He raised his hand to the knocker. Wait. He'd never before bothered to knock. *Don't deviate from normal. Be normal. Act normal. And they might believe you.*

With a deep breath and a silent wind whirling the autumn leaves around him, he pushed through the door and stood, blinking like a newborn, on the threshold of what was now his life.

Within minutes he suited up in his fencing costume and entered the grand ballroom where Roberé staged his battles. It felt familiar . . . safe somehow to be swathed in leather, a caged mask over his face, the weight of the sword at his side. He pulled forth the sword, called a small sword due to its lighter weight and shorter blade as compared to the rapier, and warmed up by thrusting and parrying with an imaginary partner. He had to imagine the familiar and satisfying *swoosh,* as he would have to imagine the *clang* when he engaged with Roberé. Where was the man? He slowed down, realizing he was breathing too hard, often turning this way and that as he could not hear his opponent, his instructor, enter the room.

It was a grand, domed-ceiling room, a former royal palace in the old days. Now it served various purposes, housing circus animals in the upper floors that the public flocked to see, meeting rooms in the lower two floors for various clubs and groups, but the ballroom had been appropriated by the aristocracy for training the elite. Gabriel had been training here for years, with the only man in England left to teach him anything, Roberé Alfieri, an Italian of varied history and reputation. No one knew who he really was, but after seeing him wield every kind of blade from dagger to broadsword, no one cared. Gabriel had been intent on besting him with the small sword for the last year.

A flash of movement from the corner of his eye had Gabriel turning toward the master swordsman as he entered from a side door. He was wearing all black, a closely fitting shirt and breeches, black stockings, and soft-soled shoes. His sword swung from one hand while he walked as if it weighed nothing and he wore the usual devil-may-care smile on his face. He said something but was too far away for Gabriel to try and make it out by reading his lips, something he still wasn't very good at.

Shrugging off the comment, he ignored it and plunged on with the ruse that nothing had changed. "Good day, Monsieur Alfieri. I'm afraid I have rather a busy day planned." He lifted his sword in salute. "Shall we?"

Roberé crooked one brow, a look of curiosity in his eyes sending a shaft of unease through Gabriel's spine. Roberé bowed his head in acquiescence though. A second later he lunged at Gabriel and the fight began.

A succession of quick parries moving up and down the ballroom floor commenced. But Gabriel knew this was just exercise to prepare them for the more-advanced moves. He took deep breaths and concentrated on the feel of metal meeting metal instead of the fact he couldn't hear the usual clangs and bell-like ringing that accompanied the sport. Like music, swordplay had a tempo, each move a beat and then double beats when an incoming attack was parried. Double-time again when he responded with a riposte. He allowed a crack of a grin.

He could still do this.

Sweat dripped down the middle of his back and down one cheek. The vibration of his opponent's sword meeting with his became a new kind of sensory experience, replacing sound. His vision seemed sharper somehow — as if he could slow the movement of the incoming blade for a brief second and respond faster and with more accuracy. They both began to breathe heavy and deep as they moved about the room.

A sudden thrust from Roberé caught his shoulder. Gabriel sank into a low squat, spun, and rose with a thrust of his own. Roberé deflected it and returned the riposte with quick thrusts, quicker than Gabriel remembered him ever doing. The man was unbelievably fast. Too fast.

Fear threatened him, beckoning him to give in to the master's skill. Then something rose within him, a greater desire than he'd ever had to best this man and prove there was nothing wrong with him. With a growl from deep in his throat, he concentrated on the cadence of the move, putting the dance back into the powerful thrusts and focusing less on the incoming blade and more on perfect footwork. It started to work. He was backing Roberé across the room, almost to the wall.

A sudden spark of yellow burst through the air with the clang of the swords meeting. It stretched into a line and then, as if exploding, turned into droplets of color in his peripheral vision. It faded before he was even sure he'd seen it, but with the next clash of steel there were more. Several quick parries and it was as if they were standing in yellow raindrops that disappeared before he could track their progress. He became distracted and clumsy.

Roberé took advantage of the moment. He thrust . . . hard . . . brought the edge of his blade to Gabriel's throat, both of them panting, Gabriel wide-eyed with shock and confusion. The colors disappeared as fast as they had appeared. Roberé leaned into Gabriel's face and grinned, pressing his sword just hard enough to prick the skin as he had done to him countless times.

Roberé cracked a smile. "Give up, Your Grace?" his lips said.

Gabriel backed away and bowed. "Well done, Monsieur Alfieri."

Roberé said something else, but Gabriel couldn't quite make it out so he only nodded again. "I must be on my way. Until next time." He didn't wait for a response, just turned to go, hoping the man didn't say anything else. Hoping he wasn't being too strange or rude.

What had just happened? He hardly knew what to think of it. And thinking of it sent prickles of a new kind of fear down his spine. He squeezed the bridge of his nose, took a deep breath, and then concentrated on putting one foot in front of the other instead of standing like a buffoon on the front lawn.

The air was crisp and windy, drying the sweat on his face as he walked back to his house. On most Tuesdays he would stop in to his club to gather the latest news after his fencing lesson. Impossible now. How long would he be able to keep up this charade? He should leave London for a while. Go back to Bradley House in Wiltshire and hide out until his hearing returned.

*What if it doesn't return?*

He ignored the question, thinking instead

of his favorite room in Bradley House: the music room. Over the years he had hired some of the most famed composers, from Beethoven to Clementi and opera singers from around the world to come and play for him. It was the one thing he'd never been able to master — music. He'd tried to learn to play the pianoforte and the violin to no success. He'd taken extensive voice lessons from famous teachers — and watched their faces wince and grimace. The one thing he loved above all else and he was miserable at it. He could manage to keep a beat, but not much else.

Thinking of beats he felt the cadence of the sword fight rush over him. Those streaks and dots of color. What were they? Should he ignore what had happened? Anxiety gnawed at his stomach. The fact that it might have something to do with his brain didn't escape him. The doctors were worthless, the lot of them. He'd studied biology and every other branch of science known to man. Something was wrong with his brain, not his ears. He was certain of it . . . in his gut. But he didn't want to be. *Big, deep breath. Just keep breathing.* No sense conjuring up demons bent on making him mad!

He picked up his pace as his brownstone came into view. Then he saw his mother's carriage in front of his house. So, the dowager duchess was here to check on him. It was a wonder he had dodged her this long. She was bound to have heard of the tragedy from the grapevine of servant gossip at the very least. Wonderful. Just what he needed.

The idea of turning around and heading to his club, or anywhere else, entered his mind but he took a bracing breath and trudged forward. May as well get it over with.

Moments later he walked through the great hall and handed over his hat and cloak to his butler. "Her Grace has called?"

Hanson bowed and nodded his head. "She is in the front salon." He pointed in the general direction of the room and spoke slowly so Gabriel could read his lips. "Would you like tea brought in?" He made the motion of holding a teacup and bringing it to his lips, which he pursed as if taking a sip. It galled him, the way the servants had changed to accommodate his "condition," but it did help him understand them.

"Yes, of course. Though I suspect she has already rang for it. Check on the refreshments, will you?"

"Yes, Your Grace." He bowed and marched down the hall toward the back kitchens.

Gabriel turned toward the salon, took a fortifying breath, and entered. He came to an abrupt stop as his mother rose, her hand to her mouth, her face gone sheet white, as if seeing someone waking from the dead, and his sisters, two of them at least, running and throwing themselves at him. His eldest sister, Charlotte, burst into tears from the other side of the room.

He was, for a second, glad he couldn't hear them.

"No need for all this caterwauling," he intoned in his best duke's voice. The sound of his voice only served to incite them, however. Mary clung to his arm while his youngest sister, Jane, looked up from her place at his other side and asked, "Can you hear me, Gabriel? Can you hear anything at all?"

It was too much. With gentle but firm hands, Gabriel pushed them back from him. "Please, ladies, sit down and let us discuss this without all the hysterics. I assure you I feel perfectly well."

Mary nodded and took hold of Jane's hand, dragging her back toward the gold-and-blue-striped settee. His mother collapsed back into her chair, dabbing her cheeks with an elegant handkerchief. Charlotte appeared unable to move, so Gabriel strode forward, held out his own handker-chief to her, led her to a Louis XIV gilded chair, and pressed her back into it. She seemed on the verge of needing smelling salts, an alarming fact as Charlotte was the stalwart one of the sisters.

Gabriel turned away from them to collect himself, walked to the sideboard, and poured a glass of water from the pitcher. He hoped no one was talking. He hoped they were patiently waiting for him to explain. Turning toward them, his gaze roved over each anxious face. His mother, a tall willowy woman who still bore the mark of her earlier beauty, was rarely prone to tears. She had collected herself, her back with the usual ramrod in it, her long neck displayed, chin up, and intelligent eyes studying him. Charlotte was still dabbing at her eyes but was doing her best to be the elder sister and a good example of how to behave even in extraordinary circumstances. Mary, the shy one of the group, who had such a soft heart that she could hardly bear to see an insect smashed, much less her brother in pain, looked at him with sad, frightened eyes. And Jane, the cheery one whom everyone loved . . . Gabriel looked away from Jane's quivering lips and cleared his throat.

Good heavens, they were wrecks, the lot of them.

"I presume you have heard of my, um, 'condition.'"

His mother said something but he held up his hand. "Let me explain what has happened and then you may ask your questions." His mother clamped her lips together.

"I was attending the opera as usual, about three weeks ago. Mr. Meade, you remember my secretary, came to my box with a letter from the prince regent. Something about a guardianship that I have inherited." He waved that away with one hand, not wanting to go into those details. "As I was reading the letter, I was struck with a great pain and dizziness, here." He tapped the upper part of his forehead. "Over the course of the next several moments, I realized that I couldn't hear any longer. It was a buzzing sound at first and then nothing."

He paced across the thick carpet in front of them. "Since that time I have, of course, seen the best doctors and tried several treatments. Nothing has *yet* worked." He swung toward them and locked gazes with each one by turns. "But know I am convinced that my hearing will return. This is a temporary condition that we need to keep amongst ourselves. In the meantime I am becoming better at reading lips if you speak slowly, not too slowly, just slowly enough and enunciate your words. Also, I have employed the use of speaking books. Rather, you write down what you want to say or ask me. Seeing that there are four of you, I suggest we use the book." He smiled at them, trying to lighten the mood. "I know how much you like to talk all at once."

Jane burst into fresh tears.

Mary clung to the arm of the settee.

Charlotte pulled forth his handkerchief again and threw it over her face.

His mother looked up and mouthed, *"The ball? You have to attend. You are the host!"* She motioned around the room.

The ball. *Excellent.* He'd forgotten that he had agreed to host one of the season's most sought-after events, hoping that in doing so his mother would stop the constant reminders that he must marry and produce an heir. A ball here, in his home, might convince her that he was at least thinking about it, even though he had yet to meet a woman of the ton who inspired much of anything in him.

His mind went blank as panic rushed over him in a wave of prickling heat.

How was he going to pull off such a thing

as a ball?

The next morning Meade handed a letter across the desk with the words, words that made his heart suddenly skip a beat, "From your ward, Your Grace. Lady Alexandria Featherstone."

He took the folded paper and motioned Meade away. Why was it that he didn't want anyone around when he read it? He wasn't sure, but Meade knew his every gesture and quickly left the room.

Gabriel lifted the letter to his nose, inhaling a faint whiff of lavender coming from the page. He opened it and read the sarcastic tone. She was upbraiding him. She was upset. It was understandable. She hated him, a little. The bearer of bad news and someone over her. He wasn't surprised but it got to him, nevertheless. She was hurt . . . grieving. And even in that state of emotion, she pledged to pray for him, to love him like family. That statement told more about her than any he'd read yet. He sighed, a strange warmth filling his insides. He would allow this little show of temper. He would let her pray for him. God knew he needed it.

He took out his quill and poised it over the page with a big breath.

My dear Lady Featherstone,

Your reluctance to come under my authority is both understandable and yet ill advised. I have taken my role as your guardian with most serious intent. I would do my duty by you in a manner that will bring you security and comfort. In effect, you may trust me. I will watch over you and your estate with the same attention that I attend to my own family and self. There is no greater promise I can give you.

It will take some time, I am sure, for us to know how to proceed with one another. In the meantime, please continue your letters. I find them refreshing and want to become better acquainted. And please continue your prayers. I have need of them now more than ever.

With much regard,
St. Easton

He reread it and then, satisfied, sanded the ink, and folded and sealed it with his ducal ring. He looked at the ring afterward, the metal still warm from the wax, and wondered if she would ever be impressed with a duke.

# CHAPTER SIX

She was doing the right thing.

Yes, of course she was.

Alex climbed into the hired coach and settled herself upon the threadbare seat as the coachman tied her trunks down to the top of the vehicle. She held the handkerchief of bread and cheese in her lap and took a deep breath. Already things had not gone as planned. She shook her head and looked out the window at the village of Beal, thinking of the small fortune she had paid Mr. Howard, a man of few words and a disapproving scowl, to drive her as far as Carlisle.

He'd not been happy to see her traveling alone, but she hadn't had any choice, had she? Ann and Henry were needed on the island to take care of the castle, the sheep, and the townsfolk while she was away, and she didn't think a long, arduous journey would do either of them any good. She'd been tempted to bring Latimere for protection but in the end had decided against it. She didn't know how long she would be gone and what forms of transport would be available to her. Her dear pet might put more restrictions on her, and she doubted Mr. Howard would have allowed him in the carriage, great hairy beast that he was. She'd had to add several coins to the bargain to gain his cooperation as it was.

A few minutes later the carriage shuddered and began down the lane. It was an ancient vehicle, large and lumbering, swaying on the rutted road. Alex looked back toward her island. The tide had come in and covered the causeway so she wouldn't be able to go back home for several hours, even if her courage failed her and she wanted to. Not that she did. She had to find her parents. No one else was looking for them. It was up to her to rescue them from whatever harm had befallen them.

She imagined saving them and then taking them to her guardian's house in London, proving them all wrong. The duke would stutter and raise his quizzing glass to peer at the three of them. The image of a fat, old man with a walking stick made her smile. Then frown. Upon receiving his last letter she'd had a moment's pause. He didn't sound quite so old and doddering as she'd first imagined. He sounded confident and . . . kind. Could he really care about her? Did he really want her to write more letters and continue her prayers?

*Dear Lord, whatever he meant by needing my prayers, I hope You'll help him. I hope he feels Your love for him in the trials of life and that Your love gives him strength and courage and peace. And help me remember to pray for him! I haven't actually prayed very much, as You know! And now I'm feeling rather guilty about that. And help me find my parents. Amen.*

As to writing more letters, she wasn't sure what to say. In a whirl of confusion she'd pulled out a worn copy of the *Magee's London Letter Writer,* a supposed guide to "the art of fashionable correspondence," and paged through it for clues as to how to write something so convincing that His Grace would send her more money. The book had been almost scandalous in its hinting that she play the coquette, something she had no experience doing or being. La! Flirt with a man to get more from his pockets? Not in this century! She would do as the widow in the Bible had done — the one with the land trouble who had gone to the judge so consistently, sweetly, and be persistent.

So, she'd written him another letter telling of the poor sheep and the well that had gone dry. Which was true. Never mind that that particular well had been dry for the last decade, they could always use a new one, couldn't they? Just a few hundred pounds more and she could at least stay as long as she needed in Ireland. She tapped her finger against her chin, deep in thought. If only she knew someone there. She was going to need some help. She bent her head and prayed for such help.

The soft rays of morning sunlight brightened as the afternoon crept by, warming the inside of the carriage. Alex leaned her forehead against the window and watched as the Cheviot Hills rolled by. Much of the grass had turned brown, but there were patches of green pastureland still to be seen. They had an undulating quality that seemed peaceful and serene. The white furry shapes of slow-moving sheep dotted one distant hill. Alex smiled. She would miss her small herd. Twenty-three in all, she had named each one, knew their various temperaments, and treated them more like pets than livestock. A fact that Ann despaired of, throwing her hands up in frustration whenever Alex had the gall to bring one inside the castle due to some malady or injury. It wasn't unusual to hear one bleating from her bedchamber. Alex chuckled and closed her eyes as the carriage dipped and swayed her into a light sleep.

When she awoke, it was dark outside the windows. The air, too, told that night had come with a deep chill that made her nose feel numb. She rubbed it with cold hands and stretched the stiffness from her back. Wondering how close they were to the town of Carlisle, she knocked at the front window to gain Mr. Howard's attention. The carriage lumbered to a slow stop.

Alex let herself down and stretched out her arms, looking around for a place to do her necessary business. There was a stand of trees not far. That should do.

"Mr. Howard, are we close to Carlisle?"

"Aye, miss. Less than an hour away if I don't miss my guess."

"Oh, good. I'll just be a minute, right over there." She pointed toward the trees and ducked her head, hoping the reason would be obvious. When he didn't say anything, just grunted and turned away, she breathed a sigh of relief and trudged through the thick grass. Clouds skidded across the half-moon causing eerie shadows to move across the grass. Alex shivered and hurried. The carriage seemed quite warm and cozy compared to the wind-whipped landscape surrounding her.

She had just turned back when the pounding of horses' hooves coming from behind her made her freeze in her tracks. Slowly, with a heart that was pounding almost as loud as the approaching men, she turned and peered into the dusky light. The white fluttering of flags and the dark shapes of the horses was all she could see.

"My lady! Quick! Get back into the carriage!" Mr. Howard hissed at her.

Snapping from her statuelike trance, Alex turned and ran back the way she had come. With a great leap she jumped inside and slammed the door shut, but wanting to see what was happening she opened the door a crack and shouted up at the driver. "What shall we do? Who do you think they are?"

"Shush, now," was his only reply, but he started the horses and they continued down the narrow road, toward the coming men, in a slow roll of the wheels against the road. Alex shut the door again and leaned back onto the seat, praying highwaymen weren't about to steal all her belongings. And before she had even made it out of England! That would certainly not be fair.

A shout came from somewhere in front of them. Alex opened the door a crack and pressed her ear to the opening.

"Stop, in the name of the prince regent, I command you."

Her heart sped up. The prince regent?

"We are the prince regent's soldiers and we patrol this road. What is your business?"

"I've been hired to take my lady to Whitehaven, sir. We were hoping to make Carlisle and an inn before dark, but alas the road has been trying and we are somewhat later than I imagined."

"A lady?" The man sounded curious and intrigued. "Who is this lady and what is her business?"

The sound of horses came nearer. Alex shut the carriage door with a soft sound, only to have it wrenched open a moment later. A sudden blaze of light came forward as another soldier lit a lantern and handed it to the man at the door. "So, what is your business, my lady?" He asked with one dark brow raised.

Alex rallied her courage and sat up as tall as she could, adopting a superior mien by staring down her nose at the soldier. She'd practiced this particular look in the mirror many times and as yet had not found an occasion to use it. This just might be the perfect time to try it out.

"I am Lady Alexandria Featherstone of

Holy Island and I have business to attend to in Whitehaven. And you, sir? You mention our dear prince regent for whom I have a great regard and friendship. In what capacity do you serve His Majesty?" It was a sad truth that lies had always flown out of her mouth with the ease of a bard telling a tall tale. She couldn't seem to help it.

The man's mouth cocked up on one side in a smile that was both insidious and admiring. He bowed with flourish, the lantern waving shafts of yellow light around the carriage. "I am Lieutenant Haggerty of the 12th Light Dragoons. At your service, my lady."

Alex dipped her head in a slight bow. "Thank you, Lieutenant." She studied his face for clues. Was he really a friend? He had dark hair and a thick mustache that tipped up in an almost comical manner on either end. His face was lean, almost too much so, giving him a gaunt look, but his dark eyes made her uncomfortable. He seemed to be looking right through her cloak and trying to judge her figure. "Pray tell, how far to Carlisle, Lieutenant? I confess exhaustion and the need of an inn as soon as may be."

"Not far. About thirty minutes yet. But my lady, do you travel alone? Where is your maid? You must at least have a servant with you?"

The disapproval in his voice was thick with accusation. His gaze flicked down again and then around the carriage as if the invisible servant must be hiding.

"She became ill at the last minute and I was forced to journey alone. I have Mr. Howard though. A true servant and guard. He is quite handy with the rifle and has bested all the local men of Beal at fisticuffs."

Her coachman made a coughing sound as that falsehood settled around them.

"I see." The lieutenant appeared to see right through her. Alex lifted her chin another notch and directed. "We really must be on our way, sir."

"Lady Featherstone, as I can see you have no idea of the dangers of these roads at night, I insist that you allow me to accompany you into town. I'm sure your *friend* the prince regent would have my head should I let trouble befall you."

Oh, dear. He wasn't buying a word of it. Alex dipped her head and pasted on a fake smile. "Very well. That is most kind of you." She reached over and grasped the door handle, pulling it firmly closed in his face.

As soon as he rode out of sight, darkness flooded the interior of the carriage. She let

89

out a big breath and leaned back against the seat with a groan.

True to his word, Lieutenant Haggerty led the small company of soldiers right into town. They passed through the town gate, saw a massive stone structure that was probably an abbey or ancient castle, and then rumbled down a cobblestone street to the main part of the town. The old carriage shuddered to a stop in front of a building. Light flooded the street in yellow squares from the windows and she could hear a bow gliding over the strings of a fiddle. The sign hanging above the door read *Black Friars Inn*. Alex wasn't sure she should trust the lieutenant's choice, but she was really too hungry and tired to care. As long as they would give her some supper and a bed, she would take it.

The carriage door swung open before she had a chance to open it herself and there stood the lieutenant, dressed in a bright red uniform. She gave him a weary smile and allowed him to take her gloved hand in his to help her down.

"The place seems quite busy, sir. Do you think they will have an available room?"

"I shall be sure of it, my lady. If you would be so good as to allow me to escort you inside and transact the business of it on your behalf?"

"Thank you, Lieutenant Haggerty, but I am perfectly able to arrange for my own room. I would not be indebted to you in such a manner."

"To assist a beautiful lady as yourself would only prove the highest honor. Please, I beg you." He leaned over her hand, still grasped in his, and brushed a kiss across the back of it.

Alex gasped and snatched her hand from his. "You do me great honor with the escort, sir. No further assistance is required." With her teeth gritted she turned away from him and marched into the inn without looking back, Mr. Howard on her heels.

Mr. Howard leaned forward toward her ear and muttered, "Sorry, my lady, but I know these types. You must give them what they want or else be the sorrier for it."

Alex cast a long-suffering look over her shoulder. Sure enough the soldiers were following them into the inn, Lieutenant Haggerty in the lead and looking none too happy. "He'll not be getting what he wants," she murmured to herself but loud enough to be heard by the coachman who only coughed and looked away.

There was a long counter with a man standing behind it at one end of the room.

Alex rushed over to him and had arranged a meal for Mr. Howard and herself and paid for two beds before the lieutenant made it through the throng and by her side.

"You rushed off so quickly, my lady. Please, allow me to share your table for dinner."

"Why, Lieutenant, I thought you must have more pressing matters to attend to than keeping me company. Are the roads safe without your patrols?"

He had the audacity to narrow his eyes at her and touch her cheek. "Nothing would give me more pleasure than keeping you safe. I fear the inns of England are no place for a lone woman. I shall sup with you and then place a guard at your door. . . . I may even guard it myself."

Genuine fear spiraled up Alex's spine. He looked serious and sounded threatening in the promising way a rapier being pulled from its sheath was threatening.

Alex backed away from his reach and turned quickly aside. "You do me too much honor, sir." Her gaze darted about the room for help if she needed it, seeing a large man with meaty arms; a group of younger, well-dressed gentlemen; and then lighting on an older man with long, white hair.

He leaned back in his chair with elegant

ease, one foot propped on a knee, his elbow braced on the table beside him, chin in hand. She looked into intelligent blue eyes and paused without meaning to. There was a confident kindness in those eyes, but when his gaze switched to Lieutenant Haggerty, it hardened like blue glass and his whole being transformed to tightly coiled strength, ready to spring. She had the silly desire to run to him and cower behind his chair but she didn't know him at all. Might be a case of jumping from the pot into the fire. Looking straight ahead she followed the innkeeper to a quieter room in the back, the coachman, Lieutenant Haggerty, and several other soldiers trailing her like a horde of bees she couldn't shake.

*Lord, send angels to protect me.* She threw the silent prayer up as she took a seat, Lieutenant Haggerty seating himself next to her on the narrow bench.

The first course of lentil soup and fresh bread was hot and smelled delicious, but she didn't know how she would swallow it around the knot in her throat. She dipped her spoon, keeping her eyes glued to her bowl and trying to ignore the lieutenant's thigh, which seemed to be getting closer and closer to hers. By the time the second course arrived, his leg was touching the folds of her skirt and his arm would upon occasion brush against her arm. She took a little scoot away, glancing at him to see if he noticed. That was a mistake. His hand reached out and grasped hold of her upper thigh like a tight, painful vise.

She gasped. Her face filling with heat. "Unhand me this instant," she hissed.

No one seemed to notice their conversation. The room was loud and they were all busy diving into the roasted chickens that had been placed in front of them.

His hand moved but slowly and with sensual intent. Alex's heart was beating so that she thought it must come out of her chest. She had to get out of there.

With a sudden motion, she stood, bowed her head to the table at large, and announced, "I'm very tired and would retire, gentlemen. Thank you for your kind escort and company, but I must bid you good night."

Several men stood and bowed, wishing her good night as she fled the room, and the lieutenant had an angry scowl on this face. Hopefully, he would give up and be gone by morning. But she wasn't so naïve as to think it likely. He seemed most determined to do what, exactly, she wasn't sure, but she had to escape him. The thought that she could be in serious trouble, packed back to Holy Island or some other alternative to her plan — jailed even, for traveling alone — made her bite down on her lower lip as she made her way up the stairs to her room.

Her room turned out to be over the taproom and was sure to be noisy, but thanks be to God, it had three other women staying in its two big beds. She would gladly cuddle up to the large woman named Trina who smiled at her with two missing teeth and took up most of the bed. Gladly!

Hopefully, such company would keep her safe until morning.

# CHAPTER SEVEN

"Your Grace."

Meade stepped inside Gabriel's dressing room where his valet, George, was putting the finishing touches on his cravat. He paused on the threshold and waited while Gabriel slipped into his waistcoat and checked his appearance in the full-length mirror.

"Good choice, George." Gabriel murmured the praise, careful not to speak too loud, causing the young man's neck to redden in embarrassed pleasure. He was dressed in a cream-colored waistcoat with scrolling embroidery of same color on the lapels and a stark white shirt and cravat. The word *snowy* did come to mind as he studied the perfect folds under his chin. Below, he wore dark blue trousers after the newest French style tucked in his boots, lighter than his usual Hessians, for dancing.

Not that he would be doing much of that.

His dark brows lowered over eyes the color of emeralds in a deep scowl. He had never minded dancing, even with debutantes. It was the music he loved, he supposed. Anything to do with music, he loved. But how could he dance when he couldn't hear the song? How did Beethoven compose without hearing the notes? He had to try. The game would be up before they even began if he didn't try.

Gabriel turned from the mirror, ignoring the fear that made his palms clammy. He motioned Meade to follow him into his bed-chamber and then spun toward him. "What is it, Meade? Have my sisters arrived? The ball started over an hour ago."

Meade bowed his head in a low nod. "Yes, Your Grace." He held out the speaking book.

Gabriel took it with a short motion of impatience, seeing the page filled with his secretary's neat hand. His hatred for the speaking book was well known, but when more than a few sentences needed to be communicated, it was more efficient despite its tedious nature. His gaze scanned the instructions and reminders for the night. He nodded and thrust the book back into Meade's hands. Yes, yes, he knew very well what to do. The plan, several small plans to be exact, to pull off the feat of the duke appearing normal before a crowd of over two hundred was neat in its simplicity. Still, it would be risky and not a little ridiculous at times, but it just might work.

It had to work.

"Let's get on with it, shall we?" Gabriel strode from the room, head held high, heart in his throat.

Before he had reached the top of the grand staircase, his youngest sister, Jane, rushed to his side. She took hold of his upper arm and smiled up at him. Was she blinking back tears? Good heavens, just what he needed right now. A simpering female to calm down. But in his heart he didn't believe it. His mother and sisters were privy to the plan and he knew she was trying to do her part to buffer and protect him. He turned his head away from her loving face — those big, brown, compassionate eyes — and swallowed . . . hard.

The house was quiet for a party. His silent party. If he hadn't seen the date on the invitations himself, he would never know another soul was here.

A sensation of being in a dream washed over him as they made their way down the long staircase, across the great, silent hall, and to the threshold of the ballroom. It was as if he could hear one thing and one thing only — the tick . . . tick . . . tick of time slowing down. The air thickened in his throat. His hands began to tremble. He grasped for control. This was not his reality. It couldn't be. He clasped his hands together in front of his stomach and forced them to stop shaking.

Jane looked up at him with concern, he could feel it in the way her spine went taut and her hand tightened around his arm, but he ignored her. If he looked into her face he might break in half, right here in front of everyone. No. Couldn't allow that. He stood at the entrance to his grand ballroom, seeing the crush of people, their mouths moving so fast, their faces hot, sweaty, animated, couples twirling to silence. The orchestra bent over their instruments, looking more like a group of land laborers than artists. Where was the beauty? Where had it gone?

*Dear God.*

He looked at Jane with silent pleading.

*We can do this.* Her lips said it and her eyes said it and he remembered who he was.

A duke. The Duke of St. Easton, to be exact.

After the first hour he actually began to enjoy himself. It was easy to float from group to group, nod, say hello and the usual pleasantries, and move on. He kept a glass of champagne in his hand but didn't dare drink it. Had to remain alert for danger. Like skirting possible land mines, he avoided those people who would question him to death over some inconsequential matter. Lord Rowland wanted to talk politics in the world after Napoleon; Randoff Yeatley, horses; and his brother-in-law, the value of the latest investment. The girls had done a good job of keeping the secret and, taking turns hanging on the outskirts of whatever group he was in, rushing in to pull him away on some urgent matter should he seem to be flailing. It was actually going quite well.

A touch on the back of his arm made him turn around, a bland smile pasted on his face. Blanche Rosenbury, the Countess of Sherwood. Rich, powerful in her own right, and very, very beautiful. His gaze flicked over her deep blue gown that openly displayed a full bosom. He took a very tiny sip of his drink, the look of the expected admiration touching his eyes. "Lady Rosenbury, how good to see you."

She turned her head a little to one side in that flirtatious way she had mastered before her debut and lowered her lashes in mock modesty. Gabriel stared at her pink lips hoping to be able to read them, but she was looking too far down and aside. As she continued talking he started to panic. Where was Mary? He'd just seen his middle sister not two minutes ago. Giving up on knowing what she said, he only let out a nondescript "hmmm" and searched those nearby for his sister's bright orange dress. They had decided it best to wear bright colors in case he needed to find them, so where the deuce was she?

A flash of orange over his right shoulder had him glancing that way. There. Wingate had her cornered, of course. The man couldn't seem to give her any leeway to move about in public without him hovering over her shoulder. "Condition" or not, he would have to check into that.

A tap on his arm brought his gaze back to the fuming redhead. Lady Rosenbury's eyes snapped with angry sparks as she prattled out some nonsense from her artificially stained lips.

Gabriel sniffed as if affronted and shook his head. "As you say, madame." He turned and strode away, hoping he hadn't agreed to something.

In his hurry and confusion where to go next, he nearly stumbled. As he righted himself, casting about to see if anyone had noticed, he found himself thrust in a group of youngbloods. They immediately bowed, one in particular turning out his leg and bowing over it in an exaggerated posture of respect. Gabriel raised his brows at the dandy. Here was a group he could handle. They would hang on any word he said.

Mr. Meade appeared in his forward line of vision prepared to make the necessary signs if needed. One finger meant "yes." Two meant "no." If he rubbed the bridge of his nose, they were asking about horses. Tugged on the hair above his left ear meant investments, and if he coughed they had brought up the topic of gambling, more coughing meant horse gambling and trading.

Gabriel watched the lips of the young Mr. Hyde, hero worship in his eyes. He said something along the lines of "your humble servant" and bowed again, then asked a question. Gabriel missed it and looked to Meade. Unfortunately Meade was wide-eyed with panic. He made a motion of holding out his arms and then bringing them in as if he were hugging someone. What the devil did that mean? Before too much time could go by Gabriel looked back at Mr. Hyde and gave him a tight smile. "Very good," he said, feeling heat fill his cheeks as he wondered if that would pass.

A look of uncomfortable confusion passed over the young man's face, but before Gabriel had time to wonder how badly he had mistepped, another young man stepped forward with a comment.

Gabriel stared at his lips and then realized how odd that looked. Most of the time when he was trying to decipher what someone said by lip reading, the person knew of his difficulty. But not here, not now. Staring at a person's mouth wasn't exactly good etiquette and might even raise some uncomfortable questions. As he was thinking this, he realized he had not been paying attention and hadn't any idea what the fellow had said. With a desperate start, he shot a quick look at Meade. Thanks be to God, he was having a coughing fit. Must be horses.

"Have you seen Lord Grant's new stud?" he asked and then hurried on before he had to read an answer. "Best stallion I've seen in some time. You all should visit his stables and get a look before he takes him off to Surrey."

The men around him paled, one coughed into his hand appearing to hide a smile, while another looked genuinely afraid. Gabriel glanced at Meade and saw that his secretary was equally ashen. He had blundered again. Time to remove himself.

Just at that moment a group of young women passed by. He didn't know any of them but that never mattered. He was the host and could introduce himself. Smiling with all the confidence he could muster, he bid the group farewell.

"I find myself ready to dance, gentlemen. And I see a lovely accomplice right over there. If you will excuse me?"

They all nodded as he gave them a small bow and backed away, disappearing into the crowd. He would have to dance now. A young woman who would be more nervous than he would be the best choice. He scanned the crowd and then saw the group and strode over to them. Four women of differing degrees of attractiveness. All in their first or second year of being "out" and still blessedly naïve. Perfect.

He stood near the group and waited . . . one . . . two . . . three.

One of them gasped and the others turned their heads toward him. Just the response he'd been hoping for. He took another step toward their group, not looking directly at them and then, as if just noticing them from the corner of his eye, he turned his face toward them and bowed his head. "Ladies."

They just stared, which was perfect.

"Do you see my sister over there?"

They gazed to where he was pointing and then nodded, still looking dazed and a little terrified.

"As you can imagine, she and my mother are insisting I cast about for a wife. Tedious business, but I'm thinking to mollify them for the moment by dancing. Any volunteers?"

The petite blonde batted her lashes, her quick breathing making her bosom rise up and down so fast Gabriel thought she might faint. Another darker blonde just stared at him as if he was a statue come to life and was asking her to dance. But the brunette, not the pretty one, took a bold step forward and had the courage to touch his sleeve. "I'll dance." She lifted her chin with a determined air.

Gabriel gave her a bland smile and held out his arm. He hoped she'd had the necessary lessons.

Once on the dance floor, he started to feel nervous again but was determined not to show it. He took the young woman into his arms in the proper stance and watched the orchestra. As soon as the man's bow touched the strings of the violin, he began to move with the crush of dancers on the floor. One, two, three — one, two, three — one, two, three — turn. It wasn't so hard. If he concentrated he could feel the vibration of the music enough to give him the timing of the beat. Astounding really, that vibration traveled through the air. Or maybe it was the floor that vibrated, he wasn't sure, but it seemed to be enough.

Round and round they swept along on the notes of the waltz. If the woman in his arms tried to talk to him, he didn't notice. He was too busy making sure he didn't misstep. When it was over, he took her back to her friends, who began babbling at her with excited faces the minute he backed away.

He needed a break, a rest, from this emotional and mental fatigue that was still new to him. He made his way past groups of smiling, waving acquaintances to the French doors at the back of the ballroom and slipped outside into the garden. The night air soothed his hot cheeks. He sucked in breaths, exhaustion overcoming him. The thought of the midnight dinner to come made his stomach twist into knots. Too much conversation. He couldn't do it. He was starting to fail and had possibly already made a spectacle of himself. Too risky. He would have to make some excuse. He would retire. Send Meade a note and let him take care of it.

Thinking of the note, he realized he could circle around to the other side of the house and let himself in another set of doors that led to his library. Feeling strangely like a thief in his own house, he hugged the brownstone and clung to shadows as he edged toward the doors under the light of a sliver of moon. There. They were unlocked. Thank God.

He let himself in and lit a candle. Sitting down at the desk, he pulled forth a blank sheet of stationery and wrote out quick instructions. He folded the paper and was about to ring for a servant when he saw a small stack of post on one corner of his desk. In all the preparations for the ball, he'd forgotten to check his mail.

He flipped through it, making piles according to importance. And then he saw it. A letter from Holy Island. A letter from the impossible, audacious creature that was his ward. His heart gave a leap of pleasure and his lips broke into a smile. He flipped it over and lifted the seal, bringing the candle closer to read. What was his lovely little hoyden up to now?

My Dear Duke,
I don't know where to begin to explain

all the difficulties this poor creature (that being myself), bereft of parents and alone in the world except for the guidance of your fine self, has so suddenly experienced. Just this morning I stepped out of my castle to more disasters. Have I told you about the island's castle and monastery? No? Dear sir, there are hardly two stones sitting next to each other to cover our heads. The ravages of time and hostiles have left us bereft of all but an occasional wall and a crumbling roof to keep us dry. Why, just the other day I had to hire ~~two~~ three men to repair another horrid hole in the roof. The constant dripping and leaking has us all at wit's end. What I really need are some workmen, and sir, you must know that a good carpenter, mason, and blacksmith will cost a great deal. I have so much work for them to do! I do lose sleep over it. Tossing and turning in my bed and wondering how I will ever make ends meet on a girl's allowance. Am I not the mistress now? Do I not deserve the funds to make this place finally habitable? I implore you, Your Grace, to reconsider the allotment of the fortune my parents left me. While they did not seem to have much regard for this lonely island, (they were rarely home long enough to feel the discomforts of leaky stone), I have been here and am yet here, making my future and way in this world the best I can. There is so much need. Shall I list some more of it for you?

The wool from the sheep could be better traded and made into cloth for our cold winters. I can't remember the last time I had a warm cloak and dress. I'm still wearing fashions from the last decade, I can assure you. My servants run about in rags, mostly. Mr. Meade can surely testify to the state of my household staff.

The well. We began digging a new one last month but were unsuccessful and the lake is so very far. Think of it, my dear duke, fresh water . . . who can put a price on that?

My servants are equally in need of provisions — food, clothing, and other necessities. My poor housekeeper is so aged that I have been cleaning the castle myself. I know your shock must be great at hearing that and do implore you to send funds for a new maid-in-training also. Your generous allowance surely didn't take into account all the souls for which I am responsible. As ward to the powerful Duke of St. Easton, you must want me well provisioned and accounted for.

I leave you with one thought.

This place has a wild, ancient beauty that is incomparable and it is my home. My parents, bless their souls, had a fleeting love for it, but I will live here my whole life as the good Lord wills. I would like, with your help, to make it all that it was meant to be. It might cost a small fortune, but I beg you to give me the time to make it what I have imagined it could be.

The time and the money.

Your most faithful servant,<br>Alexandria Featherstone

P.S. My prayers for you are often and heartfelt. Take comfort in the fact that God's love never fails. Even in the midst of life's most harrowing trials, dear sir, you can depend on Him to see you through it. If you should wish to give me the great honor of confiding in me, know I will gladly lend you my ear and my shoulder in sharing your burden. Have faith in God, Your Grace. He will carry you through.

Gabriel leaned back into his chair and

closed his eyes, imagining her face, imagining her praying for him. His intimation that he needed her prayers had struck a chord in her, he could see. And her encouragement to have faith in God made him realize that beyond praying for his hearing to come back, he hadn't really put any faith in God's love for him. If God's love never failed, then why did it feel like it had? Perhaps he would confide in Alexandria. To be able to tell someone how he felt, how this affliction was affecting him and changing him? He needed someone like that. And she needed him. She needed money, yes, but she needed *him.* He imagined the crumbling castle, the horrid condition of the fourteenth-century monastery, the poor villagers with their dry well and weak sheep.

He should go to her.

Blast the fact that he was deaf. There was too much in her letters that told him she wouldn't care. She would accept his help with open arms and a thankful smile.

Here was something he could be useful at. Here was something he could fix.

Here was a woman who might accept him just as he was.

# CHAPTER EIGHT

Alex slipped out of bed, trying not to wake her bedmate, wrapped her cape over her shoulders, and picked up her boots. Stepping lightly, she eased her bag off the room's only chair, slung it over one shoulder, and opened the door with only a tiny squeak, then tiptoed into the hall. She felt for her money bag, checking one last time before shutting the door. Perfect, it was still in the hidden pocket of her dress. She shut the door with a tiny click, then hurried from the room and down the stairs to the common room of the inn.

No sign of the soldiers, thank God. She'd risen early to try to sneak away in case they had spent the night too. The last thing she needed was to have to deal with that lieutenant. Now, to find Missy. She had asked the maid, Missy, who had brought them firewood the night before, about purchasing a horse. Alex would be riding horseback for the rest of her journey as her coachman, Mr. Howard, had pressing business to attend to in a nearby town and had to take leave of her today. It didn't matter. She would be fine on her own. It was only a few hours' travel to Whitehaven and the western shore of England, where she would board a ferry to Ireland.

A little thrill ran through her at the thought of Ireland. She'd never been farther than Alnwick, where she had once visited the famous Alnwick Castle, and here she was about to leave the country. Where exactly in Ireland she should begin her search was a bit of a puzzle, but she had one clue. She pulled the faded, much-folded letter out of her pocket and read it again.

Dearest Alexandria,

My heart despairs over how long we have been gone from you this time! Forsooth, your father and I had no idea the scope of the investigation when the mysterious Mr. Tweed (of course that is not his real name!) hired us to find our latest treasure. I fear our time here has provided only a very few clues, and thus we will be away from you longer than usual. I take comfort in knowing what an independent and resourceful young woman you are. You will do well to continue your upkeep of the castle, making your recipes and concoctions for tonics and cosmetics and such and watching over dear Henry and Ann. I must hurry, as your father is calling me that the mail coach is about to leave.

We love you, darling!
Mother

Alex sighed. It was one of her mother's shorter letters, to be sure. And the way she had referred to Alex's little hobbies of invention sounded a bit condescending, although Alex told herself she was just being silly. Her mother was always delighted to try a new face cream or hair tonic when she was home. Never mind that one of those tonics had turned her mother's blonde tresses green. She hadn't been so very upset, saying she would wash it several times a day and wear hats in the meantime. And she did look wonderful in hats, didn't she?

Alex sighed. Why did her mother always cause her such conflicting emotions? And why did she feel like she was constantly making excuses for her? Katherine was very much her own person and Alex had given up long ago expecting anything else from her, even though there were hidden moments when she cried into her pillow at night, feeling as if she hadn't a single person close enough to share her whole heart with.

The notion that "accidents" didn't deserve the kind of attention she craved made her wipe away her tears and lecture herself about how lucky she was. Counting her blessings was a task she was very, very good at.

She looked down at the worn letter and then flipped it over. There was a clue here, an important one. She raised it close to her face, squinting at the smudge. It was faint but there was a postmark that read Belfast. She had studied the old world map in the library before embarking on this journey and been relieved to see it was quite close, just across the Irish Sea and up Belfast Lough. She would start there and hopefully find someone who had seen or spoken to her parents. Now to get safely to White-haven.

When she walked outside she looked around the street for any sign of the soldiers. Seeing none, she skirted around to the back of the inn and breathed a sigh of relief to see the maid standing to one side near a water trough, holding the bridle to a tall brown horse. Alex hurried over to her.

Just as she was crossing the yard, she saw

a flash of red in the corner of her eye. Two soldiers were standing against the opposite corner smoking cigars. They must be with the lieutenant. She backed toward the corner of the inn, hoping against all odds that they hadn't seen her, and waved the maid over whispering, "Bring the horse."

Missy looked at the soldiers and nodded, understanding lighting her eyes. With casual movements, she patted the horse and then led him around the other side of the trough toward Alex.

"Is the horse for me?" Alex looked up at the tall animal with both gratitude and some trepidation. "I have to hurry away before those soldiers see me."

The young woman nodded and leaned in. "He belongs to a friend of mine. I'll fetch him later tonight. When ye get to White-haven, take 'im to me brother's 'ouse. 'is name is Paul." She pushed a rumpled paper into Alex's hand. "Here's 'is address and a note for 'im. He will take care of Sorrel until I get there."

Alex nodded and pocketed the note. "Thank you, Missy." She handed the maid a few coins.

"I'll 'elp you up." She placed her hands in a cup shape with interlaced fingers and looked up at Alex.

Alex gathered her skirt and placed her slippered foot in the maid's hands. The horse shifted beneath her weight, making her heart pound harder. "Many thanks!" she whispered, and turned the horse away from the men, going in the other direction. She pushed her heels in his side and they jerked into a canter. *Please, God. Don't let me fall off this great beast!*

An hour later Alex was beginning to have serious doubts about the entire idea of finding her parents. The horse was skittish and easily spooked. The snapping of a twig, the chirping of birds, that rodent at the side of the road. Lord help her, he had reared at the sight of the creature. Well, just the tiniest bit, but it had nearly thrown her onto her back! Now, she had no choice but to cling to the saddle with clenched thighs and the leather reins with a white-knuckled death grip. Her whole body ached with the tense muscles of pent-up anxiety. Would she ever make it to Whitehaven?

The sound of hooves pounding along the dirt road made her stop. Could it be the soldiers? Eyes wide, she scanned the road ahead and behind. There, behind her, were several horses kicking up a cloud of dirt. Panic rose to her throat as she jerked around, searching for a place to hide. She looked to the left and right, but all she saw was a lovely little valley where farmland reigned. Not a tree or building in sight.

She could try to outrun them, couldn't she? Folly. That's all that was. Why hadn't she thought to bring a gun?

Truth be known, she hadn't thought about what traveling alone would be like at all. She was so used to being on her own, though surrounded by people she knew and loved, that she hadn't imagined being alone with strangers, some possibly dangerous. It was quite different.

Having no choice but to brazen it out, she thrust out her chin, threw her shoulders back, and continued on her way. Her horse, though, had other plans. As soon as the other horses drew near, he grew even more agitated, stepping from side to side in a strange dance and ignoring her haul on the reins.

"Cease . . . whoa!" she hissed between her lips as a group of soldiers came to a stop around her. She looked up to see the dreaded Lieutenant Haggerty.

Heart pounding, she pasted on a smile and turned to face him.

"Lady Featherstone!" His face registered his shock. "Whatever are you doing on the open roads traveling alone? Why didn't you wait for my escort?"

Alex tried not to openly look to heaven for help. "My dear Lieutenant. What a surprise. So . . . good to see you again," she choked out the words.

"But, my lady, you haven't answered my question. You can't possibly be alone on the open roads! It isn't safe or fitting for a woman of your station . . . your —" He sputtered to a stop as if too aghast to finish.

Alex dipped her head and gave him her prettiest smile. "As you say, sir. But alas, my coachman was struck down with an illness and I must get to Whitehaven. I've a ship to catch. I fear I insisted. It isn't so very far, is it?"

The lieutenant's face turned an alarming shade of red and then, seeming to recover from his shock, his eyes narrowed at her. She thought of his behavior of the night before and her very real fear of him caused her blood to rush faster through her veins. But how to get rid of him?

"Since you have so little regard for your reputation, Lady Featherstone, I see that I shall have to insist on accompanying you to Whitehaven." Before she had time to protest, he turned and barked out orders to his men. "Continue your patrols on the eastern roads from Carlisle. I will meet back up with you in a few days."

"Sir, that is not necess—"

He put up his gloved hand and snapped his head toward her. "Don't. Not another word. I insist."

A deep, crawling panic washed over her. This man was offended with her and wanted to teach her a lesson . . . maybe more. The thought of what *more* meant made her shudder, but she was determined not to show him any fear. That would be exactly what he wanted. As the other men rode away, leaving the two of them alone on an empty road, she swallowed hard, very much afraid.

As soon as the soldiers were out of sight, the lieutenant chuckled. Alex looked him in the eyes, dread pooling in her stomach. Before she had time to do anything, he reached over and grasped the reins of her horse.

"Unhand him!" Alex screeched. She grasped hold of the other side of the reins and jerked to free it but he was too strong.

"You are no gentleman! Unhand my horse!"

The dark-haired man laughed, his mustache winging into a creepy smile of its own. "And you are no lady, traveling alone like a common harlot. Sit still!"

Sorrel was not taking the tug-of-war any better than she was. He skidded to one side and then the other, trying to rip the reins from both their hands.

"Ahhh!" A sudden rearing flung Alex backward where she flew through the air to land on her back with a loud *humph,* the breath knocked out of her. She lay dazed, unable to breathe, wondering if she was injured. Maybe this was it. Maybe she would never breathe again and she would die, right here and now. She would never know what had happened to her parents.

No! She sat up with a short gasp and then another and another. Dizziness flooded her but she fought it, shaking her head and trying to stand to run. The lieutenant had dismounted and was coming toward her.

"I've had enough of this nonsense. It's time to teach you a lesson."

She looked up and then beyond him. The light of the sun glared in her eyes. She must be seeing things. She blinked several times. No, he was still there.

A man stood in the middle of the road, a long wooden beam across his shoulders with a water bucket dangling from each side. He wore a long cape that swayed against his dusty boots as he walked toward them. He

121

had a bright green apple in one hand and, as if from some story of old, he took a bite of it and then casually tossed it aside.

The noise of the dropped apple caused the lieutenant to jerk around. He turned toward the stranger and took a few steps toward him. He reached for his gun, his hand lingering on the edge of it. "Hold, sir. This is none of your affair. Carry on your way."

"Do you agree with his assessment, miss?" He directed his intense stare at Alex.

She scrambled up and backed away. "No, I do not. I do not know this man. He threatened me. Please . . . help me."

"That wouldn't be wise, old man." The lieutenant took another step forward and pulled out his gun. "I have no difficulty sending you to your Maker."

Alex watched in a mixture of dread and fascination as, with catlike grace, he came up to the lieutenant. Before she knew what happened, faster than her eyes could track it, he swung one side of the wooden beam around and smacked the lieutenant against his arm, knocking the gun from his hand. Quicker yet, and before the lieutenant regained his balance, he swung the other side around and plowed wood and full bucket into the lieutenant's other side, drenching him with water.

Alex took a few staggering steps toward the scene. As she grew closer, she recognized the face. It was the man from last night. The one in the common room who had been watching the lieutenant with those hard, blue eyes. Who was he?

Admiration filled her as he threw off the beam. He looked older but moved with the strength and speed of a younger man. She watched in growing astonishment as he threw back his cape and pulled forth a long, wicked-looking sword. The sun caught the metal, the dazzling brightness hurting her eyes. It swished through the air with a voice of its own, playing with the lieutenant, making him sputter and dance and sweat.

The lieutenant tried to pull his sword out of its long scabbard, but it seemed stuck and he appeared too busy trying to avoid her savior's sword to manage it.

There was a stealthy grace in the older man's silent work. The sword said it all. Swooshing through the air it cut here and there, high and then low. He made it look like child's play while the lieutenant writhed in agony. Red started to appear on the lieutenant's shoulders, arms, thighs, and then in a sudden move that made Alex gasp, he held the blade's tip to the lieutenant's throat.

"You'll be going home now," the mysterious man said in a deep voice that held a hint of an accent.

The lieutenant nodded, short and quick, panic making his eyes wide and unblinking.

"And I don't think you will be needing your horse." The man lifted his foot and kicked the lieutenant to the ground. He then put his black-booted foot on top of the lieutenant's chest and leaned over him. "If I ever catch you near this young lady again, I will finish what we have begun, understand? I, alas, do not send men to their Maker lightly." His voice was like the sword, deadly velvet, soft and strong. He cocked his head and flashed a mirthless smile. "Be gone!"

The lieutenant nodded his agreement. The moment the man's foot rose from his chest, the lieutenant stood and backed away. He turned, his clothes in tatters, and ran in the other direction.

Alex covered her mouth with one gloved hand to keep her mirth from showing as the lieutenant ran away like a scalded dog.

The man sheathed his sword as he walked up to her. He looked at her for a long moment, with eyes that held a searching intelligence in them that made Alex both want to shrink back and rise to meet his stare at the same time. He took off his hat to reveal long, gray hair, bowed, an exaggerated movement but still, so full of grace that she couldn't help smiling.

"Thank you," she breathed. "Who are you?"

He placed his hat back on his head and pulled two apples from his pocket. He polished one on the front of his waistcoat and then held it out to her. "You may call me Montague. It would appear I am your guide to Whitehaven, for as foolish as our dear lieutenant is, he is right in one thing. It is not safe for mademoiselle to travel alone."

"Oh, I'm sure that isn't necessary."

"You don't think so?" He stared at her, waiting for her to admit the truth.

"Perhaps that would be best. I thank you, kind sir."

He reached out a hand and took her arm in a gentle grasp. "Can you eat your apple and ride? I find it a beneficial skill, eating while riding. Mayhap we can get this fearful beast of yours to take a nibble. Might calm him down too."

Alex nodded, realizing she had started to shake from the ordeal. "Yes, I find the idea of an apple quite to my liking right now."

He helped her mount and handed her the

apple. "I thought as much. Shall we, Lady Featherstone?"

She sniffed, a short and childish sound, then took a loud bite, the tart juice running down her chin. The horse stood docile as Montague fed him his apple. She swallowed hard and took a few calming breaths as they began to walk. The horse, too, seemed inclined to follow the man who held his reins, more docile than he'd ever been with Alex.

"We will go to my house for some provisions. Then to Whitehaven. It isn't very far, my lady."

Alex nodded, feeling the burden of being alone and solely responsible for her success lift from her shoulders. He was like an angel sent from above to help her.

How had he known what the two of them needed?

And how had he known her name?

# Chapter Nine

The morning after the ball Gabriel woke drenched in sweat. He turned over and then sat up, running his fingers through the pasted hair against his scalp, pulling the nightshirt away from his chest and where it was plastered against his back. What was wrong with him? Maybe he was just anxious about traveling. He would have to take Meade along, of course, and it would be quicker to go overland. There was so much planning to do. The thought brought a bout of anxiety mixed with excitement to his stomach.

What was she like?

What would she really think of him?

Should he hide his condition, or would she be the first one he told of his own accord? The thought of her, despising his weakness once she discovered what it really was, wasn't half as bad as the image of her feeling sorry for him. He drew a deep breath and closed his eyes for a moment. This was his life now and he had to keep living it, whatever her reaction. She needed him.

He swung his legs around and stood. Abrupt dizziness rushed through his head, making the room spin and tilt. He fell back on the bed with an exhale, as if all the breath had been knocked from his chest, and planted both hands on either side of the feather ticking for support. Slow, deep breaths. He concentrated on it.

But something was wrong. Something was terribly wrong.

The door to his dressing room opened; must be his valet. He turned his head. Too fast. The dizziness washed through him in another wave. "Get Meade." He directed his valet.

"Yes, Your Grace. Right away."

Gabriel's head shot up despite the need to sit very still to control the dizzy sensation. Had he just heard the man speak? Hope flared, so bright within him he dared not breathe for fear of mistaking the moment. The sound had been dim and as if he were under water, but it had been a sound nonetheless. He wanted to stand and rush over to his valet, grab him by the departing shoulder, spin him around, and demand he speak again, but he felt so dizzy and nauseous. Instead he yelled, "George, wait. Come back!"

His man turned back to him, alarm on his face as he hurried over. "Your Grace, please get back into bed. You look pale. Do you feel faint?"

Gabriel allowed him to plump up the pillows and pull the coverlet over his legs. He closed his eyes, trying to block the sensation of the room tilting. "George, I do believe, if you speak loud and clear, that I can make out what you are saying."

"Sir!" The excitement in his man's voice was unmistakable.

"I feel terrible. Dizzy, my stomach rolling, especially when I open my eyes. The room, it tilts back and forth. Call the doctors and Meade. Tell them to hurry."

George's hand reached out and grasped his arm in a comforting hold. "Praise be to God, Your Grace. It is a miracle!"

Gabriel shook his head as the words came together in his mind. Miracle. It's what he'd been praying for, begging for God in the quiet hours of the night when no one could see how ravished he felt by this new fate. Yes. A miracle. God had listened. He had really answered his prayers. Or maybe it was Alexandria's prayers? He would be able to hear her!

Fear dogged his fledgling faith. Fear said it wouldn't last. That he knew something was not right. If his hearing was coming back, even if it remained this strange, clogged form of hearing, he would be eternally grateful. But if he couldn't open his eyes without feeling like he was going to fall on the floor — that was almost worse. A miserable thought, that. But the fact that something was changing, shifting inside, might be a good sign. Meade had better hurry. Gabriel clenched his fists and breathed hard through his nose. He had to see those doctors.

It seemed an eternity waiting for them. George brought coffee and toast and then tea and then a cup of steaming chocolate, trying to tempt his palate, but just the thought of anything on his stomach made it churn all the harder. He could only cling to a precarious state of balance by remaining very still with his eyes closed.

Suddenly he heard the door slam against the wall. He *heard* it!

"Your Grace, is it true? Can you hear me?" Meade's voice was an exultant shout from across the cavernous room.

Gabriel held out one hand, eyes still shut. "You sound ten leagues under the sea, but I can make it out." He couldn't help his grin.

"Only problem now is an overwhelming dizziness. Can't seem to open my eyes without feeling the urge to retch. Get those ear doctors from Moorfields down here — Saunders and Curtis, wasn't it? And tell Bentley. The family doctor won't want to be left out of any credit for a cure."

Sweat trickled down his face at the exertion. "And get me a chamber pot in case I'm sick. God, help me, this dizziness is almost worse than not hearing." But he had a smile in his voice as he shouted out the orders. He was hearing again! The other symptoms were temporary, of course. No one suffered from permanent dizziness. Did they?

Meade said something but it was too low and muddled to make out, and he dared not open his eyes yet. "Say it again, Meade. Loud and clear."

"I said right away, Your Grace. Just sit tight and I will get the doctors."

The man was probably shouting, but Gabriel didn't care. He could hear him. His face broke into a great grin. He started to laugh with the joy of it, but the movement made the falling feeling worsen, like he had jumped from a tall cliff and was falling, falling, falling. He grasped at the blanket with both fists as if to stop his fall.

Within the hour, he had three doctors leaning over him, pressing and prodding and inserting metal objects into his ears. They were talking among themselves, but he could only catch a word here and there, as they were speaking too low and fast. He tried to tamp down his annoyance while fighting the fear. It seemed he could only hear when there was one person talking at a time, and then only if he spoke very slowly and clearly. Finally, he'd had enough.

"If you please, doctors. What is the diagnosis?" He knew his voice was loud, but he didn't care.

He cracked his eyes open and peered at them through the slits. They all stopped talking at once and took a step back. Dr. Bentley cleared his throat and looked to be shouting. "It seems you have some of your hearing returning, Your Grace. We are still consulting on the vertiginous nature of your current situation. Dr. Saunders recommends a hot tea made from linden, taken three times a day. It may help if you have water behind the ear."

Water behind the ear? Gabriel pictured the anatomy of the ear and what he had read on vertigo. He'd done a study on anatomy years ago, one branch of science in a long course of study during his twenties, even going as far as visiting the famed La Specola Collection in Florence. He thought of the delicate makeup of the inner and outer ear. It was possible that a diuretic could help. He would try just about anything, of course.

"Yes, yes, get the tea. Meade, send someone to Apothecary's Alley posthaste. Buy it all if you have to." He turned his head in a slow and careful movement toward the doctors. "How long will this infernal dizziness last? And will the hearing yet improve?"

Dr. Curtis stepped forward. He was a young man with the Napoleon hairstyle of forward-combed waves that was all the rage in France and immaculate in his dress. "We don't know, Your Grace. Cases like this are rare. However, it looks promising and, in the meantime, you can use an ear trumpet to help facilitate the sound."

An ear trumpet. *Wonderful.* Like an old man. But he shouldn't complain. He should be on his knees thanking God he could hear anything at all. And if the tea helped control the dizziness and nausea, well, he would be almost as good as normal. Good enough, by the Lord's grace and mercy. He would go back to church. Most sermons sent him into a dozing state of boredom, but now he would pay close attention to every word.

And the opera! The faint hope that he might be able to hear music again gripped him in a sudden euphoria. He rubbed his face with a hand, hoping his lips weren't quivering. Just the thought of it made his heart pound in excitement. He would take the ear trumpet to the opera and not care how it looked. It would be worth it. He would go this afternoon if he could get out of this infernal bed and walk!

But he couldn't leave his bed. The dizziness plagued him for three more days, sometimes so badly he did lose the contents of his stomach. He was growing thin and dehydrated — a new source of fear. If nothing else, he had to keep the liquids down, including the linden tea that made him run to the chamber pot more times than he could count, which was not helping his body's ability to hold enough of the water he was drinking. It was a cycle that wasn't working. Taking a diuretic for the inner ear and then not able to keep down enough nourishment to give him strength. He was fading . . . he could feel it. Little by little, no energy. He started to think he just might die of it.

Then, the fourth day, the dizziness stopped as quickly as it had started. He woke up one morning and found he could turn his head without the room spinning. There was a dull ringing in his ears that made hearing a bit more difficult but still, he could hear if the person speaking was slow and concise in pronunciation and loud. It was a far cry from normal, but it was an improvement.

Another two days of nourishment and his strength began to return. By the end of another week he was moving, slowly, through some of his routine. Now for a test. Before he could even consider the long tedium and endurance required to travel across half of England to Holy Island and his recalcitrant ward, he felt he had to successfully attend the opera. The place where the nightmare had begun.

The night air was chilly as he threw his greatcoat around his shoulders, the ear trumpet in one pocket, and strode toward the high carriage with the St. Easton coat of arms emblazoned on the side. The motto, *his motto,* stood in bold, scrolling French underneath the unicorn and bull. *Foy pour devoir* — "faith for duty." He paused as he thought of it. He certainly knew the duty part. Settling himself inside the carriage, he leaned his head back against the high seat and closed his eyes. The carriage started with a jerk down the street toward the Theatre Royal in Drury Lane.

It was difficult, the anticipation, the half hope, half dread of facing people and more, facing the moment of whether or not he could hear the music well enough to be enjoyed. The carriage pulled up in front of the grand building and stopped. He didn't wait for his coachman to open the door but, rather, sprang out and clamped down on his hat in the stiff breeze, eager now, desperate almost, to have it over with.

The crowd was thin, a deliberate calculation as he was quite late. Head down, he rushed through the elegant reception room toward a back staircase, avoiding the wide, curving stairway where some of the elegantly clad members of the ton still loitered, hoping to see and be seen. He met a servant on the way up but ignored the questioning stare. He strode down the darkened hall where the boxes of the most affluent flanked the balcony that overlooked the crowd below. Almost there. Just as he thought it, a rush of satisfaction filled his chest and an acquaintance stepped into his path.

He looked up in time to keep from crashing into the man. There was an elegant woman on his arm but her name escaped him.

"Your Grace, so good to see you again. It's been some time since you've visited the opera. We were all beginning to worry."

Gabriel watched his lips and tried to keep up with the steady, inane chatter. "Lord Berwin." He inclined his head to the man and then the lady. "I've been rather occupied of late, but I'm eager to hear tonight's performance."

The man had the gall to clap him on the shoulder, which made his ears start to ring in that annoying way that blocked more of the sound. Despair and anger filled him, flagging heat into his cheeks. He blew out a breath and gave the man a stare that warned him not to touch him again.

Berwin seemed to take the hint in a tirade of mumbled apologies and a backward step. With a bow toward Gabriel, he turned the woman aside and scurried away, coattails flapping.

Gabriel pressed his fingers against the bridge of his nose and took a deep breath. His box. He just needed to sit down in the quiet of his box.

A few moments later he settled himself into the dark shadows of the back of the small enclosure. He pulled out the ear horn and held it loosely in his lap. Every muscle in his body strained as the curtain went up and the woman on stage opened her mouth to sing. It was faint, dulled, wavy.

He rubbed his temples and then the aching spot between his eyes. God help him. His head began to ache and his heart pound. What if it happened again? He stared at the stage, willing himself to hear the beauty of the notes, willing the experience to produce the same emotion it always did.

*Dear God, I need this!*

The sound dulled further, as if falling down a long, narrow tunnel. It grew dimmer and dimmer. Gabriel pressed the ear trumpet further into his ear, mounting desperation gripping him. He was losing it again. He would leave this place deaf again. *Oh, God.* He gripped the trumpet in his fist, squeezing, hard. In some faraway place he felt it crumble into pieces in his hand. He opened his hand and looked down at the tortoiseshell. It lay in beautiful shards of blue-green in his palm, some falling to the floor.

*God, please. Don't let this happen.*

He had to get out. Run.

He was just rising, panic thick in his throat, when he saw something from the edges of his vision. He fell back into the chair, afraid his head would burst open as it had the last time he'd attended the opera.

He closed his eyes and took long, deep breaths. There was no pain. He couldn't hear more than a faint shadow of the music but there was no pain. His eyes fluttered open. Pinpricks and then faint streaks of color — blue, purple, green — streamed across his vision. He blinked, the colors pulsing in time with the music. It was coming from the stage, from the orchestra and the woman singing. The colors waved and undulated, pulsing around each other, streams of living color.

*God, what is happening to me?* A strange, unknown fear washed over him. So beautiful. It wasn't the same as hearing the music, but . . . it was terrifyingly beautiful.

# CHAPTER TEN

The October wind blew gusts of chilly air in her face and down her cloak as Alex rounded the bend in the road toward White-haven. It was a coastal town known for its coal and its harbor, Alex knew that much. Ships traded coal, tobacco, and rum from here, making it a crowded and growing little city. She drew out the note with the address Missy had given her and glanced aside at her traveling companion.

He'd not said much since rescuing her, just trotted beside her on the lieutenant's horse as if he'd been riding him all his life and they were bosom mates. She was hesitant to be the one to break the silence, but there was nothing for it so she pasted a bright smile on her face and waved the note toward him. "I have to return this horse to a man named Paul Keys. His sister loaned him to me for this journey."

"Ah." His striking blue eyes flashed toward

the note and then back on the road.

"I have the address here, but I must confess as to having no idea where to find . . ." she glanced down at the scrawled address, "43 Lowther Street. Do you know Whitehaven?"

"Well enough." He grinned at her, a brief, almost humorless action that made wrinkles break out across his face.

"Oh, good. I was dreading searching it out. One never knows the best place to stop and ask questions in an unfamiliar town." She smiled at him, trying to encourage a response.

He looked at her, a long and considering glance this time. "What makes you take this journey? It must be something important for you to be taking such risks alone."

Alex nodded, gazing down at her gloved hands. He would think her stupid. She should come up with some reasonable explanation for her journey to tell people, but her mind was blank of any excuse except for the truth. "Well, I received a letter that the regent and some other people believe my parents are . . . have perished." She swallowed hard and looked over at him. "I believe I'm going to find out if it's true."

"You have reason to believe it's not?"

"Well, yes. You see, my parents are often

far from home on some adventure or another. They are something like treasure hunters, sleuths you might say. People hire them to find things or to solve a puzzle. It's true," she asserted when his eyebrows came together in a puzzled way. "They are quite famous for it."

"Hmmm. And how long have they been away this time?"

Alex bit down on her lower lip. "A year. And yes, that is longer than usual, but I've had letters from them. And . . . I just know they're alive. They may be in trouble. They may need me."

"So, you are going off alone to find them?"

Put like that, it did sound rash, ridiculous really. She didn't even have a weapon or the knowledge of how to use it should she magically discover one. "I didn't see any choice," she muttered back toward her hands.

"When did you receive the last letter?"

Alex grimaced. "About ten months ago." She rushed out the rest. "The postmark is from Belfast in Ireland. I may find clues as to what happened to them there. They must have spoken to people. I know I can find out what has happened to them. I . . . I have to try. I can't go back and just sit and wait. I can't." Tears threatened her eyes.

Montague cleared his throat. "Well, you've

made it thus far, haven't you?"

She sniffed and faced the wind and the edge of town. "Yes, I suppose I have."

He didn't say anything for several minutes and then abruptly, "I have a nephew who lives in Dublin. Perhaps now would be a good time for a visit."

Alex swung back toward him, her eyes widening. Was he offering to travel with her? Keep her safe? It was as if God had sent her an old, warring angel as her guard. "I'm sure your nephew would be most happy to see you." She gave him a bright smile, which made him clear his throat and look away.

A little happy thrill ran through her. He had all but agreed!

They turned down a narrow street, Montague motioning for her to follow him, and soon stood outside what looked to be a quaint little shop of some kind. It had large windows on the ground floor and smaller windows, probably where the proprietor lived, on the upper floor. The sign on the building read Keys Pottery with the number 43 above it. This must be where Missy's brother lived.

They dismounted, saw that the horses were secured to a hitching post, and then went through a green door. The interior was a bit dark and it took Alex a few seconds for her eyes to adjust. Once they did, she smiled. There were shelves and cupboards on every wall with rows and rows of bowls and cups and pitchers and pipes. Many had designs of ships on the water in pretty colors. How she wished she could take something home to Ann. She would just swoon over the large pitcher with its soaring birds circling on it.

A voice interrupted her. "May I help you?"

She looked up to see the male copy of Missy. Dark curly hair and big brown eyes. She smiled at him. "I'm looking for a Mr. Paul Keys."

He flushed and cast a glance aside. "That would be me."

"Oh, wonderful. You see, I've just come from Carlisle and your sister loaned me a horse to ride. His name is Sorrell and he belongs to your sister's friend. She asked if I would bring him here, to you, while I continue on my way to Ireland."

Paul glanced at Montague standing beside her. "You want me to keep a horse?"

"Just for a few hours. Your sister is coming to fetch him later tonight when she finishes her work for the day. It was so kind of her as my carriage broke down." She paused, realizing her story had changed, and tried to remember if she'd said something

144

different to Montague.

"That is, my coachman took ill and had to go to the next town and do some business and —" Her hands waved in the air like a ninny. She really needed to stop making up things so readily! "Anyway, she loaned me the horse and said to bring him to you. You don't mind, do you?" The fact that her lashes started involuntarily batting just a bit faster made her feel wretched but she waited, letting the silence grow in a way no one had taught her but always seemed to work.

Paul flushed a deeper color of pink and looked around the room. "I'd be glad to take him off your hands, miss."

"Oh, how silly of me!" Alex held out her hand. "I'm Alexandria Featherstone and" — she turned to Montague and gestured toward him with a gloved hand — "this is my kind escort, Mr. Montague."

She gave him a sunny smile and raised her eyebrows. "I do wish I could purchase something from your shop to take back home. You have so many fine things! But, alas, I shall be traveling for some time and shouldn't add to my baggage if I can help it."

"Thank you, Miss Featherstone. Perhaps on your way back?"

"Oh yes. That is a very good idea. I shall have to remember that."

Paul hesitated. "I do have something rather small." He turned and scurried away, his tall form darting through a door and then around a corner, and then he was back with something in his hand. He opened his hand and held out a small white duck with two tiny yellow ducklings.

"Oh, how cute they are! Did you make them yourself?" Out of the corner of her eye she caught Montague rolling his eyes, arms crossed in front of him.

"Yes, and I would like you to have them. They won't take up much room at all."

"I couldn't just take them. How much do they cost?"

"I insist." He held the trio out until Alex allowed him to drop them into her hand.

"Thank you so much. You are too kind, sir."

He smiled at her, pointedly turning away from Montague. "Perhaps they will remind you to stop here on your way back home."

"Oh, yes. It has been a pleasure, sir."

They made their way outside and delivered Sorrell over to the eager-looking young man. She mounted the lieutenant's horse and Montague swung up behind her. She leaned around him and waved good-bye until Paul was out of sight, saying, "What a nice young man he was!"

"Humph."

Alex faced forward, ignoring the comment. Just ahead she could see a glimpse of the water. They were so close. After going about two more blocks toward the harbor, she just barely heard Montague mutter, "Nice young man, hmmm? The real danger is the men falling all over themselves around her. Doesn't need a protector. A muzzle would do just fine. A muzzle and a potato sack over her head."

Alex gasped. "A potato sack! You wouldn't dare! Maybe your nephew doesn't need a visit from you after all. Maybe he's busy!"

Montague gave her upper arm a little squeeze. "Don't forget whose horse we're riding. You don't think he'll come after it? I wonder at his mood when he next sees you."

Instant fear struck Alex's heart at his words. "Sorry. Perhaps I was a little hasty. I do appreciate your company. Thank you, Montague. I'll try and not encourage unwanted attention."

"That would be wise, my dear. Whenever on a mission of any importance or secrecy, one must learn to blend into the background."

Alex let the words sink in, knowing their

truth. "Montague, how did you learn these things? And how did you learn to fight so well?"

"I was a soldier for many years," his deep voice murmured. "And I've traveled on the king's business throughout the world. It took many years to subdue my nature and train my body into submission. My goal is that of the apostle who said, 'Be not conformed to this world: but be ye transformed by the renewing of your mind, that ye may prove what is that good, and acceptable, and perfect, will of God.' "

Alex thought about the Scripture. She wasn't sure if tearing off to find her parents was God's will or not; truth be told, she had been too afraid to ask Him and hear something she didn't want to hear. But the Scripture Montague quoted seemed a much bigger picture than asking for a specific answer for God's direction. It was almost as if asking no matter what she did or where she went, He would use it to prove her, to make her into what was good and acceptable. She had to only be not conformed to this world and renew her mind. "How does one renew the mind to prove out the will of God?"

"Through Scripture and trials." Montague chuckled. "Your journey should give you plenty of trials."

"Oh, dear," Alex murmured. "I'm not sure I like the sound of that."

Montague barked out another laugh. He didn't say anything else, just nudged the horse's sides and hurried them along to the harbor and the ferry that would take them across the Irish Sea.

The ferry, *Saint Patrick,* rocked along on the Irish Sea, crowded and cold, wet and windy. The wind that had seemed harsh on the road was like a cutting force driving its cold fingers through Alex's clothes on board the deck of the ship. She stood at the rail, looking across at the choppy, gray water while Montague had gone off on some unknown errand. She was learning it was better not to question him too closely about his affairs. His frown when she overstepped his invisible privacy boundary was enough to send a dog scurrying away with its tail tucked between its legs. He would find her when he was ready, she was sure of that. And more, he wouldn't have left her unless he thought her safe.

She glanced around at the people squeezed in beside her. More women and children than she would have thought. The journey was to take four hours to the Isle of

Man, the destination of some of her fellow passengers, and then another three to Belfast. It had cost them seventeen shillings each. She'd offered to pay Montague's way, but of course he'd given her that look and she'd let the matter drop like a hot potato fished from the coals.

Thinking of him must have conjured him up, as he came up from behind her. He was holding out a piece of paper.

"After I bought our tickets I went to the post office to check for any correspondence. Seems you have someone of importance writing to you."

Alex bit down on her lower lip and took the letter. Only the duke would be important enough for someone to forward it on to Whitehaven. She had instructed Ann to speed any letters to her along the route to Belfast while she was gone. What if her parents wrote? She had to have her mail.

Taking the letter, she glanced down at the long, bold lines of the duke's familiar handwriting. She thought back to her plea for more funds. Had he believed her? Had he sent it? "Thank you, Montague." She turned away and peeled up the ducal seal. Swallowing hard, she opened it and began to read.

Dear Lady Featherstone,

It has become apparent from your letters that you are in need of guidance and direction. I shall be traveling to Holy Island posthaste to assist you in the calamities that have befallen you since the death of your parents. Fear not, my dear, I shall take care of everything.

Could you relay your measurements in your next letter? I understand you are in need of a new wardrobe, and I would like to have London's best modiste make up the latest in fashionable attire for a young woman of your status. No ward of mine will be found traipsing about the countryside in rags. A description of your coloring might be advantageous as well.

I confess that I am looking forward to the pleasure of meeting you in person and putting a face to the impression you have made in my mind. And I find myself thankful for your prayers and offer to confide in you. We will talk more of this on Holy Island.

Yours,
St. Easton

Alex leaned back against the railing with a groan, her heart sinking with dread.

"Something amiss?" Montague asked, one brow cocked.

Alex nodded and pressed her gloved hand to her mouth. Oh, dear. Yes, something was going to be very much amiss.

# CHAPTER ELEVEN

Gabriel stumbled through his front door, slammed it shut, and leaned against it. He was breathing as if he'd run from the opera house instead of riding in his comfortable carriage. His driver had taken one look at what must have been the wildness on his face and hurried them through the London streets to home. The whole way Gabriel tried to convince himself he was not losing his mind. Worse, was the feeling that something was not right with his mind.

He remembered an essay he'd read long ago by Jonathan Swift on matters of the brain and wondered if he still had it. Swift and others had written about experimentation with electrical current to correct the brain's function. Maybe Gabriel should start thinking of more alternative methods to gain back more of his hearing. Yes, that was it. He needed to pull out books and old manuscripts he'd studied years ago and find his own cure. He was more educated than the physicians anyway.

There had been a time in his life when he'd wished he was not a duke and could study medicine and become a physician, not that he'd breathed that thought aloud. A short bark of a laugh escaped his throat as he pushed away from the door and imagined the look on his father's face had he dared mention his many interests over the years. Dukes were supposed to conduct themselves in the powerful realm of politics, social politics mostly, but in times of war a duke's influence could, and many times did, impact history.

And it wasn't that he didn't cultivate the appropriate relationships, he did. But it was all so easy, and the only thing to keep the numbing boredom at bay was a constant challenge. He'd always craved intense study and then, after learning all he could on a topic, he became bored, despondent for a while, until the next stage of interest surfaced. The pattern repeated itself all through his life — diving into study and discovery with heady glee and then plummeting into despondency when he'd learned all he could on the topic. By his thirtieth birthday he had studied every branch of science, history, geology, agriculture, languages, mathematics, philosophy, and religion, not neglecting the physical challenges of swordplay, the mastery of all sorts of weapons, wrestling, horse breeding and racing; the list was nearly endless.

When all that failed to impress him any longer, he turned to the last unknown — the arts. Avenues of endless creativity. Painting, sculpting, drawing, he tried his hand at poetry and even inventing. But music had become the only passion he knew would never fade. He had one of the most elegant music rooms in the world back home in Wiltshire. He'd spent hours there, trying to learn the pianoforte, the violin, voice. And he'd failed, miserably failed. He saw the natural ability, the genius of Mozart, Beethoven, Bach, and Handel and knew he would never, not if he studied the rest of his life, master a miniscule piece of score as they had.

Seeing his butler approach, he pulled himself back to the present and took off his coat, handing it over.

"You have a caller, Your Grace."

"Eh?" Gabriel said the word and then bit down on his tongue. The butler's voice was probably loud enough to wake the dead, but Gabriel had to pay close attention to hear him. He watched the man's lips move as he repeated the phrase.

"A caller? Who is it?" He couldn't imagine seeing anyone right now, except maybe for Albert, but he'd gone back to the country, the place where Gabriel *should* be — hiding out, not attending operas and planning trips to Northumberland.

"Sir Edward Brooke, Your Grace." The butler held out a calling card.

Gabriel took it and read the name. Edward Brooke. One of the prince regent's advisors and a friend to the prime minister, Earl of Liverpool, a most powerful man. How the deuce was he supposed to carry off a full conversation? He had to face facts. By taking this meeting he would risk everything. Once the royal court knew of his fate, it wouldn't take any time at all for the gossips to inform the whole of English society.

Gabriel pictured the crumbling of the empire he'd spent the last nine years building. They would lose faith in him. If he showed any weakness, they would not trust him. It was all a house of cards anyway, investments based on relationships based on other investments. But what could he do? Brooke was obviously bent on seeing him if he had waited for his return from the opera. Gabriel couldn't avoid him forever. One did not refuse the regent's men when they called. It was tantamount to refusing the prince regent, and that kind of behavior could lead all the way to treason and the tower.

Taking a bracing breath, he nodded to his butler and turned toward the front salon where guests were received. He reached for the door handle and paused. His hand trembled, fear pounding like a shadow against his soul. *Stop it.* He could still hear well enough to help. Between that and reading the man's lips, he might muddle through. He turned the handle and pressed open the door.

"Sir Edward, what a surprise. I am sorry to have kept you waiting."

The man, a stocky gentleman with deep sideburns and a head of black hair heavily threaded with gray, stood and gave Gabriel a brief bow. He said some polite trifle about inconveniences with a hand motion of brushing them aside. Gabriel walked over to the sideboard and motioned toward the crystal decanters.

Brooke nodded in response. Gabriel turned his back to him to pour the drinks but glanced over his shoulder as he did so to see if he was speaking. He was not. Gabriel took the glass over to him and held it out. He turned and seated himself across from Brooke and then tapped his ear, inspiration coming to him. "I fear I am suffering from a dastardly cold that has clogged my ears up something terrible. You may have to speak up, and if that doesn't work, write down the nature of your visit." He waited, breath held, for the reaction.

Brooke's eyes narrowed but he nodded and spoke louder, his lips clearly enunciating the next words. "I'm sorry to hear that, Your Grace. Have you seen a doctor? The prince regent's own physician may be available if you would like me to put in a request."

"No, no, it's nothing." Gabriel waved away the concern. "I have excellent physicians on the case. Should just be a matter of time and then" — he tapped his temple three times — "good as new."

"Oh, well, that is a relief, isn't it?"

"What can I do for you?"

Brooke looked off to one side for a brief moment, as if collecting his thoughts, and then his intense, intelligent eyes met his. "I have a favor to ask of you. Actually, the prince regent has a favor to ask."

"The prince regent? I hope I haven't done anything to displease His Majesty." Gabriel took a bracing drink and set the glass on the table. Just what he needed. The prince regent wanting a favor from him.

"Not at all." Brooke assured with a wave of his hand. "I know you are a member of the Antiquities Society, yes?"

Unease coiled within Gabriel like an awakening snake. The fellows of that society were an odd lot, feverish with their passion for the earth's treasures. "Antiquities, you say?"

"Yes." Brooke nodded.

"I am a member of the society, as with most of London's societies and clubs, but I've been little active of late. My collection is far inferior to most of the members' collections. It was one of my passing phases of diversion, I'm afraid. Why do you ask?"

Brooke pressed his lips together and breathed deeply from his nose, his barrel-shaped chest lifting in and out as he regarded Gabriel with alarming intent. For some reason the prince regent needed him. And Brooke wouldn't want to write it down; he wouldn't want that evidence, Gabriel was sure. Pinpricks of unease mixed with curiosity caused him to lean forward toward Brooke. Gabriel rested his elbows on the perfectly tailored breeches and lifted his brows in interest.

Brooke leaned forward as well, speaking slowly. "Have you heard of Hans Sloane?"

Gabriel looked away, thinking. The name rang a distant bell. Ah, the physician for King George II, wasn't it? A century or so ago? And the foremost collector of antiquities of his time. He nodded at Brooke. "An avid collector of antiquities, if I recall. Wasn't he the recipient of the famed collection of William Courten?"

"Yes, yes." Brooke's eyes took on an enthusiastic gleam. "Cabinets full of books, manuscripts, prints, drawings, flora, fauna, medals, coins, seals, and all sorts of curiosities."

"And with King George's library, they started the British Museum with the lot of it, yes?"

Brooke nodded with a small smile. "I had hoped you would know of it."

"Well, as I said, I am no expert on the topic. Most people know of Sloane." What could Brooke want with him on the matter? There were men far more knowledgeable than he on the subject.

"Your Grace, there is a manuscript long missing from the collection. It has come to the attention of the Crown that we must find that manuscript." He paused, took out a handkerchief, and dabbed at his forehead. "Many months ago I was assigned that task. I hired investigators, treasure hunters you might say, very well known for finding missing or hidden things from all ends of the earth." He paused again and waited, probably to see if Gabriel heard and understood.

"Yes, I understand. It's an interesting story but why involve me? I am not an expert at such things."

"No, but you are connected, recently, and the prince regent felt you should know. Actually, the prince regent insisted you know."

"Know?"

"Your ward, Lady Alexandria Featherstone."

Gabriel's head jerked up, a protective instinct rising inside him. "Yes?"

Brooke took a long drink and then set the empty glass on the table in front of him. He looked Gabriel in the eyes. "Her parents were the treasure hunters I hired. They had been looking for this manuscript for nearly a year, and then they disappeared. It seemed best to the prince regent to declare them dead, to throw off any others looking for them, but we are . . . not sure what has happened to them. We needed Alexandria to be under protection, and the prince regent thought it time to put you to good use, for you to do your duty to the Crown, so to speak. In truth, you are no relation to the

Featherstones, but it was the best way to explain your involvement. Alexandria could be in danger. Until we know the fate of her parents and find the manuscript, she will need your powerful protection. Do you see?"

Gabriel swallowed hard, thinking of her silly letters that brought an unexplainable joy to his heart. He'd been so caught up in his own tragedy . . . God forgive him, he hadn't taken care of her at all. He nodded. "I understand. I will bring her here and she will stay with me until this is settled. Please assure the prince regent that her well-being will become my utmost concern."

Brooke smiled, pleased. "Thank you, Your Grace."

He started to rise from the silk sofa but Gabriel stopped him with one hand. "One more question, if you please."

Brooke sat back down and folded his hands in his lap.

"If the danger is so fierce, I should know something of it. Something to look for, don't you think?"

Brooke pursed his lips and then laughed. "The prince regent said you would not be so easily put off and has given me permission to say this. There are three countries — Spain, France, and England — who have acquired a part of the manuscript, the same part. We believe the original was stolen as it disappeared from the museum's collection many years ago, but a partial copy has been found and what it appears to be is very . . . interesting to these kings. They all want the original, badly, to complete the picture, so to say."

Gabriel started to speak but Brooke held up his hand. "I can't tell you any more. Just know that very powerful people want to get their hands on this. They will do anything to have it. Alexandria is in grave danger and we are depending on you to keep her safe until it is found."

Gabriel nodded as the implications fell into place. This was far more serious than anything he had imagined. He had to get Alexandria to safety.

He had to get her home.

# CHAPTER TWELVE

The *Saint Patrick* rounded a bend in the channel as they approached Belfast Harbor, where gulls and other seabirds soared above the quay. Sea craft of all sizes, from great sailing ships to fishermen's boats, lumbered and bobbed alongside them. Tall buildings bathed in mist came into view, dotting along the streets in a sprawling little town, and beyond were rolling hills of green. Alex took a long breath of the sea air and smiled softly at the scene. It was just as she had imagined it.

"What do you think of your first look at Ireland?" Montague asked.

"The Land of Ever Young," Alex murmured. "It's magical."

As people began to disembark, they made their way to the shore. Montague kept her close by his side and seemed to be on alert. Alex looked around them, seeing a dark man, tall and rail-thin, with the hood of his black cape pulled over his head, standing just behind her, watching her. Alarm made her look at Montague. He nodded but said nothing. Someone was following them.

They walked down the quay of Belfast, the crowd thinning out and going each their own way. She continued to feel the sensation of being watched in a spine-crawling tingle. She looked to the left, over her shoulder, and saw that the strange man had fallen back. She had a sudden longing for a long black cloak and dark dress instead of the bright red one, which covered the blue dress that was her best. Her mother's armoire of plain dark clothing took on new meaning. Her parents knew such things, didn't they? Memories of mysterious visitors, closed doors, and whispered conversations swept across her mind. They had taken cases for as long as she could remember. As she grew older she'd asked to be included, but they always insisted it was too dangerous. She was too young. But what Alex really felt they were saying was, "You do not have the talent. You are not worthy of it. We don't want you around."

She'd decided to show them, taking on the local mysteries and even some in nearby towns. She might not have the fame of her parents, but she'd begun to be known and eventually she'd thought they would hear of it and take her with them. Now she would save them and that would prove her worth more than anything could.

Determination forged through her with the thought. She shot a quick look over her right shoulder and saw a dark shape move further into the shadows of a building. His face was still in the depths of his hood, but his eyes had been staring at her. She turned forward and looked up at Montague.

"Did you see that man? He was staring at us, I'm sure of it."

"Aye. He has been following us since boarding at Whitehaven. I left your side to see what he would do, and he moved ever closer until I finally returned to you." His gaze scanned the crowded port of Belfast as they hurried into the bustling town. He stayed close to her side, muscles taut and ready, one hand caressing the hilt of the sword that swung from his belt.

Alex swallowed hard and kept her head down, hiding as much as possible behind the hood of her cloak. Thank God for Montague. She was glad all the way to her toes that she wasn't alone.

Montague reached for her arm with an abrupt tug. "There." He pointed and squinted up into the light. "See that place?

McHugh's. A good place to get some dinner and hear the latest news. Popular with travelers. Your parents may have gone there as well. Let's see if our friend follows us inside."

Alex nodded and quickened her steps to match the more-hurried gait of Montague's long stride. She looked back, a brief glance toward the ships in the port area, the gray water of the channel and cold Irish Sea was behind them. The man was nowhere to be seen.

The brick building of the inn loomed in front of them, taking up the corner of the street, three stories high with long, narrow windows on each floor. The first story had a false front with an awning made from whitewashed timbers and more timbers flanking the door. It looked a pleasant enough place and busy with people coming in and out. The door opened as they approached, spilling light and music onto the street. Alex took a quick look around before scurrying by the man exiting, Montague remaining just behind her.

She stopped inside and drew in a breath. Music came from a lantern-lit stage, music that gained her full attention at once. A woman with long, auburn hair stood at the front of the stage. She wore a pale green dress that glittered and fluttered around her with the moving air of the room. When she opened her mouth and began to sing, Alex's mouth dropped open. It was the sweetest, purest sound she had ever heard. The melody whispered and rang against a backdrop of violins, bagpipes, the tin whistle, or *feadóg,* as she later learned it was called in Gaelic, and the bellows of the concertina. Alex found she couldn't move. She hardly remembered to breathe.

"Struck by the *sidhe,* she is," a low voice above her said with a chuckle.

"Aye, and who can blame her?" Montague responded. "The woman sings like a fairy come to life."

"Oh, alive she is, and not alone if you've eyes to see." The man assured them. " 'Tis the festival that's brought the fairies out."

Alex finally turned away from the singer and looked up at the man. Up and up her gaze traveled to reach his face. He was over seven feet tall and three times Montague's width — a giant, a giant of a man and standing right next to her. She took a breath and held it, fear mixed with awe. She locked gazes with him and blinked in wonder. His eyes were light green ringed in a darker green, giving him an otherworldly look, but they twinkled at her as if he knew some great secret and had been standing at this very spot waiting to meet her and share it with her.

His bulbous nose took up the middle of his face, a face framed in flaming red hair with a long beard that reached his massive chest. His beard had been braided in the middle, the end tied with a tiny strip of bright green ribbon. The perfectly tied bow on the ribbon made Alex release her breath in a rush and grin up at him. He wasn't what anyone would call handsome, but there was something bright and astounding about him. Something that transformed what could have been an ugly face.

More incredible was the brightly colored green and yellow bird perched on his finger. Alex looked at it and made a clucking sound, mimicking the seabirds from home. "What a beautiful bird." The bird cocked its head back and forth, looking at Alex, and then, in a flurry of color, flew from the giant's hand to Alex's shoulder. She squeaked but stayed very still, blinking at the bird's owner.

"I see you've a bit of fairy magic about you, lass." He grinned, revealing big, strong teeth.

Alex's eyes widened, a happy flush filling her face, her mind still struggling to keep up with the world she'd suddenly stepped into. "What should I do?"

The giant reached in a pocket and brought out a little black and white seed. "Feed him this and you'll make a friend for life."

"What's his name?"

"Roscoe. And who might I tell him you are?"

Alex very carefully dropped into a small curtsy. "I'm Alexandria Featherstone and this gentleman behind me is my friend Montague."

She took the seed and very carefully offered it toward the bird's curved beak. Roscoe reached for it, grabbed it with the tip of his beak, and crunched down on it.

"Many thanks!" the bird said as clear as day.

Alex gasped. "Your bird talks? How can this be?"

"He's a parrot from the Amazon. My brother is a physician who loves to travel. He brought him back as a present for me." He grinned broadly. "I didn't know he could talk until he started repeating after me. His first words were 'yes, my dear.' " The giant threw back his head and roared with laughter. "That's what I say most often to my wife, don't you know."

As if to prove him right, the bird mimicked, "Yes, my dear. Yes, my dear. Yes, my dear."

Alex shook her head in wonder. Then, as quickly as he had landed on her shoulder, Roscoe flew back to his owner's finger.

"Did you say there is a festival?" Alex asked the man.

The giant nodded his massive head. "Oh aye, the likes of which you've never seen. We've come for the music . . . and the dancing" — he paused and wiggled his bushy eyebrows up and down — "and the games."

"It sounds wonderful. The music already . . . I can't describe it." Alex looked back at the woman on stage. "I've never heard anything like it."

They all paused and listened as she began another haunting melody. The giant leaned down and murmured into Alex's ear, "She practiced that one for hours."

Alex swung her gaze toward his. "You know her?" The shock was unmistakable, making him laugh deep from his chest in a rumble she could feel though he didn't touch her.

"Aye, I know her. Would you like to meet her?"

"Could I? I would love to."

"Come then. Let us sit over there with my friends, and I will call her over when she's finished with her entertaining." He threw back his head and laughed again, causing Alex to look to Montague for clues as to what to do.

Montague leaned toward her ear. "He's safe enough, I think. You should try to make a few friends while you're here."

Nodding, she followed in the wake of the giant, wondering what his name was and why she hadn't thought to ask him yet.

Once seated between the man and Montague, the music changed, happy now, with the bow of the violin skipping up and down the strings. People rose to dance, filling the aisles and the middle of the floor with tapping feet. Alex could feel her heartbeat begin to race with the excitement of the crowd. Her foot tapped under the table, her hands itched to clap, and her whole being strained to join the dancers, even though she couldn't match their steps. She hardly knew any dances, only a few local ones that were popular with the young people, but there'd been no dancing instructor, nor any occasions to need the knowledge. Suddenly she wished that hadn't been the case.

"I see you'd be wantin' to dance, lass?"

Alex looked into the giant's grinning face and nodded. "But I don't know how!"

"Never stopped me!"

Before she knew it, he had dragged her out of her seat and onto the cleared area made for a dance floor. People moved like the parting sea out of their way, some complaining and others laughing but all clapping and dancing, their feet moving faster and faster to the quickening music.

Once they reached the front, right by the stage, he stopped and spun her around. His big hands enveloped hers and then she was lost. He swept her into twirls and foot movements as if she were a rag doll. Her hair came loose from its pins, flying out like a long, brown cloak as they spun. Her face heated, sweat trickled down her back, her chest gasped for air, but the smile on her face felt frozen with pure joy.

The song ended abruptly and she collapsed against the giant's arm, panting to regain her breath. But it didn't matter; everyone around them was doing the same.

"Well done, lass. I knew you had it in you."

"Thank you, sir." She curtsied and leaned back, still laughing, unable to contain it. "What should I call you?"

"The name's Baylor."

"Thank you for the dance, Baylor. I — I —" She shook her head, suddenly shy. "I've never danced like that before. It was wonderful."

He grinned and leaned down toward her ear, shouting above the crowd. "There will be plenty more fun tomorrow." He burst into another boom of laughter. "I'm to compete in one of the games. You and your lad should come and cheer me on!"

"Yes, I would love to. Just tell me where to be."

"The festival is up High Street, just around the corner. You won't have trouble finding it, what with all the crowds a goin' there."

Alex was just nodding her agreement when a soft voice came from behind her. "And here you are. Flirting with a pretty woman, I see."

Alex watched Baylor's eyes grow round and a look of pure panic cross his face. She spun her head around to see the beautiful woman who had been singing, hands on her hips, eyes narrowed at the giant.

"I was only bein' friendly to the newcomers, my dear. There ain't room in my heart for nary a one but you." He turned to Alex with a sheepish smile. "Well, I promised you'd meet her. This here is one of the most famed singers on our fair isle, Maeve, my wife."

"This is your wife?" Alex couldn't help the exclamation of shock and then felt her face flush for showing it. "I mean, you're so talented. I haven't ever heard music like this. It's simply the most wonderful thing I've ever heard." Oh, bother, now she was rambling like a pea brain.

"Thank you . . . ?" Maeve raised her brows in question of a name.

"Oh," Alex held out her hand to the ethereal creature. "Alexandria Featherstone. So honored to meet you both."

The woman smiled at her, the first real smile since meeting her. "A charming child." She looked up to her husband. "Wherever did you find her, under some rock?"

Baylor pointed to the table where his friends and Montague were sitting. "She's with him. She was fairy struck by your singing so I invited them to our table."

"And then you couldn't help but to dance with her. Ach, I know. Never mind that. I will join you in a few moments."

She turned and seemed to float away toward the dark recesses of the back of the building. Alex looked at Baylor and covered her mouth with her hand at his stricken look. "Is she terribly angry?"

Baylor smirked at her and let out a big breath. "You wouldn't have to ask had she been angry. Just testing me. I believe we've scraped by. Come now, let's sit with our company."

Alex followed his looming form back to the table.

What a place, Ireland! And what people she'd met already! She turned around and gasped. There, near the door, stood the dark, mysterious form that seemed to be following her. He turned his head and glared at her. It was him. A spike of fear thrust through her as she hurried after the giant and sat in the safest spot between him and Montague. She leaned toward Montague's ear. "He's here. By the door."

Montague flicked a glance at the man and then looked away. "I know. I've been watching him."

"What do you think he wants?" Alex breathed, resisting the urge to sink under the table and hide.

"Alexandria, if your parents were looking for something valuable and they've disappeared . . ." He stared into her eyes, more serious than she'd ever seen him. "It would stand to reason that you might be in the same danger, would it not?"

"But I don't know anything. I don't even know what they were looking for."

"Yes, but he doesn't know that. To him you are following the same clues your parents followed. To him, you may be the only link to this treasure your parents sought. We must be very careful, my dear. I shall sleep outside your door tonight."

Alex didn't know what to say. He was right, of course. But she had to shake this man from them. She couldn't risk leading him right to her parents. Maybe she should give up, go home where she was safe. The first real trial had begun, as Montague had warned would happen on this journey.

*Dear God, what shall I do?*

# CHAPTER THIRTEEN

Gabriel neared the little village of Beal in the northeastern most part of Northumberland with a sense of relief. Upon hearing of Gabriel's intention to go and fetch his ward himself, the prince regent had insisted he be accompanied by a cavalcade of soldiers during the five-day journey, and the company was, quite frankly, wearing on his nerves.

He rode toward the front on a big bay stallion, flanked by officers in red-coated uniforms and led by a captain who relished his temporary command over the duke. "Regent's orders" was a favorite phrase of the captain, which he used in short barks of sound, eyes round and heady with power.

Gabriel mostly ignored him, which infuriated the little man. Thank God Meade was with him or he'd really be bad tempered. His secretary had balked at the idea of riding all the way to Holy Island, not having any skill to control a horse, but Gabriel refused a carriage. Alexandria might be in danger. They didn't have time for anything but fast horses and hard riding. Meade would just have to bump along behind them as best he could.

On a positive note, his hearing had improved a bit again the farther north they traveled. Did the change of altitude have anything to do with it? If it did, he would have to pack up and move to Scotland. Perhaps he should try some healing waters. There were those in Bath, but they were in the south of England. He would have to find out if there were any in the more northern climes.

Gabriel turned and looked over his shoulder at his stalwart secretary. Poor man, he appeared ready to slide off to one side or the other at any moment. Mayhap he should tie him to the saddle. The picture of it brought a half-cocked smile to Gabriel's lips.

"How's the sore bum faring, Meade?" It had been obvious by the way Meade had been walking bowlegged and wincing with every step that he was sore from head to toe from the unfamiliar exercise.

Meade groaned and looked down at the death grip he had on the reins. "I shall be most hardily glad when this trip is over, Your Grace. Now you see why I insisted on sailing to Holy Island the last time I traveled there," he shouted.

"Ah. Yes, but it took you twice the time. The way you extol her virtues, surely you believe the lady worth all this trouble?" Gabriel's voice held an obvious note of amusement.

Meade smiled back through gritted teeth. "It's the only thing keeping me on this beast, I assure you."

"She must be something indeed to produce such sacrifice." Gabriel mused. His horse had slowed to a trot beside Meade's so he could better talk to him. "Tell me again . . . what exactly is so special about this young lady?"

Meade once again turned tongue-tied. He sputtered and shrugged, started to say something, and then clamped down on the words.

"She's cast a spell on you. I do believe it's so. You cannot even speak of her." Gabriel's chuckle lurked just behind the words.

Meade nodded in eager agreement.

"A beauty, surely?" Gabriel raised his brows at his secretary, immensely enjoying the man's discomfort.

Meade nodded again.

"Prettier than Jane, even?" The fact that Meade had a terrible crush on his youngest sister was well known to the family. He turned mute in her presence, something Jane found bewildering and her husband, Lord Matthew Rutherford, found annoying.

Meade's face turned bright red and his throat worked as if he were about to choke. Better to lay off and take it easy on the poor man. He was, after all, the best secretary Gabriel had ever had, and he didn't intend to let him die of apoplexy on his horse over a little teasing.

"Very well, keep your secrets." Gabriel's voice softened as his gaze swept to the road ahead and the dark smudge on the horizon that must be the sea. His heart leapt at the sight of it. "I shall meet her myself soon and see what's smitten you so thoroughly." His voice lowered even more so only Meade, if even he, could hear him. "Let's see if you have any magic for me . . . Lady Alexandria . . . Featherstone."

A short time later they arrived in the ancient little village of Beal. They stopped at the local inn, a sprawling, squat building made from local stone, and dismounted. Several of the soldiers rushed to take the reins of his mount while Gabriel adjusted his coat and, ignoring everyone save Meade, strode for the door of the establishment. Some hot food to warm up from the bracing autumn wind should put some spring back into his step, if not his mood. Hopefully the place could accommodate the needs of fifteen hungry men without advance notice.

The inn's owner, Mr. Gerald, was a squat man with a balding pate who nodded and scurried and rubbed his head with a mixture of awe and glee as the captain explained their needs. Gabriel soon found himself at a wide plank table with the best the house had to offer — rabbit with black pudding, smoked salmon and fresh oysters, platters of goat cheese and bowls of potatoes thick with butter. For dessert there was bread pudding with custard and plum tarts. A feast, to be sure, and a fine example of a seaside village's harvest.

When the soldiers appeared to linger with their after-dinner port, Gabriel became impatient, stood, and directed his stare at the captain. "I would like to reach Holy Island before nightfall, Captain."

The captain sputtered on his mulled wine but he rose, glaring at his men. Before he had a chance to command anything, Mr. Gerald waved his arms for the attention of all. "My good sirs, and Your Grace," he bowed toward Gabriel, "I'm afraid you must wait until the tide goes out. Holy Island is truly an island except for twice a day when the tide is low enough to reveal the causeway. To reach Lindisfarne you must cross the causeway."

"Can we not reach it by boat?" the captain asked in his clipped tones.

"Oh no." The innkeeper shook his head emphatically. "There are sand dunes and mudflats. The tide comes in very quickly. It is very dangerous water. You must wait for the tide to go out, which happens twice daily."

"How long until the next crossing?" Gabriel asked.

"Not long. Another hour at best." The innkeeper smiled. "Please, might I bring you more port while you wait?"

Gabriel pressed some coins in the man's hand and motioned for him to follow him out. To the captain he said, "Wait here with your men. I would like to see the town . . . alone." He turned his back on the man when the captain started to protest.

"Mr. Gerald, please see that these men are amply taken care of. Several bottles of wine will be required, I'm sure. They will require several hours of rest from our long journey, you see?" He raised his brows while the request sank in.

Mr. Gerald grinned broadly, his head nodding up and down. "I'll see to it, Your Grace."

That should take care of one problem. The last thing he wanted was to arrive at Lindisfarne Castle with an army. He hoped to convince Alexandria to come with him willingly, but her letters and the knot in his gut told him that was going to be a challenge. She would be headstrong and obstinate. A little charm may be in order, something a scarlet-clad army and a short-tempered captain with the prince regent's authority riding high on his face would be sure to ruin. It wouldn't be Gabriel's fault if they missed the tidal timing and became stranded on the mainland for the night. Not his fault at all.

Gabriel motioned for Meade to follow him out. They would ride to the shore and await this tide, following the water out to the island as soon as they were able.

Having escaped the soldiers, Gabriel and Meade rode the short distance over rolling farmland to a pretty pebbled beach. The water was as the innkeeper said — marshes of mudflats with tall plants and teeming with creatures. Gabriel saw a rabbit here and there nibbling on some plants and flocks of brent geese on the tidal flats between the mainland and Holy Island. There were many species of birds that must winter here from the northern climes of Scotland. It was a gray and brown, windswept place with an air of mystery about it. Alexandria professed love for it, and as he stopped and soaked in the subtle beauty he thought he could understand why.

Lifting his gaze toward the island he saw a hill and on that hill, a castle. Lindisfarne Castle. Her home. A crumbling old place as he had expected, but it still had a grandeur about it, at least from this distance. Eagerness to see it, to see her, tensed his muscles.

He thought of one of the letters he had written to her and flushed hot with embarrassment and desire. It had started to sound like a love letter so he'd balled it up and thrown it into the fire. Fantasies, that's all it was. She would end up being like all the other women who eventually bored him. And anyway, who would want a duke who might become deaf again? Of course there were any number of women who had married worse for the duchess title, but he would never marry from that ilk. His mother would turn to a pillar of salt if she knew how much he abhorred the idea of marrying any of the women of the ton.

Of course, he hadn't met all the women of the ton . . . yet. Alexandria's lineage certainly qualified her to be among those elite circles, but he doubted she knew it or cared. That fact alone made her different, very different and interesting. And she prayed for him. No one had ever done that.

He doubted even his mother had ever prayed for him, his family's religion being attending church as expected and leaving God at the door when they left. They'd thought Gabriel daft when he'd studied philosophy and religion and became a believer in Jesus' sacrifice on the cross as the only way to salvation. He'd been a bit of a zealot for a while, he supposed, but like all things he studied, the excitement had worn off and he'd fallen back into old patterns. Maybe prayer, like Alexandria said, would rekindle his love for God.

*Alexandria. Just a little longer and I will see your face.*

He stared at the castle's dark silhouette against the gray sky. The thought of finally seeing her had him sweating as he paced the shore, waiting, cold and hot at the same time, for the water to lower. What if she *was* everything he'd dreamed, someone who felt like his other half, someone who knew him soul deep and loved what she had discovered, and he for her, their love chasing away the boredom forever? What would he do then?

A motion from Meade snapped him from his reverie. "Your Grace, look." He pointed toward the muddy path being revealed little by little as the water receded.

A grin broke out on Gabriel's face. "Shall we?"

Meade looked as excited as he was. "As you know, I arrived by ship when I was here before. I heard about the causeway but didn't have a chance to see it. It is quite remarkable, isn't it?"

"Enchanting," Gabriel murmured as he mounted his horse and took the first step. The tide was going out faster now, revealing a gravelly, muddy path. Within the hour they would set foot on Holy Island. Within the hour he would finally see her face.

The road to the castle wound its way through the village of Lindisfarne, an obvious fishing village with small colored boats lining the shore and sheds made from two boats propped up together for shelter against the constant sea wind. The village houses were of stone lining up and down the main street. At the end of the street was the monastery Alexandria had written about. It was in a shambles, half-knocked-down walls, a graveyard full of tombstones and parts of the original building. It sprawled back from the road as if the earth had rolled and spit up some stones in uneven lines that made little sense. A familiar sight in England's countryside though, ancient and full of stories. Gabriel liked it immensely.

A little farther on, through sheep-grazing pastureland, the castle came into full view. It looked as if it had grown out of the top of the hill, taking up the entire flat top. The road turned steep as they started up the hill, winding around toward the top like a spiral staircase. At the end was a large wooden door, faded with age.

"Allow me, Your Grace." Meade stepped up to the door and picked up the brass knocker. He banged it several times and then stood back and grinned. "Let's hope she doesn't have her pistol."

Gabriel gave a bark of laughter and then composed his features. In a moment's hesitation he took off his hat, felt ridiculous, and then hurriedly replaced it. If Meade noticed, he was wise enough not to comment.

The door finally gave a groan and then creaked open to reveal a small, wizened old man, skinny enough that the wind looked to bow him back a little. He squinted at the two of them and then broke into a toothless smile. "Mr. Meade, you've come back!" His voice was as thin as the high notes of a pennywhistle. His watery eyes slid to Gabriel and he frowned. "Now, lookie here, we don't need no fancy visitors. Can't hardly keep body and soul together as it is and ain't got nothin' to offer the likes o' some fancy gentleman."

Meade hurried forward and took the old man's hand. "Oh no, Mr. Henry. This is His Grace, the Duke of St. Easton."

Mr. Henry eyed Gabriel with a suspicious gleam.

"This is Lady Featherstone's guardian. He's come to help Lady Alex with her troubles."

"Troubles?" the old man barked. "We've troubles enough for a duke, all right. I suppose you must come in then."

Gabriel swallowed back a chuckle. The man hadn't even bothered to bow, just stood a little aside and gave them enough space to squeeze by. Once inside Gabriel studied the room and what must have been a great hall with interest. The castle had not been updated much since medieval times. Cold stone floors, drafty cracks in the walls, an enormous fireplace that housed a pitiful little fire, and a scattering of shabby furniture. So this was her beloved castle. He couldn't imagine what she would think of his palatial London town house or, God forbid, his own monstrosity in Wiltshire. He should, perhaps, keep those details to himself.

"As I was sayin' we haven't nothin' to offer ye but some tea."

Gabriel took a step toward the man and locked eyes with him. "We've not come for refreshments. I have come to see Lady Featherstone. Fetch her . . . if you please."

"Well, it ain't no nevermind if I please or not." The old man rankled. "She isn't here."

Gabriel took another step, towering over him, and frowned. "Well? Where is she?"

Before Henry could answer, an equally old woman rushed into the room. "Now, Mr. Duke, we're under strict orders not to tell a soul where she is and we're not tellin' you neither."

Gabriel turned his glare on the old woman. He ground his teeth. He'd known this wasn't going to be easy. . . . Something had told him Alexandria would be trouble and here was the beginning of it.

"As her guardian and here under the direct orders of the prince regent himself, you will tell me — immediately — where she is."

The old man crossed his arms over his chest.

The old woman pressed her lips into a stubborn line.

Gabriel threw off his coat, flung it with his hat on a chair, and sat on the only decent-looking furniture in the room. "Meade, you may as well make yourself comfortable. It looks like we shall be here for a while."

# CHAPTER FOURTEEN

High Street in Belfast swelled with people of all shapes and sizes, all of them jovial — laughing and shouting, the children racing through the crowds in the midmorning light. The air smelled of roasting meat over open fires and barmbrack, an Irish fruit-filled bread Alex had sampled just that morning at breakfast at the inn. There were stalls selling meat pies, fish, oysters, and all sorts of Irish fare. Other stalls hawked brightly colored linen and woven wools done up in warm shawls, shirts, dresses, and petticoats. There were shoes and striped stockings and lace for any number of uses. So much to see! Alex wanted to stop and just gawk, but Montague kept a brisk pace and she didn't want to lose sight of him.

He had mentioned drawing out the man following them as a possible source of information as to what, exactly, Alex's parents had been looking for. Alex hadn't been able to answer many of Montague's questions, leaving wide gaps in their knowledge. But he was convinced that if they were being followed, it had something to do with whatever her parents were hired to seek. And that put their mission and their persons in serious danger.

They followed the crowd, as Baylor had directed, down High Street where the games were to begin. Alex rose on tiptoe and scanned the merrymakers for the giant — he couldn't be missed, so tall and with that hair the color of flame. A great crowd had gathered at the end of one corner.

Alex shouted toward Montague and pointed. "There! I think I see him." She grinned with excitement. "It's Baylor!"

"Aye."

"Come on! Let's get a closer look!" When Alex didn't get very far through the crowd, Montague clasped her elbow tight to his side and fought their way toward the front.

There, in the middle of the street, flanked by the tall buildings of Belfast, stood three men. They were all large and muscular, but Baylor was the tallest and strongest looking by far. They each held a metal ball of different sizes.

"Montague, do you know the rules of the game? What are those heavy-looking balls?"

Montague chuckled. "Those are cannonballs, my dear. Solid iron."

"But Baylor's is so much bigger than the others. Is that fair?"

"In Baylor's case it is probably more than fair. The others look to be throwing a twelve-pound ball, but I would wager that Baylor's is a twenty-four-pound shot."

"So they actually throw these cannonballs down the road?"

"I've not seen the game, but I believe they throw them as far down the road as possible and the first one to reach the goal, a few miles hence, is the winner."

Before Alex could ask another question someone shouted, "Clear the way!" The first man stepped to the center of the road. He was a younger man, more her age. He looked serious about the business though, dressed in brown breeches and a heavy shirt, shoes of sturdy leather. But it was his face that made him seem a contender. His dark brows studied the road ahead in a way that said he meant to win. The crowd quieted as he ran forward and then heaved the ball with an underhanded throw into the air. There was much cheering and clapping and Alex saw money changing hands as the spectators betted on their favorite competitor. Some shouted advice as the next man moved to the center of the road.

"Keep to the lee side, laddie," someone beside her shouted.

"No! Straight down the middle!" the man in front of her boomed.

Alex gathered her cloak more tightly around her and studied Baylor's next competition. The second man was middle aged. Gleeful was the word that came to mind when looking at his broad, happy countenance. Alex laughed and looked up at Montague. "I do believe he is excited to be playing this game."

"You've the right of that, my dear," Montague nodded.

They watched as the second man's ball flew down the street farther than the first player and then rolled to one side. It went out of sight in the tall grass.

The crowd went wild as Baylor stepped to the center of the road. With a great leaping run and a mighty roar, he wielded the cannonball around in a full circle and then thrust it into the air.

"But it's so much heavier, it's not fair," Alex complained.

"Just wait," Montague murmured.

The crowd had quieted, holding a collective breath as the ball landed with a loud *thwack* and rolled and rolled and rolled down the road, out of sight.

A great cheer burst from the crowd as they all surged forward toward the spot where the shortest throw had landed. It was impossible to tell where Baylor's ball had landed until the second man's turn because his starting point was so much farther down the road.

As the road curved and changed from cobblestone to dirt, Baylor remained in the lead but only by a few yards. The second man got closer and closer with each throw.

"Do you think he's tiring?" Alex asked after another twenty minutes. The first competitor was behind the crowd now without a chance of winning. When it was his turn, the crowd parted to the sides of the road and had to watch out for the flying ball not to hit them. It was funny to see them scatter as a cannonball came right at them. The second man had outthrown Baylor on the last turn, causing a great scowl to linger on Baylor's face. If Alex didn't know what a softhearted man he really was, his fierce face would be frightening indeed.

"He is getting tired, but the end is near. It will be a close game and please the crowds." Montague winked at her. So that was it! Baylor was holding back so it would be an exciting game.

As if to prove her right, on his next turn Baylor let the ball go with such force that it flew through the air so fast she couldn't track it with her eyes. The crowd surged forward to follow it and see if it had crossed the finish line.

Jostled and bumped along with the swelling fans, Alexandria lost sight of Montague. Panic washed over her as a big man practically ran her down. She tottered and would have fallen except for the fact that someone grasped her shoulder and swung her upright.

She turned to look at the person. "Thank —" Her stomach dropped as shock ripped through her body. Oh no! It was him — the man who had been watching her. The breath whooshed out of her as he leaned toward her. He was thin, his face gaunt, his eyes hungry and haunted.

His face snapped toward hers, eyes like a ravenous dog. He smiled a slow, ghoulish smile and took her arm in his bony fingers. What had she done letting herself get separated from Montague? Where was he? She wanted to scream out for help, but it wouldn't do any good against the cheering throng.

The man grasped her arm in a tight hold and rasped into her ear, "What is your business in Ireland, *señorita?*"

His accent was decidedly Spanish. She tried to twist out of his grasp, but his bony fingers bit into the tender flesh of her upper arm. "Who are you? Unhand me this instant!"

"Your name, *señorita.* Only give me your name and I will release you."

"Her name is my daughter and none of your concern." Alex turned her head to see Montague and Baylor standing behind her. Montague had unsheathed his sword and Baylor was lifting the heavy cannonball above his head, staring with a pleased smirk at the Spaniard's forehead.

The man abruptly let go of Alex's arm and backed away, hands outstretched. "Gentlemen, gentlemen. I mean her no harm. I am searching for a distant relative who was described to me such that she looks very much like your daughter. Her name is Louisa Martinez and her father is Antonio. You are not Antonio Martinez?" he asked Montague.

Montague took a step closer and then another until he stood toe to toe with the man. Alex slowly backed up until she was safely behind Baylor but still able to see around his massive side. "And what if I am this Antonio Martinez?" Montague taunted in a soft and deadly tone. "What would you do then, *señor?*"

The Spaniard's eyes narrowed but he backed up another step. "You are not him. I apologize. I will take my leave." With a short bow and a flick of a sinister smile toward Alex, he turned and slithered away.

Alex let out her breath. "He was lying, wasn't he? He wanted to know my name. I think he wanted to know if I am a Featherstone."

"You may be right." Montague flicked the sword through the air, making a hissing sound, and then slid it back into its scabbard. "You are in more danger than I thought when I first joined you. I fear he will not give up easily."

"We have to hurry and find clues." Guilt at being sidetracked from her mission by the festival gnawed at her stomach. "Baylor, can you tell me where the post office is located? It's the only clue I have."

"Not far at all, lass. Back toward town. On Church Street. I will take you there."

"But you've won the contest. Don't you want to stay and celebrate with the crowd?" There were several groups of people who appeared to be waiting to talk to him.

"Don't worry your pretty head about that; it's just a game. I will join Montague in protecting you whilst you are in Ireland." He turned toward Montague and raised his brows. "If you'll have me."

"We would be honored to have your help. We need someone who knows the land, as I have a feeling we'll not be in Belfast much longer."

Alex had to agree that Baylor would be a fine addition to their party. "But what of your wife? She won't be pleased by this, I think."

"You've the wrong of it there. She'll be mighty pleased to stay in Belfast a wee bit longer. Gives her a chance to sing. We live in the cliffs of Blackhead. 'Tis a lonely place with only the whistling wind to accompany that fine voice of hers. She bid me to watch over you just this morning."

"She did? But I thought she didn't like me."

"Oh, she took a shine to you well enough. You would know it if she hadn't." He shivered as if just the thought of it caused fear to snake down his spine.

Alex shook her head in wonder. "Give her my thanks. Shall we go to the post office?"

Baylor turned back toward town, tucked the cannonball under one arm, and held out the other toward her. She grasped the huge forearm and smiled up at him. "While we walk, why don't you tell me what you know about your parents' mission in Ireland. What were they looking for?"

The three of them turned from the hills surrounding the city and returned to the rows of thatched houses on High Street and then on to Church Street while Alex told what she knew. "My letter has a postmark from the Belfast Post Office on it. I'm hoping the postmaster will remember my parents."

"Aye, he might. Mr. McCracken is the nosy sort. Let's see what we can learn here."

They came to the door and entered to find a quaint little parlor and an office with a long desk. Alex rang the bell on the counter, which soon brought a white-headed man with thin legs and arms and a round stomach. "Ach, what have we here but a pretty young thing? Do you need to post a letter?"

"Not exactly, sir." Alex pulled the letter from her pocket and held it toward the man. "I was wondering if this postmark came from here. It's a letter from my mother and I am desperate to find her."

"Your mother? She's missing?" He took the letter, pulled a wiry pair of spectacles from his pocket, and adjusted them over the bridge of his nose. Peering at the corner of the letter, he nodded. "Yes, indeed. I

201

stamped this myself." His keen eyes studied Alexandria's face. "I remember your mother. Your resemblance is very easy to see." He stared off into space for a moment, thin lips working. "She was with a man."

"That would be my father."

"Yes, she seemed very much in love with him. He made her laugh — a distinctive laugh, that. Loud and happy."

"Did they say anything about where they were going or where they were staying? Anything at all?" Alex strained toward him.

"Hmm. Something about a castle if I remember rightly."

"There's castles a plenty in Ireland, man. Can you remember which one?" Baylor inserted in a booming voice.

"Yes, yes. Now give me a moment. I'm thinking." He turned away from them and paced over to the long desk, stopped, and then tapped his fingers on the top. "That's it! Killyleagh Castle. They asked for directions." He smiled at the three of them in triumph.

"Killyleagh Castle," Alex breathed. They would have to go to Killyleagh Castle. "Was there anything else? Did they say why they wanted to go there?"

"No, no, even though I probed a little." The postmaster grinned like a mischievous schoolboy. "They seemed to be in a hurry. But that was months ago. You don't suppose they are still there?"

"I don't know." Alex's voice turned soft and sad. "But I must speak to whoever lives there. They may know something important."

"Godspeed to you then." The postmaster nodded at her. "If something comes to me, I'll send word to the posting house in Killyleagh. It's not more than twenty miles from here."

"It's close then. Good. Many thanks for your help." Alex turned toward the door, Baylor and Montague behind her.

Belfast was an exciting town and a place she would like to visit again someday. But now it was time to get back on the search. It was time to find her parents.

# CHAPTER FIFTEEN

Gabriel sat in the cramped library at Lindisfarne Castle on Holy Island, leafing through a book that told the story of St. Aiden and the Irish monks who had built the monastery of Lindisfarne and brought Christianity to Northern England. He laid it aside, stopped, and stared at the bookshelf, frustration making his temples pound.

Where was she?

What if she was in trouble?

Feeling restless, he paced to the long, narrow window and looked out. He'd toured the place and surroundings earlier that day and had been astonished that she was living like the people who lived here centuries ago, without any modern comforts. The castle was a cold, drafty hodgepodge of rooms, many of them uninhabitable. There wasn't a nearby water supply and the animal shelters were falling down in disrepair, not that he'd seen any animals aside from some wandering sheep. Her bedchamber was a stark place that somehow made him both angry and appalled on her behalf. There was a small bed with thin, lumpy bedding, a faded coverlet with no pillow, a set of drawers that he'd opened and found empty save for one pair of worn stockings.

Ann had caught him snooping and started screeching, which brought that beast Latimere around. What in heaven Alexandria did with a dog as big as a small pony was another curiosity to ponder. Upon arriving he'd been anxious to meet her. Now he was growing desperate. What if these servants of hers had sold her off to someone? Gabriel turned from the window and scowled. He had to convince them to talk.

Taking a seat at the small table, he closed his eyes and leaned his head back onto the hard wooden chair. *Dear God, please keep her safe.* He opened his eyes and looked up. There, in the dusty light of the library, was a book poking out from among the others on the bookshelf. He hadn't noticed that before. Maybe he'd done that rummaging through their books. He rose to push it back into place and then stopped, his fingers hovering over the spine. It was a book of poetry. There was a scrap of paper hanging out of it. He carefully pulled it free and opened it.

The familiarity of the handwriting slammed into him like a battering ram. Alexandria had written this.

He sat back down and smoothed out the pages, the first words caused the breath to whoosh out of him.

Dear Mr. Duke,

I find myself thinking of you often, wondering about your life and what it must be like. It must be the opposite of mine. You must attend glamorous parties and balls, surrounded by beautiful women and men who are powerful and wealthy. What do dukes do with their days, I wonder? Mr. Meade said only glowing things about you, but there is still so much I don't know. How old are you? What do you look like? I've poured over the copy *Debrett's Peerage* that my parents often refer to in their investigations, but I fear that I cannot find you; perhaps you were not born yet, as it is sadly out of date.

Gabriel's breath paused with the fact that she had thought of him thus. It was how he had been thinking of her. Wondering her age and what she looked like, wondering if the connection he felt for her through their letters could possibly lead to something more. She'd never hinted at it, and he'd tried to ignore it, but now. Now he knew what had really been lurking in her heart. He quickly turned back to the page.

Your tone in your letters makes me think you must be above forty at least, and I assure myself that you are too old and crotchety for my daydreams, but perhaps you are just used to bossing people around? You are a duke, after all, and must be used to people bowing and scraping wherever you go.

I shan't post this, of course. I couldn't let you know how truly alone and afraid I sometimes feel. My parents weren't here very often, but they've never been gone this long. What if I am truly alone in the world? I can't let myself think it. I won't believe it. But I wish I had someone. I wish I could someday meet you and see your face.

It ended there, abruptly, and he was chagrined at how badly he wished there was more. Gabriel turned to the next page where she had started another letter:

Dear Gabriel,

He liked that address the best of all the ones she'd given him so far. Only the nearest and dearest to him called him by his given name — hardly anyone.

I've found this poem of Shakespeare's and thought of you. Have you read it before?

Let me not to the marriage of true
  minds
Admit impediments. Love is not love
Which alters when it alteration finds,
Or bends with the remover to remove:
O no! It is an ever-fixed mark
That looks on tempests and is never
  shaken;
It is the star to every wandering bark,
Whose worth's unknown, although his
  height be taken.
Love's not Time's fool, though rosy lips
  and cheeks
Within his bending sickle's compass
  come:
Love alters not with his brief hours and
  weeks,
But bears it out even to the edge of
  doom.

If this be error and upon me proved,
I never writ, nor no man ever loved.

His breath whooshed out of him and he leaned his forehead into his hand, bent over the flowing words. It was one of his favorite poems, a poem he'd studied and memorized the lines of years ago. The beginning spoke of marriage and the wedding vows, and then it went on to describe an ideal form of love that was constant despite changing circumstances, a love that stood the test of time until death parted the lovers. A light, a star, of incalculable worth.

At the end of the poem, Shakespeare bet his entire body of work on his statement of love. And then there was the elegant simplicity of the words themselves. Unassuming words put together in such a way as to state humankind's most complex commission — love. Had Alexandria seen that? That she might have and had thought to have such a love with him flooded his body and mind with warmth and joy. He closed his eyes and let the feeling fill him.

Could one really fall in love through a few letters?

He folded them as if they were made from spun gold and put them into his pocket. He placed the book back on the shelf and walked back to the room's only window, staring out at the rolling countryside. If only she hadn't run off he could have shown her how much he cared, how he only wanted to take care of her and make her life happy. He looked around at the shabby room and curled his hand into a fist.

She deserved better.

Who were these parents who left their only child alone in such a dilapidated home? The tide of anger he felt when he thought of them washed over him again. How dare they leave her here as if she meant nothing to them. What kind of parents could do that?

Meade suddenly appeared at the entrance. Gabriel had sent him to the village to question the inhabitants about Alexandria's whereabouts. Hair askew and cheeks red, he looked as if he'd been running all the way back to the castle.

"Well? Did you find out anything?" Gabriel beckoned him into the room.

"She stopped at the market house just before leaving and posted a letter. The shopkeeper said it was addressed to you, Your Grace. That's the last time they saw her. No one knows where she went when she left the island. They thought she was just going into Beal for something. She often went there to visit or help someone in need, I'm told. And it wasn't unheard of for her to stay several days. No one thought to question her whereabouts until she'd been gone some time, and then her servants would only say what they told us — that she's gone on an exploring trip."

"Rubbish." Gabriel paced back to the window and stroked his chin in thought. "They know more than they will tell us."

"With all the whispering they do, I would have to agree."

Gabriel could tell that Meade said the words louder since he was facing away from him. He turned back toward his secretary. "I will question them again. Ask them to meet me in the great room. I'll beg if I have to."

"Yes, Your Grace." Meade gave him a quick bow and turned to fetch the servants.

The thought of going back to Beal and telling the captain that the Lady Featherstone was missing was not pleasant. The captain would go straight to the prince regent and the regent must not know that his prize had already gone missing. The prince regent would be furious with all of them, including Alexandria, when he learned she had run off by herself, tricking a duke for money. He had to protect her from the prince regent and this little army with which he was currently riddled. He would have to get rid of the army to search for her. *He* would be the one to find her and bring her back safe and sound.

Who knew being a guardian would be so much trouble?

But he couldn't deny that it was a wonderful sort of trouble. The emotions he felt as he imagined finally finding her, seeing her, holding her in his arms — *God help me* — it made his heart pound in an odd way and his body flush with heat as if he'd been standing next to a roaring fire. He needed to get ahold of himself.

A few minutes later he entered the great room relieved to see Ann and Henry sitting in chairs by the fire. He pulled up another chair and sat across from them. Ann had an obstinate fold to her lips and Henry wouldn't look him directly in the eyes.

"Ann, Henry, I understand that you are trying to protect her, but I have a story to tell you. It's a great secret told to me by one of the prince regent's men, and I wouldn't tell it to you if I didn't know from experience how good you both are at keeping important secrets."

Henry flashed a disgusted look at him. "You'll not be tricking us into saying somethin' so save your secrets, Duke."

Gabriel acknowledged the threat with a nod and smoothed back his smile. What he wouldn't give to have the old man working for him. He'd not seen such loyalty since his navy days. "Regardless, I will tell you." He proceeded to tell them about the missing manuscript that Lord and Lady Featherstone had been hired to find. And he told of his guardianship and how the prince regent had given him the task of keeping her safe.

"So you see, Alexandria is in great danger. If she has gone off alone and unprotected, I fear for her life." He let the words sink in a moment, noting the softening of both their faces. "If there is anything . . . anything at all that you know . . . I beg you to tell me. I can't protect her if I can't find her."

The silence thickened in the room. Gabriel waited, watching them by turns, seeing their internal debate. Finally Henry looked at Ann and murmured, "I didn't want her going off alone anyway. Told her it was a fool thing to do."

"She had the coachman," Ann hissed. "When have you known her not to have a plan? She's always been able to take care of herself."

"She ain't had enemies before. Not real

ones, anyway. We need to tell him what we know."

Ann gave a great sigh and looked at Gabriel. "It ain't much but she hired a coach to Whitehaven."

Whitehaven. A seaport town. "To leave England?" Gabriel felt a shifting of panic. Had she really left the country?

"She had a letter from her mother . . . last one she ever got from her. It was from Ireland. We figured that's where she'll start her search."

"Her search?"

Henry's voice was full of pride. "For her parents, of course. The girl never believed them dead. She said she'd feel it if it was true."

Gabriel reached up and covered his eyes with one hand. He should have known. He should have read between the lines of her letters and guessed. She'd been redirecting his attention to the state of the castle, fleecing him for funds, not for repairs, but to hie off to Ireland of all places! He had underestimated her. Clever minx. Clever and determined. All she cared about was finding her parents.

Not that he really blamed her — it's exactly what he would have done. He even admired her for it. But the fact that she might be right, that they might be alive, and if they were alive then they were undoubtedly in very real trouble . . . trouble his ward seemed determined to place herself in the middle of, made him groan aloud. Stubborn, impetuous girl! If she had only asked for his help. But she didn't know him. She didn't know about the inexplicable place in his heart she'd already carved out. Now he would have to track her all the way to Ireland.

"Do you happen to know where, exactly, in Ireland? It is a rather large place."

They both shook their heads. Of course not. She wouldn't make it that easy.

"Meade, find this coach she hired and the identity of the driver. He should be of some help."

"That would be Mr. Howard from Beal. He's the only one with a coach in these parts," Henry said.

"Very well, find Mr. Howard if he has returned." Gabriel rose, impatience humming through his veins. "Thank you for confiding in me, Ann." He nodded to the old woman. "Henry." Another nod in his direction. "Meade will send you a letter when I find her. In the meantime, I give you this." He took out a pouch and dropped it onto the chair with a heavy *clink*. "Lady

Alexandria did not overly exaggerate your need to have this place repaired. I'll send more when I'm able but at least stock the larder and get the leaky roof patched. You might have someone work on the sheep shed; it's bound to cave in soon."

Ann stood and stretched out her neck toward him, her old eyes intent. "You said you aim to protect her and I want you to keep your promise, Duke. You take care of that girl." To Gabriel's astonishment, her lips began to quiver. "She ain't had much in this life what with her parents gallivanting all over the world and hardly noticing her and what with all the responsibility she's had . . . but she's a rare soul, she is, and I'll not have the likes of a fancy duke swooping in and changing her. You promise me you'll protect her precious spirit, not just her life. Don't take her off into your world and let them change her and make her believe she's less than she is." Her voice fairly shook as her meaning, her real concern, hit him in the stomach like a punch. "Protect the real her, you promise me."

And suddenly he knew exactly what she meant. It was why Alexandria's letters had come to mean so much. It was how he knew for certain that she was different from anyone he'd ever met. That quality she had, that generous spirit that was so full of joy and laughter, a beautiful soul. "I promise."

Ann must have seen his seriousness because her lips curved up into a thin smile. "I've been praying for you to come." She said it quietly, but Gabriel read her lips. With a pounding heart he bowed toward her, grasped the side of Henry's frail arm, and then turned to go.

It was shocking how life could change so suddenly.

# CHAPTER SIXTEEN

The road from Belfast to Killyleagh was in good condition, making for a comfortable carriage ride. Well, for Montague and her, Alex revised, looking over at Baylor hunched in the middle of the seat across from them. He had to slouch down to keep his head from touching the roof and upon occasion he would grow tired of the cramped space and demand to walk alongside the carriage in the open air for a while. Poor giant. But he took it as a natural occurrence so he must be used to it.

Montague, as usual, hadn't said much, just pulled his hat low over his eyes and promptly fell asleep, softly snoring beside her. How she had ended up with two such champions she still couldn't quite figure out, but she was excited to be following their first real clue. Someone at the castle must have spoken with her parents.

A little while later, they rolled into Killyleagh. It was a pretty little town situated on the blue waters of Strangford Lough, a sea lough dotted with islands and rocky outcroppings. The thatched cottages that lined the main road were painted green and yellow and a soft blue. Alex leaned her nose against the window, a smile spreading across her face as the silhouette of the castle came into view. It looked like it had come straight from a fairy tale with tall towers and round turrets. It was built from gray and tan stone that gleamed with a bluish purple color in the afternoon light. The facade brought to mind medieval knights and ladies with brightly colored conical hats.

"Oh, Baylor, isn't it grand?"

Baylor leaned down toward the window and peered out. "That it is, lass. That it is."

As they neared it, Alex saw the rock wall surrounding it and the gatehouse with an iron gate. "We have to visit the castle to look for clues. Do you think they'll let us inside?" She hadn't thought about the gatehouse and soldiers who might be guarding the place.

"Once you flash your bonny smile at them, they're sure to let us by." Baylor grinned. Montague sat up and joined them looking out the window. "We should stop at the inn first and find out about the owners."

"And get some supper." Baylor patted his round stomach. "I could eat a sheep with the wool still on, I'm so hungry."

Alex laughed. "It's a good plan. Let's find out the situation before we approach the gate. And my parents must have stayed in the town. I can question the innkeeper."

The carriage continued up a long hill and then stopped in front of the Dufferin Coaching Inn.

It was a pretty building, painted a pale blue with stone on the bottom half. They entered to find a neat sitting room and off to one side a long dining room where groups of tables and chairs sat mostly empty this time of day. A woman with a wide apron and a friendly smile came from the dining room, a platter in her hands.

"Well hello, there," she greeted them. "You've just arrived on the coach then, I see. Wouldn't you like to freshen up and have some tea? I have fresh barmbrack just from the oven."

"Thank you, ma'am. We'll be needing beds for the night too," Alex ventured. She hoped Baylor and Montague could share a room even though Baylor was so huge. She needed to watch her spending and she'd insisted on paying their way as long as they were helping her. If only the duke would send her more money. The thought of him arriving on Holy Island and finding her gone made her stomach drop. What would Henry and Ann tell him? And what would he do next? There was no way to get his letters now. Henry and Ann didn't know where in Ireland she'd gone. She hadn't been able to risk it, even knowing how tight-lipped and loyal the two were.

Well, it couldn't be helped. She needed Baylor and Montague and had to trust that God would help her coins stretch. He'd done it with the loaves and the fishes and so many times when needs were too great for her allowance on Holy Island. She was sure He would make a way this time too.

"There's plenty of room, dearie. Just go on in to the dinin' room there and have a seat by the fire. I'll bring some cider and barmbrack for your men there."

"Thank you."

Alex led the way toward the dining room, stepped one foot inside, and then stopped cold. There, sitting with his head bent over a book of some kind, was the Spaniard and he wasn't alone. Had he followed them here, or had he come before them for clues of his own?

Alex backed up, motioning for Baylor and Montague to back quickly away too. The three of them hugged the corner of the room, just outside the door to the dining room.

"What is it?" Baylor asked, trying to whisper but still too loud.

"Shhh," Alex warned. "It's him. The Spanish man who was following us, and this time there are two of them."

"It cannot be," Montague intoned and then stealthily crept to the doorway and glanced in. "It is him."

Alex motioned him away from the door. "They have to be after the same thing we are looking for. It's the only explanation."

"What are we looking for? I thought your parents," Baylor whispered.

"Yes, of course. But my parents were hired to find something important. I don't know yet what they were searching for, but it must have been very valuable. These men must be looking for it and following us to see if we find the clues first."

Baylor and Montague exchanged glances. "We need to turn the tables on them, spy on them for a change. But they'll recognize us; they know our faces."

"We could make a disguise," Alex suggested. "Montague, if you shaved off that mustache and beard and we powdered your hair —"

"No." His answer was immediate and definite.

Alex looked up at Baylor. Impossible to disguise his size. She had an image come to mind of him dressed as a woman, which made her press her lips together to keep from laughing. "I can't imagine any disguise working on you."

Baylor shrugged.

Montague turned toward her. "You're the only one who could do it and quickly enough to get in there right now."

"But how?" Alex looked around the room, seeing tablecloths and lace doilies. What could she do with them?

"We'll dress you as a man. I've an extra pair of breeches and boots in my bag. They'll be too big, but with some rope tied around your waist to hold them up and a hat to cover your hair . . . we could use some soot from the fireplace for a little shadowing around your beard."

"My beard?" Alex nearly choked between shock and laughter. "Do you really think it will work? We have to hurry!"

Montague laid his bag onto the floor and dug through it. He tossed articles of clothing at her until there was a pile around her feet. "But where will I change? The serving woman could come back at any moment!"

"Baylor, quick, take off your cloak and make a screen here in the corner. Alexandria, we'll turn our backs but hurry."

Baylor made the screen and Alex scurried into the borrowed clothing, stuffing her skirt into Montague's bag. By the time she was finished, Montague had come back from the fireplace with dark smudged fingers. "Here now, hold still."

The smell of ashes burnt her nose as he tapped the blackness against her upper lip and chin. She stood mute, with lips together in a half panic. "What if they recognize me!"

"We'll be right here, should you need us," Montague assured her.

Baylor leaned down and gave her a broad grin that took up his entire face. He patted her cheek with a quiet chuckle. "Ach, but you're a pretty lad. Never fear. They'll think you too young to have much sense yet."

"He's right. Sit close enough to hear them but with your back turned toward them."

"What about the serving woman? She's sure to recognize me and wonder where you two are!"

"We'll take care of her. Now go." Montague turned her by the shoulders toward the door to the dining room.

Alex took a deep breath and steadied her nerves. She could do this. Just keep her head down and her back to the Spaniards as much as possible. When her feet didn't move, Baylor nudged her into the room.

The scuffle of her overly large boots brought the gaze of everyone to her face. There was one other couple having what looked to be a light repast and a serious conversation. Alex looked at them with a polite nod in their direction and then made for the table by the fire. She glanced at the men, one tall and skinny with a thin mustache and line of a beard; the other one, the one she hadn't seen before was his opposite, short with a round stomach, black hair, and a chubby-cheeked face.

The short one looked up. Alex hurriedly looked at the floor, sidestepped around a table, and went to the fire as if to warm herself. A glance at them gave her a sigh of relief. They were pouring over the book again. She slowly made her way to the table beside them and sat down, her back to the Spaniards. They didn't look up from their book, they were so intent on it.

"The answers must be in here," the tall, bony man hissed.

"I am a slow reader, my liege." His voice was high and full of fear.

Alex heard a quick *thwack* and jumped in her chair.

"What was the king thinking? Sending *you* with me. I might as well have a stone tied around my neck."

"Ouch," the short, stout man replied. "You hit me!"

"And I'll hit you again if you don't stop being so stupid. We finally have the upper hand on that Featherstone girl. Our first stroke of luck was getting into the castle and finding Sloane's journal. We must find out if it says anything about the manuscript."

A sudden clatter of dishes had the diners looking up toward the doorway. A young serving girl came into the room. She went to each table and set down tea and the sweet bread. Alex kept her head down and waved the girl off when she came to her table, sighing in relief when the girl moved on. When Alex looked up, her heart sank. The Spaniards had abandoned their table. She'd heard so little! She hurried from the room to find her friends.

She was more than a little shocked to see Montague in the parlor, standing close to the serving woman they'd first met, stroking her plump cheek and laughing in a way Alex had never seen him laugh. The woman was blushing, tilting her head with a coy glance while Montague murmured phrases to her in a low, husky voice. So that was what he meant by taking care of it.

Thinking to rescue him, she made her way to the pair. "There you are, Montague. Goodness but I'm tired. Have you managed rooms for us?" She looked up at him and then smiled at the serving woman, brows raised.

Montague frowned, his gray brows coming together over azure eyes. "Mistress Tinsdale has been all that is accommodating. She was just telling me that the Hamilton Rowans reside in that castle you are so keen to see."

"Oh yes. My sister is the housekeeper there and will give you a tour, she will," the plump woman promised with an adoring smile at Montague.

"That would be lovely! When can we see it?" Alex clasped her hands together for added effect. Crafty old fox. His talents were vaster than she'd realized.

"I've sent a note round to my sister. We should hear back shortly, but it will most likely be on the morrow . . . to work around the family's schedule, you see. They don't like to be disturbed."

"Of course."

"In the meantime Mistress Tinsdale has ordered cook to prepare her finest for us.

227

You should go and" — he lifted his brows and looked askance at her strange clothing, which Alex had forgotten about — "freshen up."

Alex gazed down at the breeches she was wearing and flushed. Mistress Tinsdale must think her daft for changing from the skirt she'd recently seen her in to men's clothing. "I was going to play a prank on our giant friend." She shook her head like it would be hard to explain. "I'll just go up to my room and change before dinner. Where, exactly, is my room?"

Mistress Tinsdale didn't seem too appalled, only distantly confused. "Up the stairs. The first door on the left. You've a room to yourself, dearie, as we only have two other occupants aside from your fine selves."

Alex nodded, giving Montague a side glance. "I will see you shortly then?"

Montague winked. "I'll be right here, my lady. Entertaining this lovely woman with my tall tales."

Alex smirked, one brow raised, and then turned to go.

At the top of the stairs, she felt a hand on her shoulder. She stopped, heart pounding as a voice said in her ear, "We'll be watchin' your door, lass, never fear."

She turned with an exhale of relief to see Baylor's tall frame.

"They have a journal. . . . I think it's Sloane's journal."

"Shhh. Let's not speak of it here. Wait until after dinner. We will all take a little walk and talk where it is more private."

Alex nodded and turned the knob to her door. "Thank you, Baylor. For everything."

"I wouldn't miss it for the world, lass. Not for a leprechaun's pot of gold neither."

Alex laughed. "That, I don't believe."

"Well," Baylor shrugged, "you may have the right of it there, lass. It's a fine thing, the end of a rainbow."

Alex pictured it in her mind as she opened the door to her room. At the end of her rainbow wasn't a pot of gold. No, at the end of her rainbow stood her parents, alive and very happy to see her.

# Chapter Seventeen

The captain of the troop traveling with Gabriel looked as if steam might come from his ears as he and Meade rode into Beal and the inn's grassy yard. His white hair was standing on end as if he'd shoved his fingers through it too many times, his face was an unbecoming red, and his eyes bulged out the moment he saw them. He started to speak, sputtered, and then clamped his lips closed as Gabriel dismounted and walked over to the short man. What was it with diminutive men and their tempers?

"My dear captain, I am so relieved to see you standing here in good health. I could not imagine why you weren't right behind us when the tide went out."

A vein in the captain's forehead pulsed purple, and when he finally choked out words, they were hissed between his gritted teeth. "We were served strong drink, Your Grace, and I have feeling you knew of it."

"Strong drink? How should I know of it when I wasn't even here? Besides, I'm not in charge of what your men drink. You are."

The captain inhaled as though he'd been struck and then turned his back on Gabriel and walked a few steps away. When he turned back around, he seemed more composed. "And where is the young lady, Your Grace?"

Gabriel gave him a shrug and a half-hearted smile. "It would seem the lady has gone on a little journey. Problem is, no one knows where."

"Impossible! How could she not be here?"

Gabriel slapped his gloves against one leg and moved toward the warmth of the inn. "It's hardly impossible. She hired a coach."

"The prince regent will be furious. This is your fault. You didn't control her."

"Perhaps." Gabriel motioned the captain inside and clasped him on the shoulder in a friendly manner. "Perhaps we'll all be in the soup. But let's not be too hasty. It has occurred to me that we might not tell the prince regent. We might find her and bring her to safety instead."

"Sir, do you speak of deceiving the prince regent?"

"Deceiving is such a strong word, Captain. I am only suggesting that we continue to do

231

what we've been ordered to do. Find Lady Featherstone and bring her to London. Should the prince regent learn that she wasn't home where we all expected her to be, she will be the one in dire straits. I would spare her the prince regent's wrath if we can, don't you think?"

"But my orders and provisions are only within the perimeter of this trip to Holy Island and back."

"Don't fear the added expense, my good captain. I shall be glad of your help and pay accordingly. We'll need to spread out, some going south, some north into Scotland, and some west. And someone, preferably someone I can trust with her life, will need to stay here and lead the operation as it is most likely that she will come back home soon."

"I would insist on staying here in charge of the home base." The captain sat across from him at a low table by the fire.

Gabriel allowed a small smile to touch his lips. The captain was falling right into his hands, making it easier than he thought to rid himself of the soldiers. "I was hoping you would take the lead, Captain. You shall be handsomely compensated, be assured. Now" — Gabriel leaned forward and lowered his voice in secrecy — "Meade and I will go west as we've learned that a coachman left for Whitehaven about a week ago." He hurried on. "But another coach left for Newcastle upon Tyne a day later, so send your best two or three men south in that direction. The northern postal route is the least likely, but she may have smuggled herself on board a postal coach. It bears looking into."

The captain nodded, chewing on the end of his thumbnail in concentration. "I know just the men to send north, Bobby and Carter, they'll get into too much trouble sitting idle here."

"Good. That leaves Benjamin and Georgie to go south. If someone discovers her, they are to bring her back here so she can stay under your protection while the other teams are alerted. We can meet in a convenient place and then make our way back to London as planned, no one knowing we had a little hiccup, eh?"

"It's a sound plan. I — ah — apologize, Your Grace, if I've seemed short tempered on this mission. It's just that it's my first one directly from the prince regent and I've been anxious to please him. You understand, don't you?"

"Of course, Captain. The prince regent is not someone we want to displease in any way, which is why we must find our little bird and bring her safely to nest before he hears of her disappearance."

"You don't think she's in trouble, do you?"

"I hope not." Gabriel mused, looking off into the distance. "I think she's a precocious passel of trouble. But that will be my problem once I have her back in London. I, too, don't want to disappoint the prince regent. So, it's all set then?"

"Yes, Your Grace. We have an understanding."

Early morning the next day, Gabriel and Meade successfully crept out of Beal before anyone, even the scullery maid, had arisen. Meade had learned that Mr. Howard had indeed taken Alexandria west toward Whitehaven. He had not returned, according to Mrs. Howard, because he had business in a nearby town, which might take a fortnight to complete. His wife didn't know why Alex had gone or if she would return with her husband, but she leaned in toward Meade, wiggled her eyebrows, and said she doubted it. Everybody knew the young mistress didn't believe her parents were dead and everyone knew how much she thrived on solving mysteries. Was it any wonder she'd gone off looking for them? She thought not.

Gabriel was convinced of it. The letter

from Ireland was cause enough to head in that direction and so he persuaded Meade to get back on his horse and gallop off toward the Emerald Isle. The thought of seeing it again after so many years actually brought a jolt of joy to his heart. A beautiful land, Ireland, but with a history rife with conflict and the struggles of the poor. The people, though, were rich of heart, living in a place that had a wealth of mystery and magic, if he believed in magic.

It was hard to describe the feeling when he'd been there last. A land of green and brown and blue so deep it made your throat ache to look at it — as if it had jumped right from the pages of a fairy tale. And the stories, so many stories that the bards of old still kept alive. Had Alex made it there yet? And if so, how was she faring?

He imagined her boarding a ferry, all alone. The coachman wouldn't follow her that far, he was sure. Maybe she'd had the wits enough to attach herself to another group, a group with women in it. The possibilities for danger made his stomach churn.

"Come, Meade, we must ride faster."

His poor secretary groaned but tapped his heels against his horse and tried to keep up with Gabriel. If they hurried they might make it to Whitehaven in three days, three days of torture for Meade, but what didn't kill him would only make him stronger.

True to his word, Gabriel and Meade rode into Whitehaven on the evening of the third day. They went first to the post office on the slim possibility that Alex had left him a letter. Had she received his last post? Ann had said she had sent it here. If it was missing, then she'd picked it up and they would be certain they were on the right track.

Sure enough, when he asked the clerk if his letter had arrived and whether Lady Alexandria Featherstone had picked it up, he'd been told yes, well, sort of. The man was hard to hear, his voice was thin, which didn't carry well. It rankled to ask him to write down his words, but Gabriel did it, not giving any explanation as to why he couldn't hear him.

"A man came by and picked it up. He said he was traveling with her, a servant of some sort, though he didn't look like a servant."

"And you just gave it to him? He could have been anyone," Gabriel barked, panic washing through him. "What did he look like? What, exactly, did he say?"

Another man entered the post office and stood behind Gabriel. The clerk glanced at him, wrinkled his nose, and stammered, "He, er, looked like an older man, long, gray hair and a weathered face. He had a sword and comported himself like a — a leader of some sort. He barked orders at me, much like you are doing now, and I just — I just did what he asked."

The description sent Gabriel's level of panic up a notch.

"Did he say who he was? Did he give a name?"

"No, that is, I don't recall one. He just said he was here to pick up any correspondence for Lady Alexandria Featherstone."

"Did you see her at any time?"

The man shook his head. "He took the letter, glanced at it but didn't open it to my knowledge, and left. He seemed to be in a hurry."

Gabriel rubbed one eyebrow with a finger and sighed. Either she had this man with her, which could be for her protection if he was going around carrying a sword, or someone was following her. *Dear God, let it be the former.* Gabriel looked back at the clerk. "Did the man post any letters? Anything for the Duke of St. Easton, perhaps?"

The clerk pulled forth a box. "I do believe so, Your Grace. Yes, here it is."

Gabriel's heartbeat sped up at the sight of

it. What was she up to? "Thank you. Where's the best inn in this town? I will ask if anyone has seen her there."

"The best inn would likely be the Queens Arms on Market Place, right in the middle of town, Your Grace. But there are over one hundred public houses in Whitehaven, due to all the shipping done here," the clerk said proudly.

"Wonderful," the duke intoned. He turned to go. His gaze met that of the stranger behind him for a brief moment. The man bowed his head, which Gabriel ignored. He would rather word didn't get out that the Duke of St. Easton was in town.

The chance of finding where Alexandria had stayed was too depressing to contemplate. They would rest tonight and question the shipping office first thing in the morning. She must have bought a ticket and there would be passenger lists. It might take some time, but unless she'd changed her name, he would find out where she had sailed.

He stepped out the post office door to the street where Meade held their horses.

"Any luck, Your Grace?"

Gabriel mounted his horse as he spoke. "Not much. A man picked up my letter to her."

"What sort of man?" Meade looked

238

alarmed.

"The trained sort, it would seem. An older man, but strong and capable, used to giving orders."

"Do you have any idea who it might be?" Meade struggled to hoist himself back into the saddle.

"Unfortunately, no. Do you? Were there any other servants at the castle when you visited her?"

"Not that I saw. No one of that description, anyway."

"He's either with her or against her. Let's pray she's been smart and hired a protector."

"Uhm," Meade grimaced, "it doesn't sound like something she would do."

"You know her so well, do you?" Gabriel barked like a snarling dog. Meade's face registered shock as if he'd been slapped. "I apologize, Meade," Gabriel lowered his voice. "It's just that I can't abide thinking of her all alone. Surely she has more sense than that."

Meade clamped his mouth shut but looked doubtful.

"Well, let's get a move on. We sup at the Queens Arms and then an early day tomorrow. We'll find her, Meade. We'll find her."

■ ■ ■ ■

The candle flickered in Gabriel's room as he sat hunched over Alexandria's latest letter.

My Dear Guardian Duke,

Oh, dear. You must be angry. If you are reading this letter, then you have discovered that I am not, presently, at my home on Holy Island. And you've tracked me to Whitehaven, which means you are determined to find me. I would ask that you give up, but from our acquaintance through these letters we have been writing, I would guess that you won't. Please, Your Grace, I beg you to allow me to search for my parents undeterred. When I find them, I promise to bring them directly to you in London. And I promise to give up should the trail of clues grow cold. In my darker moments I allow myself to question if they are really alive. I believe they are, wholeheartedly, but if they are not, I will then willingly come to you and be your most biddable ward. (To the best of my ability, of course.)

Yours,
Alexandria

Most biddable ward, ha! He liked the sound of that, but he knew her better than to believe it. She would always give him trouble. Why did the thought of it bring him excitement instead of dread? Perhaps he would have a lifetime of such excitement.

Folding the letter and adding it to his pile, he rose, blew out the candle, and climbed into the big featherbed. The Queens Arms was a most comfortable inn indeed. He closed his eyes, drifting off to sleep with visions of her in his arms.

# Chapter Eighteen

True to her word, Mistress Tinsdale's sister, Helen, was waiting for them at the gate-house to allow them entrance to Killyleagh Castle. They'd walked the short distance from the inn away from the harbor, passing the colorful rows of shops and houses on either side of them. A two-wheeled cart with a horse pulling it passed by. The lone driver lifted his hat with a smile and a good-day. The air was brisk with the feel of the sea in it, but the sun was shining and they were going to the castle. A day full of promise. Alex tried to temper her excitement as she told Montague and Baylor of the strange conversation she'd overheard from the night before.

"I have to get that journal and have a look at it too," Alex stated for the third time. "I just wish I knew what I was looking for."

"Don't you worry your pretty head about that. I'll get the journal for you."

Montague frowned at the giant but remained silent.

"Perhaps I can sneak away from our 'tour' and get lost. It's such a huge place . . . perhaps Helen won't notice I'm missing for some time."

"The Irish charm can help with that." Baylor grinned and wiggled his thick eyebrows.

"As long as your wife doesn't hear of it," Montague replied in a dry tone.

Baylor's face blanched at the thought. "I'll not overstep my bounds." His tone turned defensive.

Montague chuckled. "Seeing as how I've applied some *English* charm to the Mistress Tinsdale, I suppose I shouldn't overly regard her sister."

Alex stifled a laugh as they came to the gatehouse and then choked it off with a cough. Helen was coming toward them with a big smile on her face. She looked a great deal like her sister, round in a motherly way, brown hair with wisps that curled around her face. A big, open smile with dimples. "Hello." She held out her hands in welcome. "Helga told me about the wee lass with her giant guard and handsome admiral. What a blessed child you are."

The gatehouse was built into the stone

wall that enclosed the courtyard and the castle. On either side of the gate were tall towers, four stories high with windows framed with a lighter-colored stone. Helen unlocked the padlock on the great iron gate with a long key and pulled the gate open. It creaked and moaned with its weight. "Come along, then." She motioned them inside.

As they followed her swinging skirt up the wide pathway to the front of the castle, Alex leaned toward Montague and whispered, "Admiral? You never told me that."

"You never asked." Montague winked at her.

"Well, I won't forget to ask about it later," Alex assured him.

A sense of awe grew apace with her excitement as they neared the castle. It was perfect with its conical-shaped spires, waving flags with the family's crest and the flag of Ulster. They went up wide stone steps to a massive, arched wooden door.

"If you'll look above the door, carved in the stone is the coat of arms of Charles I. The Hamiltons were royalists, and for their support they were granted the right to display the king's arms. Now, if you'll just follow me inside, I've many a tale to tell you about the castle."

They followed Helen down a long stone

corridor and then into a surprisingly cozy drawing room. The furniture was thickly upholstered and comfortable, done in soft shades of brown and green. The fireplace was big, with a nice warm fire burning in it. Above the elaborate mantel made from marble was a painting of a beautiful woman. Nearby were landscape paintings, one had the rolling green hills of Ireland, lavender heather blooming across the hills in the foreground, and a sky of azure blue. The dark silhouette of a castle stood far off in the distance. It wasn't Killyleagh, but it was magical just the same.

"I've permission to take you on a short tour, but I thought you might like to warm yourselves and have a cup of tea first." Helen smiled her broad smile at them and then left to fetch the tea.

"It's not at all like Lindisfarne Castle," Alex murmured in wonder.

"Is it not? What's your home like then?" Baylor sat carefully on a pretty chair that creaked under his weight.

Alex shook her head, embarrassed. "Not as cozy and nice as this."

"Castles are a cold and damp place to live if they haven't been renovated such as this one," Montague agreed.

"Have you lived in a castle, Montague?"

She realized that she hadn't gotten to know very much about him and perhaps that was her fault as much as his.

"Oh, I've stayed a spell in a few but never lived in one. My wife wouldn't have stood for that."

"You have a wife?" Alex sat across from him. Why hadn't she asked him about his family?

"I had one. She died over two years ago."

"I'm sorry. Do you have children?"

He shook his head, a faraway look in eyes that had turned darker blue. "No children." His voice was low and Alex let the subject drop. Before the silence that followed could become uncomfortable, Helen returned with her tea tray. She glided over to a table in front of Alex and set it down. After pouring, she perched on the settee with Montague, and with her brown eyes twinkling, asked Alex, "Would you like to hear about the ghost that haunts the castle, Lady Alexandria?"

"A ghost? Oh yes. Please tell us." Maybe there would be a clue in the story.

Helen clasped her hands together and became very still. "Very well. A long time ago, around the time of the Earls of Clanbrassil in the 1600s, the second Earl of Clanbrassil married the Earl of Drogheda's daughter, Alice Moore. The match was a disaster and Lady Alice only had one child, who died as a babe, God bless it. The earl's father decided to write up a new will that said if his son died without an heir, the entire estate would go to five Hamilton cousins.

"Well, Lady Alice wasn't having that, I can tell you. She broke into the safe, found the will, and threw it into the fire. Then she convinced her husband to write a new will with her and her brother as the heirs. He did it, he did, even though his own mother warned him that he wouldn't live three months after signing it. And wasn't she right about that? The earl was poisoned not three months after he signed the new will."

Alex gasped. "Was she caught?"

"Nay, my lady. They never proved it, at any rate. But God or fate intervened as the Blue Lady died two years later, leaving the castle to the Hamilton cousins after all."

"Why did they call her the Blue Lady?"

"That's the name of her ghost. It is said that Lady Alice haunts the halls of Killyleagh Castle and everyone who has seen her says she's wearing blue." Helen paused and set down her cup. "Be on the lookout as we tour the castle. She does like to appear now and again." She laughed then in a way that said she enjoyed telling the story.

Alex shivered as she stood and gazed around the room. It was too bright for ghosts! But she edged over toward Baylor for protection. When she peered up into his face though, his eyes were wide with a look of wariness that said he believed the tale. He took her hand and squeezed it. When she tried to let go he held on, looking as if he wouldn't let go the entire time they were there. Finally she had to jerk her hand away. Why, he seemed more afraid than she was!

The rest of the tour, through the grand, high-ceiling rooms with their Jacobean motif plasterwork, rich fabrics on the windows and furnishings, and thick rugs to keep feet warm against the polished stone floors was pleasant enough, but Alex was hoping to find the owners.

They climbed a spiral staircase and entered a library that smelled of books and pipe tobacco. Helen seemed suddenly ill at ease. "Just have a quick look through the window there, you can see all the way to Strangford Lough, and then we'll finish up back in the sitting room where we began."

Alex took a peek out the window but noticed some odd tables and shelves scattered around the dome-ceiling room. She backed into the shadows as the men commented on the view. *Here. This has to be where the Spaniards found the manuscript. Maybe there are others.*

As Helen waved them back down the narrow spiral stairway, Alex lingered. Baylor glanced back at her and winked as he started the long descent.

Turning quickly to the task, she read the spines of the books on the shelves. She pulled down the few volumes about the castle and the town and paged through them with darting eyes. Dates . . . names . . . most of them unfamiliar crossed the pages. There were a few mentions of Hans Sloane but nothing about a missing item from his collection.

"Did you find what you're looking for?" a deep male voice said from the top of the stairs.

Alex started, inhaled, and twisted around to face him. He was an older man, probably in his sixties, with white shaggy sideburns and a mostly bald head. His eyes were intense, intelligent, with a spark of humor that gave her courage.

Alex turned her attention from those piercing eyes down to the table where her hand was splayed on the opened book. She'd been caught and there was nothing to do but tell the truth. "The stories of the castle are so fascinating. I was looking for more stories."

"Ah, the stories." He chuckled and moved farther into the room. He walked over to one bookshelf and took down a sheaf of papers. "I know the allure of stories. I've written some of my own, you know."

"You're Archibald Hamilton Rowan, aren't you?"

He turned, the smile on his face genuine. "You know me?"

Alex shrugged. "Just what I've heard from Helen."

He laughed out loud. "What do you seek, my dear?" He walked a step closer and looked down at her. "I've a mind to help, if I can."

Alex took a deep breath. "I am Alexandria Featherstone of Holy Island. My parents came here some months ago, almost a year ago," she amended with a downward glance. "They were searching for something but . . . I've not come for that." She looked back up. "They've disappeared and the prince regent has declared them dead. But they are not dead. Something has happened to them and they need me. I have to find them." She took a step forward. "Please, did they come here to the castle? Did you see them?"

He took a deep breath and motioned for her to take a chair. "Sit down, my little owl. Such pretty, questioning eyes you have." After she sat and settled her hands into her lap, she gazed up at him in expectancy. "You've the look of your mother, you know. Yes, they were here. They wanted information as to the collection of Hans Sloane."

"Yes, I've heard that name. Who was he?"

"He was born here in Killyleagh. He moved to London and became a great physician. Eventually he became King George II's physician. But that's not what he was really famous for."

"What then?"

Sir Archibald walked toward the bookshelves and plucked off two volumes. He set them down in front of her with sentimental flare. "He was a collector of antiquities."

"Antiquities?" Alex looked from the books up to his face.

"He liked old things and puzzles. Anything from old relics to manuscripts full of poetry, drawings, inventions and such, coins, medals, just about anything you can think of that is old and important. He amassed a great collection and then bequeathed it to the British Museum. That is, it became the British Museum with his collection and King George's valuables."

Alex motioned toward the old, leather-bound volumes. She opened one of the books and paged through it, not knowing what she was looking for. "What do you think they wanted . . . my parents, that is?"

He let out a little exhale with another gentle smile. "I don't know, child. Except that it was something Sloane had found. The question is, if they couldn't find it in the British Museum, then what happened to it? What is missing from Sloane's collection and, as important to ask, who wants it?"

Alex nodded. "There are others searching for it."

"They were here. They got off with one of my books, I'm afraid, but I doubt it has the answers any of you are searching for. Your parents took that journal with them."

Alex gasped. "They stole a book from you?"

Sir Archibald chuckled. "They borrowed it."

"What kind of journal was it?"

"It was from the fifteenth century, some obscure Italian sculptor and inventor. It was his story."

"Do you remember his name?"

"I believe it was Augusto de Carrara, but that is all I know. I never read the book."

He bowed low and turned to go. At the top of the stairs he turned and gave her a thoughtful glance. "Take your time, my dear, but I doubt you will find anything of much use."

So her parents had the only manuscript with any real clues in it. "Thank you, sir." She looked down at the books before her, discouragement weighing her down. She'd promised the duke in her last letter that she would go to him in London and be his most biddable ward should she come to a dead end with the clues. Just the thought of giving up made her grind her teeth, but she hadn't promised it lightly. She laid her forehead on her clasped hands.

*God, lead me and direct my path. Light my way. Don't let me be faint of heart and give up too soon nor be too stubborn. I can be so stubborn . . . show me the way.*

The thought of giving up was almost more than she could bear.

Her parents needed her. Until she had proof that they were dead, she had to keep trying.

# CHAPTER NINETEEN

Gabriel woke in his room at Whitehaven's Queens Arms to a piercing, ringing in his ears.

He sat up in a sudden move, pressed his hands over his ears, and broke out into a sweat. "No. No, no, no." He gasped as the sound echoed inside his head, louder and louder and then snap. Nothing. A dull, aching nothing.

He stood on shaking legs and fumbled with lighting the candle. Panting, sweat streaming from his face, he stumbled to the bowl and pitcher of water on the room's small table. He poured some water into the bowl, splashed his face, and wiped it on the nearby towel. Then he braced his hands on either side of the table and leaned over the bowl, just trying to breathe and trying to keep the contents of his stomach where they belonged.

After a few minutes the roaring of his

heartbeat slowed and he was able to stand upright. He swallowed, turned from the table, and made his way to the window. He opened the curtains and leaned his forehead against the cool glass. It was still dark but with the beginnings of a sunrise in the east. Gabriel concentrated on the pink hues for a long time, waiting for his panicked body to calm. He didn't have the courage yet to speak into the stillness. He knew what he would hear.

Just thinking it made his heartbeat speed up. He breathed, deep and slow, and concentrated on the widening glow of pink and yellow. Like a flower blossoming in slow motion, the sunrise grew across the sky until it lit up the roofs of Whitehaven and glistened against the top of the water.

God made this, he thought. God made every sunrise and every sunset. He knew just how the light would bend against the horizon of a circular earth. God knew who would be watching each one and what they would think and feel about it. He knew *everything.*

Then why did He let this happen? Was it something Gabriel had done? Was there some test he hadn't passed? Anger and fear enveloped him in a nauseous cloud.

"Why did You let this happen to me?

Again? It was coming back!" He spoke the words out loud but he didn't hear them, not even a little. *Oh, God, what if it is permanent this time?* He'd begun to really believe that the northern climes had done him good. That his hearing would soon be back to normal. But no. Anger filled him as he'd never felt it.

"Why give it back only to take it away again? You are cruel." He turned away from the sunrise. "You may know everything, but You are cruel to give me hope and then snatch it away again."

Gabriel hit the post on the end of the bed with his fist. The bed shook with the force of the blow. Pain radiated up his arm but he welcomed the feeling. He had to get out of here.

Trembling with anger, he dressed and packed up his belongings. They were to board a ship to Ireland today. Dare he go now? He was dreading getting on any kind of ship, having had to battle seasickness in his navy days. Humiliation that a duke's son, a person of his rank, was curled into a wretched ball of misery and then the accident he'd had . . . well, they'd moved him to land duty and kept him there. But now, he had no choice. Alexandria was coming home to London with him whether she liked it or not and if he had to cross a hundred seas, he would do it.

Minutes later he pounded on Meade's door and waited. He finally opened it, his hair sticking up in all directions and eyes squinting against the light. It must be early. "I'm going down to the taproom for coffee and breakfast. Meet me down there as soon as possible."

Meade nodded and said something but his head was down and Gabriel couldn't make it out. "I've lost my hearing again," he blurted out in angry staccato. He might as well tell him, as he'd find out soon enough.

Meade's head came up and his eyes widened. His lips clearly mouthed that he was sorry. "How do you feel, Your Grace?"

"I feel like pounding someone into a bloody pulp, that's how I feel. Now, we'll use the speaking book again when necessary, but we must get on that ferry and find Lady Featherstone. You will have to question the men at the customs house. Find out if they have any record of her, what ship she sailed on, and where she disembarked. Also, try and find out the name of the man traveling with her, if indeed he is traveling with her and not following her." He waited for Meade to nod his understanding and then turned and stomped down to order breakfast.

Gabriel paced the dock area while Meade went inside the customs house to find out about Alexandria. It was humiliating that he couldn't ask the questions himself, humiliating and infuriating. Anger hummed through his veins like wildfire. It wasn't good for him, he knew that readily enough, but he was afraid what would happen if he let go of the anger. The despair waiting for him at the other end of this rage was too terrible to consider. So he paced, switching his gloves back and forth from one hand to the other.

A hand on his shoulder stopped him mid-stride. He spun around to find a gun pointed at his chest. His heart leapt to his throat. Dear God, was this it? Was he about to get murdered in broad daylight by a couple of footpads?

The two men flanked him and he had a flash of memory from the post office the day before. The man in line behind him . . . it had to be . . . yes, he was the same man as the one with the gun standing right in front of him. He'd overheard them talking. He knew Gabriel was a duke.

The man shouted something but Gabriel had no idea what it was. The other man reached for him. Instinct took over and Gabriel spun to the side, but he wasn't fast enough. The gun went off, a silent explosion with smoke that surrounded them like thick fog. The air smelled of burning powder. It was too close! Too close. Pain burst through his shoulder in a shocking wave. Had he really been shot?

He stumbled as the other man dove on him, rummaging through his coat. He grasped Gabriel's purse in a tight hold. They were both breathing hard as the first man held him while the second patted down his body. They spoke to each other and then shoved him to the ground and turned to run.

"Help!" Gabriel shouted. He started after them, the pain from his shoulder radiating down his arm. Wasn't anyone around to help him? He ran a little farther, stumbling, blood dripping down his arm and to the street. A black curtain started to veil his vision. He fell to the ground. He was going to faint.

He woke to find Meade's face hovering over him. "Thank God, Your Grace. I've called a doctor. He should be here any moment."

Gabriel struggled to sit up, finding himself in his bed at the Queens Arms. "They got off with my purse, Meade. We have to find

259

them. We need that money."

Meade's hands fluttered nervously around Gabriel's good shoulder, his reed-thin body blocking Gabriel's attempt to rise. "But sir, the blood. Doctor first."

Gabriel glanced at his shoulder and gave in, lying back down. He looked at his blood-soaked shirt, a wave of weakness overwhelming him. "Very well, help me get this shirt off. Is it still bleeding?"

Meade set to work on the shirt, a tortuous process that made the wound leak fresh blood. Gabriel knew enough about bullet wounds to direct him to press on it and hold the pressure until the bleeding stopped. They discovered that the bullet had passed directly through the upper part of his shoulder, which was good news, a clean shot with no bullet to dig out. By the time the doctor arrived, they had the bleeding stopped and had cleaned the area around the wounds, both front and back. The doctor spoke with Meade and then set to work stitching the one in the back.

"The wound is more ragged in the back, Your Grace," Meade explained as Gabriel breathed hard through his nose and concentrated on staying conscious. How had he let this happen? He would have heard them approach had he not been deaf. He could have fought them off if he'd heard them coming. Would he have to have someone with him at all times now, like a child in leading strings? The frustration gave him something to concentrate on as the needle poked in and out of his shoulder. Finally the torture was done.

The doctor made a poultice of some kind of strong-smelling concoction, applied it to both wounds, and bandaged it with a wide strip of linen around and around his shoulder and under his arm. The doctor held out a bottle of laudanum, which Gabriel refused. It was just a dull ache now and it kept him awake. Meade paid the man, Gabriel wondering how much money his secretary had on him, and then the doctor left with the promise of coming tomorrow to check on him and change the bandage.

"Meade, you must alert the authorities of the theft. There was over five hundred pounds in that purse. I recognized the man from the post office. He came in and must have overheard my conversation with the postmaster. He knew I am a duke. Tell them to check the post office for the identity of the man. If they recover the money, they can send it to us."

"Yes, Your Grace."

"How much money do you have? And

what did you find out about Alexandria?"

Meade took out the speaking book.

"Alexandria's name was on the passenger list of the *Saint Patrick*. It left 2:00 p.m. on a Wednesday, almost two weeks ago. Its destination was Belfast — directly across the Irish Sea. She was not seen with a man, but when I questioned the clerk he said he did remember a striking older gentleman who carried himself with authority and the man did have a sword, which I thought sounded like the same man described by the postmaster. The clerk couldn't remember for sure, but after studying the list of names on board at that crossing he thought it might be James Montague."

Gabriel looked up, startled. "Admiral James Montague?"

Meade's eyes widened. "I had not considered that," he mouthed. "Could it be?"

Gabriel thought back to what he'd heard about the man. He was certain he hadn't met him in person and so had no face to put to the name. He had heard though that the admiral *had* gone north upon retirement from the Royal Navy. He must be in his upper sixties by now. Hadn't his wife died? He'd turned into something of a recluse after that, the gossip papers had said. But what could one of the most famed military

262

leaders in British history possibly be doing with Alexandria? God save them, she was impossible to second-guess.

"If Montague is for her, she couldn't be in better hands. But if he's against her . . ." Gabriel tried to get up. "We've no time to lose. Let us get aboard the first ferry to Ireland. Do you have enough money for the fare?"

Meade took out his leather purse and emptied it onto the bed. It wasn't much but it would get them across the Irish Sea and then, in Belfast, Gabriel could make a visit to the Bank of Ireland.

"But sir, the doctor warned of infection. You need to stay in bed and rest for a few days at least. You shouldn't travel until it is somewhat healed."

"There is no time to coddle my shoulder. We leave day after tomorrow."

The cold breeze blew back Gabriel's hair as they skimmed across the choppy waves that crashed against the bow of the ship. He swallowed hard against the rolling of his stomach and set his teeth, a sheen of sweat forming on his face. Just a few hours . . . and if he kept his gaze fixed on the horizon, it helped a little.

What a mess he was! His hearing gone

again, his stomach revolting against the rocking of the waves, and his arm in the sling under his coat aching with the damp air. He felt like the walking dead and hoped desperately that no one recognized him. He wore his collar up and his hat pulled low over his eyes. His anger had diminished into an imperceptible hum as they'd passed the inhabited Isle of Man with its quaint cottages, stone castle, and wide rocky beaches. A little while later, he saw the grandeur of the Emerald Isle coming into view. Land. Blessed relief. Rocky cliffs gave way to rounded hills of green. Those then sloped down into an inlet valley with the buildings of Belfast making black and white smudges against the green.

He'd never been to Belfast, only Dublin and some smaller towns in the south. The northeast of Ireland was said to be more Protestant, more British from all accounts. He would be afforded more respect here as a peer of the British realm, not that it mattered much with his hearing gone. Meade would be doing most of the questioning from now on. He would lend his weight as duke when needed, but otherwise he hoped to stay in the background where the curious couldn't seek him out.

*Alexandria, couldn't you make this easy,*

*sweetling? Leave a wide path? It would be ever so helpful.* He cracked a smile at the thought. Grasping tight hold of the handrail, he clung to it and tried to think as she might think. She was looking for her parents so she would be searching for clues. Where might she go to find such clues was the question. The letter from her mother had led her to Belfast, so she knew of one place her mother had gone. She must have visited the post office and inquired after her parents there. It was the best place to start.

An hour later they traveled up the channel and docked. Thanks be to God, he could get off this bobbing ride and plant his feet on solid ground. His knees wobbled and his thighs quivered as he followed the crowd off the boat. Once on shore, Gabriel took a long breath, his eyes shut as his body readjusted yet again, and barked orders for a carriage for hire, giving directions to the driver to take them to the post office. It was something of a comfort knowing that if someone said something he should respond to, Meade would take care of it. His secretary was becoming ever valuable, he reflected none too happily, settling back for the ride.

Thatched houses and shops lined the streets with pubs and churches on every corner. After a rocking ride that did little to help the nausea he was fighting, they stopped at a building with the British Union flag flying from the eaves. Gabriel followed Meade out. "You know what to ask, Meade?"

"Certainly, Your Grace."

"I'm trusting you to take charge of this mission and it's well . . . difficult," he murmured as they neared the door.

"I understand, Your Grace. I shall do my best."

Meade's lips were easy to read and his response expected. "Yes, well, see that you do. And if you get into any trouble, just bring out the speaking book. We'll deal with questions about that as they come."

Meade nodded, opened the door, and allowed Gabriel to precede him.

Gabriel watched in tense frustration while Meade struck up a conversation with the postmaster. The man looked at them both with obvious suspicion, a fact that boded ill of getting any information out of him. Gabriel tried to read his lips, understanding only that he'd been introduced as the Duke of St. Easton here on the prince regent's business. Risky that, but perhaps it would put the fear of God into the man. They proceeded to have an animated conversation with hand gestures and facial expressions Gabriel fought to understand.

Blast! Meade wasn't winning him over, Gabriel could tell. He didn't know how. What came as easily as nature, this golden charm, a velvet voice that he, instinctively, knew just how to use — thrust and parry, like a game of chess or swordplay. Every man had to be willingly conquered; women in a different way, but it had an easy flow to it, like satin against satin. One only need know how to react and counter.

Poor Meade was at sea. After several minutes Gabriel couldn't stand it any longer and interrupted. He leaned over the thin desk that he could easily break with his weight alone. "Tell us everything you know about Lady Alexandria Featherstone and her family, her parents, or see the prince regent's own men at your doorstep, my friend." He tilted his head and gave him an easy smile. "I mean only to protect her. I mean her no harm."

The man looked visibly shaken, but his chin raised in such a way that told Gabriel something important, told him that Alexandria had gotten to him. In their brief encounter, Alexandria Featherstone had won this man's allegiance . . . and that said a very great deal indeed.

Gabriel backed a little out of the man's face and smiled, a genuine smile. He stopped a laugh, knowing it wouldn't be understood. *Look what's she's done. She is everything I am imagining she is.* The thoughts pounded with the beating of his blood. He had to look away as a sharp sensation struck his eyes. He brought his fingers to his nose and squeezed, still smiling, unable to stop it.

"My good man." He looked back at the postmaster, leaned toward him, and infused his gaze with a penetrating onslaught of belief. "Please tell us what you know. I will, I swear to you, protect her with my life."

They held there. The gaze of the old postmaster's brown eyes and Gabriel's green. Like two swords meeting and testing, they held for a long, silent moment.

"She went to Killyleagh." The postmaster breathed deep as if coming from a battle. "Killyleagh Castle."

Gabriel blinked once, took a deep inhale, and stood back. He'd read his lips. And he knew of the place; he had heard of it from some distant place and time. "Thank you." He touched his forehead with a nod of respect.

Turning to Meade, he quirked a brow. "Come, Meade, the pieces of the puzzle are beginning to make a picture."

Meade looked at him with eyes full of admiration.

Gabriel led them back to the street, both excited and terrified that they would soon be looking into the face of his ward.

# CHAPTER TWENTY

"So, did you find what you were looking for?" Baylor asked as they walked from Killyleagh Castle back to the inn.

Alex sighed. "Even with the good fortune of Sir Archibald's help, I only learned that yes, my parents had been there and they were looking for something that was missing from Hans Sloane's collection, something to do with a sculptor from the fifteenth century named Augusto de Carrara. I couldn't find anything in the books that mentioned his name. I am sorry to say I'm at something of a dead end."

"If only we knew what was stolen, that would help." Montague's blue eyes scanned the horizon in thought as they walked.

"Yes, I agree. But what could it be?"

"It must have been something of great value making it tempting to a thief."

"Yes, but how would one sell a stolen work of art without being caught? Unless the person who stole it didn't want to sell it. Perhaps he just wanted it for himself."

"Pirates have been selling stolen treasure for centuries. There are ways in which it can be done — middlemen and underground methods and such. I would not count that out of your theorems."

Alex nodded, her mind whirling with possibilities. "Sir Archibald said that Sloane was born here. I wonder if we could find more about him from his descendants, if any of them are still here. He might have told stories about the antiquities he'd found, particularly something of such fame that would have to do with de Carrara."

"That is an excellent idea," Baylor chimed in. "You've the mind of a great sleuth."

Alex grinned over at the big man. "Another thing. We should find out everything we can about this Augusto de Carrara. There may be records of missing art. A newspaper or antiquities society might know of any disappearances. There might be important rumors we can pursue."

"I have some old friends who belong to the London Antiquities Society. I could write to them, if you'd like," Montague suggested.

"Oh yes, would you? That would be wonderful!" She looked back and forth at the men on either side of her. "If I haven't said it recently, I do thank you both. I don't know what I would do without you."

"Ach, this is the most exciting thing I've done in a long time, lass. I wouldn't miss it for the world." Baylor put an arm around her shoulders and squeezed, causing the breath and a gasping laugh to whoosh out of her.

"I'll bet your wife is missing you though."

"Good for her, I say. She'll appreciate her man all the more when I return." Baylor's bushy eyebrows shot up with glee.

Released from Baylor's hold and able to walk again, Alex cast a shy glance toward Montague. "Many thanks, Montague. I'll not forget your kindness."

"Ah, well, it's as the giant says. It has done me good to get out of the pitiful hole I was digging for myself." He cleared his throat and glanced away, his voice so low she could hardly hear him. "It was hard to know how to go on after my wife passed. You've given me back some purpose, Lady Alex."

Alex laid a gentle hand on his arm. They didn't say anything but there was a deeper companionship amongst the three as they walked down the windswept hill toward the inn and dinner.

There was no sign of the Spaniards when

272

they returned to the inn and sat in the dining room where dinner and a musical performance were promised. Alex thought that must mean they'd been seen. It was rather hard to hide a giant, so not surprising, but still, there was something to the saying of keeping your friends close and your enemies closer. What if they were hiding and watching her again? Her flesh prickled at the thought. If she could just turn the tables again and spy on them, she might learn something more. They certainly knew more than she did about whatever it was her parents had been hired to find. She pushed her plate back and rose from the table.

"Gentlemen, I believe I will find Mistress Tinsdale and ask her some questions about our dear friends, the Spaniards." Baylor started to rise, so she hurried out, "Please, don't bestir yourselves. I will only be a little while. Stay and finish your meal."

Montague narrowed his eyes at her as if judging the truth in her words. "I do have some letters to write." He rubbed his whiskered chin. "You'll not leave the inn?"

Alex bristled. "I'm not a child."

"Not far from one."

"Montague. I will be careful." She crossed her arms over her chest and stared at him.

"I'll keep an eye out." Baylor nudged Montague with his elbow and winked at Alex. "I'll be right here with my tankard and listening to the whistle that lad is about to play. You give a holler if you need me, promise?"

"I won't need you. It's just Mistress Tinsdale," Alex assured them both.

"Very well." Montague rose and adjusted his sword belt. "Give Mistress Tinsdale my regards, will you?"

Alex shook her head at him in exasperation and hurried away before they could think of more ways to waylay her.

Mistress Tinsdale was just where Alex thought she would be, in the kitchen. She was stirring something in a big pot, her back to the door. Alex lingered just inside and cleared her throat. "That smells wonderful. What is it?"

The lady started, spinning around with a wooden spoon clasped in her hand. She brought it to her chest with a gasp. "Goodness gracious, child, you gave me a start."

"I'm sorry. I was just . . . looking for some female company. The inn seems full of men."

"Poor lamb. Take a seat there and I'll dish you out some fine Irish stew. Best stew in the world, it is."

"Thank you." Alex sat at the long wooden table and clasped her hands together over the top. "How long have you been at the inn, Mistress Tinsdale?"

"Oh, call me Helga, dear. My husband and I took jobs here when we first married. We saved our coins, we did, and bought it outright not two years later." She brought over a steaming bowl and a spoon, placed them in front of Alex, and sat across from her, a broad smile on her face. "How excited we were! Still young, with a passel of babes that were always underfoot and in the way, but didn't we love them? A true family business we had."

Her eyes turned sad and misty as she stared across the room, a gentle smile on her lips. She turned and looked at Alex, who was taking her first bite of stew. "I can still feel him near sometimes, you know. The dead, they linger sometimes after they've gone, especially here in Ireland, what with all our leprechauns and fairies and such. It's a magical land, Lady Alex. Where magical things happen."

Alex nodded, caught in the woman's tone and the faith she had in it. "I believe you are right."

Helga gave her a broad grin, her cheeks rosy, her eyes alight with laughter. "Aren't you a fine thing. So tell me your story, my dear. What's made you come to Ireland?"

Alex wondered how much to tell her and decided it couldn't hurt to tell the truth. Helga might know something useful to help her. "Well." She took another bite and swallowed, thinking it *was* the best stew she'd ever had. "I live on Holy Island, in Northumberland."

"I've heard of Holy Island. Our Irish monks were there once upon a time, were they not?"

"Oh yes. Lindisfarne Castle is just up the road from the old monastery. The barony went to the Featherstone family about a century and a half ago. My parents are the current Lord and Lady Featherstone."

"So you've lived in a castle all your life, have you?" Helga's face beamed with fascination, making the telling of the story a pleasure.

"Yes, but I must say after seeing Killyleagh, my home is not so modern nor so comfortable. It still reminds me of the medieval castles of the past." She didn't mention that her parents didn't seem at all bothered by that fact and were rarely home to endure the discomforts of it. Brushing that thought aside, she hurried on. "My parents are something like treasure hunters;

they are famous for it, actually."

"Treasure hunters! Upon my word, that is exciting. What have they found?"

"Oh, all sorts of missing or stolen items — family jewelry, valuable coins, journals full of secrets. Once they were hired to find the tomb of a mummy in the pyramids of Egypt!"

Helga pressed her hand against her ample bosom. "Good heavens, did they find it?"

"Yes." Alex grinned and took another bite. "They never failed in finding what they were looking for."

Helga took a deep breath with a slow shake of her head. "I've never heard of such a thing."

Alex looked down at the delicious stew. "They never failed until now, that is. This is why I'm in Ireland. My parents disappeared some months ago and the prince regent thinks they're dead. I don't believe it, of course. They're too smart for that." She looked up at Helga, stared into her kind brown eyes. "Something has happened to them and they need my help. I have to find them."

"Well, of course you do."

Alex breathed a sigh of relief at her reaction.

"Did they come to Ireland, then? Is that

why you're here looking for them?"

"Yes. They came to Killyleagh several months ago. They visited the castle and possibly some other places. They might have even stayed here."

"You don't say?" Helga leaned back and pressed her hand against her plump cheek. "About a year ago? I think I might know of them. A very elegant couple from England? They didn't say much, kept quietly to themselves, and she often wore a veil, but I saw her once . . ."

"And?" Alex prodded.

"She was lovely, with eyes much like yours. We don't get many guests from England. Wait. I'll run and fetch the guest book. They would have signed in, don't you know." She hurried from the room before Alex could respond.

When she came back, she sank onto the bench and opened the book. Back and back she went through the pages. Suddenly her finger stopped. "There it is, just as I thought. Ian Featherstone." She turned the book around and pushed it in front of Alex.

Her heart sped up as she leaned over the lines of names. She saw it instantly, her father's elegant scrawl. Tears leapt to her eyes. It was him. They'd stayed here. She looked up at the top of the page and saw the date: 7 November 1817. Just a few weeks less than a year ago.

"Did they say where they were going next? Can you remember anything about them?"

Helga leaned back on the bench with a frown of concentration on her wide brow. "Give me a moment, dear. Finish your stew now, you look white as a ghost."

Alex obeyed, shoveling in the delicious lamb, potatoes, and carrots and washing it down with a cup of tea while she waited.

When she finished she pushed aside the bowl. "Wonderful stew, Helga. Thank you."

Helga nodded at her. "Best stew in the world, it is. I'll write out my secret recipe for you. Now then, I do remember a thing or two about them. Firstly, they did visit the castle a time or two and seemed pleased by something that happened on those visits. I recollect that they asked my son, who works here, where they could find the house where Hans Sloane was raised. The family has all gone to England now, but they visited someone there."

Alex was pleased beyond measure that her hunch to go to Sloane's childhood home was so perfectly matched to what her parents had done. "Anything else?"

"Just one more thing." Helga's brow wrinkled. "I don't know what it means, but

I heard your father tease your mother about getting her some warmer clothing. Something about traveling somewhere cold, I think he meant."

"A cold place? No idea as to where?"

Helga shook her head. "Sorry, dear. You might ask the coachman where they went when they left here. They were traveling by rented coach."

"An excellent idea. Thank you so much, Helga. You have helped a great deal."

"I have? Well, isn't that something! Me helping on an investigation." She paused and leaned in. "It's dangerous though, isn't it? Is that why you have those two fierce men traveling with you?"

Alex nodded. "God has blessed me greatly to find champions for my cause in my travels."

"Yes, indeed. That Montague! Oh, bless me, he's a fine man."

"He said to give you his regards," Alex teased with a grin.

"He didn't!"

"Oh yes, he did. I think he's quite taken with you. His wife died not too long ago and he has been rather lost since."

"The dear man . . . he's in need of comfort then? I remember that, when my poor Cormac passed. I'll have to bake him a pie and see that he gets it before this night is out."

"What an excellent idea." Alex stood to go. "Oh, can I ask you one more question?"

"Of course, dear."

"I have a feeling that the two Spanish men who were here yesterday are looking for this object that my parents were hired to find too. They've been following me and one of them grabbed me in Belfast and demanded to know what I was doing in Ireland. He was quite frightening. Do you know anything about them?"

Helga slowly shook her head back and forth. "They settled their account and left right after you arrived. I haven't seen them since."

"They saw us then. Just as I thought. Well, if you see them, could you please alert me? I'm keeping my eye out for them in case they mean us harm."

"Oh yes, dear. I'll be keeping my eye out too." She came around the table and enveloped Alex in a big, motherly hug. One of her hands patted Alex's back. "You're a right brave thing, Lady Featherstone. I pray God's grace upon you."

Alex swallowed back the sudden lump in her throat. Had her mother ever hugged her like this?

"Thank you, Helga. I think God's grace is on me and covering me and going ahead of me as I take each step. I can feel it in the people, like you, that He has sent to help me."

Before she could break into a cry, Alex gave her a tight squeeze and then turned and hurried from the room.

# CHAPTER TWENTY-ONE

When they got back to their Belfast inn, Gabriel was told that he had a visitor who had been waiting in the private drawing room for some time. It was Lady Claire Montgomery, a woman he'd met some time ago during a London season of balls and soirees. An image of her stunning face, blue eyes, creamy skin, and that little pointed chin that lent an elfish air to her came to mind. She'd had lush blonde hair that was elaborately dressed in a sleek, upswept style and cultured speech that told of a good education. She'd made her splash and then married a baron, Lord Montgomery, who had whisked her off to Ireland some years ago. Gabriel hadn't heard anything about her since. How had she possibly found out that he was here?

Turning to Meade, he sighed. "You'll have to accompany me, Meade, and bring out the speaking book. There is nothing else for it."

As they entered the room, a delicate woman turned from the window. She was even more beautiful than he remembered — dressed in black, at the height of fashion, and dripping with jewels. What little she had aged had only given her face more loveliness. Gabriel sucked in his breath, a mixture of chagrin and admiration churning in his stomach. The fact that he'd been recently shot and had one arm in a sling wasn't going to help matters. She would feel sorry for him. It would be ghastly.

"Lady Montgomery! How lovely to see you." Had he yelled it? *Calm down, man.* He walked over and took her hand, then planted a light kiss against the silky skin. She blushed, a delicate pink that colored her cheeks, and stared up into his eyes with a vulnerability he hadn't seen in a woman in a very long time. Pink lips gushed out words that he couldn't read and he couldn't stare at for too long. He took a step away and looked to Meade for help. He didn't know if he could bear to tell her outright, *I'm deaf.* He hadn't said those words to anyone.

He swept his hand toward the settee and seated himself across from her. "I'm afraid I must ask my secretary to write down what you say in a speaking book, as I'm having difficulty with my hearing."

Her eyes widened and her mouth opened but she quickly recovered. She looked down at her lap as if she didn't know what to do next and then over at Meade.

"Just say what you normally would say and Meade will write it down." Gabriel gave her a self-deprecating smile. "It takes a bit longer, and I may seem to be staring at your lips outside of all that is respectable, but we'll muddle through."

She spoke much slower then, looking often at Meade for signals that he was keeping up.

Gabriel read the page.

It is so good to see you, Your Grace. I am sorry that you are suffering with this affliction. You look well, but what has happened to your arm? I hope that you are not in pain.

"It's a long story. I was robbed and shot, if you can believe it, but I am mending nicely." He smiled and shrugged one shoulder. "Tell me, I've only been in Belfast a few days. How did you hear I was in Ireland?"

Meade took the book back and wrote as

she spoke.

"Oh, Your Grace, I have just gone through a great trial myself. I have been in Belfast these last days dealing with my husband's estate. You see, he died a few days ago and after the burial at Ballymena, where our home is, I had to come here to see his solicitor. It's been dreadful. I can't make heads or tails of all his many business dealings. There are decisions that must be made, and I was at a loss and didn't know who to trust or advise me . . . then I overheard a guest at my solicitor's office say your name. And when I asked, they said they had heard that the Duke of St. Easton was staying at the Ostrich Inn."

She paused and took a deep breath. "It was like an answer to my prayers. If anyone could guide me during this difficult time, I knew you could. Pray lend me some of your time and assistance, Your Grace. I've taken a room here so it might be more convenient."

Gabriel's pulse hummed through his veins. He couldn't possibly say no, and yet he had planned to leave this very afternoon for Killyleagh. It would be a risky delay. What if Alexandria left town and he couldn't find out where she'd gone?

The lady was waiting patiently for his

answer. He looked up and nodded. "I am sorry for your loss, Lady Montgomery. I will, of course, lend you what aid I can. My own business here in Ireland is of a timely nature but perhaps I can arrange different plans."

"Oh, I would be so grateful." She clasped her hands together in her lap as tears shimmered in her blue eyes. "I can have Mr. Donovan, the solicitor, bring all of the documents here. What time would be good for you?"

"Give me an hour to take care of some business and then we'll meet back here, if your solicitor is available then."

"I will make sure that he is, Your Grace." She rose and Gabriel stood too. On clouds of grace it seemed she floated toward him, reaching out and taking his hands. She looked into his eyes, at his lips, and then back into his eyes and very clearly said the words *thank you.*

As she left, Gabriel had to remind himself to breathe again.

"Meade, I have an idea to buy us a little more time here. I will write a letter to Alexandria demanding that she stay in Killyleagh until we can get to her. You hire a man, find a good one and pay him well, to see that the letter finds her and that he gets her response. The town is small and we know she's been to the castle. The people there should know where she is staying and help our man find her."

"But, Your Grace, what if she doesn't want to be found? We may be tipping our hand that we are so close with a demanding letter, don't you think?"

"It is a possibility." Gabriel rubbed the stubble on his chin. "But as I control her purse strings and I know she must have run through most of what I've given her so far, I think the promise of enough money to track down her parents will keep her in one spot."

"Ah yes, that may work. But do you really plan to give her permission for such a dangerous trip?"

"Once I have her back in London and have hired the best investigators to track these clues she thinks she has, I am hoping she will be satisfied and remain under my protection as the prince regent has ordered. A visit to the prince regent might be enough to convince her of obedience."

Meade pressed his lips together and said nothing. It boded ill, but Gabriel ignored the look, went to the desk, and took out paper and quill. He thought for a long moment and then hurried out his instruction to his recalcitrant ward.

My dearest Alexandria,

I have just come from your home at Holy Island. You can imagine my surprise when upon entering your (yes, crumbling) castle, you were nowhere to be found. I'm sure you will be happy to know that it took a great deal of persuasion to convince your stalwart servants to give up what they knew about your location. Only my assurance of my mission to keep you in all that is health and my genuine concern for your welfare made them change their minds. I have since been on something of a wild-goose chase and finally discovered you'd actually gone to Ireland. I am here now, in Belfast, and know from the postmaster (another difficult conquest of information) that your next clue led you to Killyleagh. The fact that you are reading this letter tells me that I've found you, which is to both our good fortunes as the prince regent has ordered me to bring you back to London.

However, there has been a delay in my coming to you, and I will need to remain in Belfast for a few days. I order you to stay where you are until I can come to you. Now, my sweet ward, I understand that this news might not be happy for you, but I assure you that if you obey, I will give you a large sum of money to hire trained investigators to find your parents. We have reason to believe you are in danger and I pray you are being cautious. Do you happen to have Admiral Montague with you? I must say, I am astounded by the possibility but it gives me some measure of comfort that you had the sense to hire someone as protector and didn't attempt to do something so rash as to travel alone. I daresay I only sleep at night with the image of him standing guard outside your door, however you managed it.

I await your reply and look forward to finally putting a face to all your cherished letters.

Yours,
St. Easton

Gabriel sanded the letter and gave it to Meade, hoping he could locate a good messenger within the hour. He wasn't looking forward to the tedious task of going through Lord Montgomery's accounts, but the presence of a lovely widow would be some compensation. Now, to tidy his appearance and order refreshments to be served in the private drawing room when they arrived.

There was a lightness to his step that surprised him. Lady Montgomery had been sympathetic more than pitying. Perhaps he was making more of his "affliction" as she put it than he needed to. People of all classes and origins since time began had suffered far greater distress than his deafness. Perhaps he should be thankful for what he did have, which was quite a lot. It had been something of a relief to tell someone, anyway. Keeping it a secret was draining and depressing. Maybe his world wouldn't fall apart after all, should he let it be known that the Duke of St. Easton was human too.

An hour later a maid scratched at his door and informed him that his visitors had arrived. Feeling refreshed, Gabriel strode down the long hall of rooms to the private, second-story drawing room for the inn's more important guests. Lady Montgomery was there, seated next to a surprisingly young and handsome man dressed in the height of gentlemanly fashion.

The man leapt forward when he entered and bowed almost until his nose touched his knees. After Gabriel greeted Lady Montgomery, she asked with slow, overstated facial expressions of someone trying to be easily read where Mr. Meade was and would he be attending them.

"Meade is upon an errand, at present." Gabriel motioned for the maid in the room to pour the tea and serve the crumpets, cheese, sweetmeats, and delicate little cakes. "Please, have some refreshments." He drew out the speaking book and turned to a new page, some of the comfortableness from his last conversation leaving him in having to do this in front of the young man. God certainly knew how to take the pride out of a man, he reflected morosely.

Looking up, he pushed the feeling aside and directed his question to Mr. Donovan, the solicitor. He could well understand why Claire had not been restful about trusting him; he was entirely too pleasing. "Well, Mr. Donovan. What is the condition of the estate?"

Donovan took the book and scribbled down several pages. Gabriel scanned it, leaning to one side of his chair in a position of ease and confidence, one elbow propped on the arm, his thumb under his chin, occasionally stroking it in concentration. It was as he thought and he doubted this was even the worst of it. Montgomery had been on the brink of bankruptcy. The final collapse had occurred just days before he died. Poor Claire. The creditors would soon be pounding down her door and there was little to sell.

"Claire," he said her given name in a tone filled with kindness. "You never said. How did Carrick die?"

She blanched as white as the plasterwork on the walls. Gabriel slowly handed her the speaking book. They waited, Donovan sipping his tea and averting his eyes, Gabriel watching with sincere sorrow as tears dripped down Claire's lovely face and splattered onto the not-yet-dry ink as she labored over her lines.

He'd noticed something about the speaking book. People generally spoke with little thought, just spewing out whatever was in their heads at the time, but when they had to write it down, they paused, some of them at least, and they spoke more from the heart than the head. He'd gotten to know his best friend, Albert, better in the last few months because of the speaking book. It was harder to be glib on paper. And it had made them closer, something he hadn't bothered to be thankful for.

Claire handed the book back, took his offered handkerchief, and dabbed at swimmingly beautiful blue eyes ringed in dark, wet lashes. What a dear thing she was.

He tried to read the smeared lines. She'd found him in the stables, hanging from the high rafters. A black bird had been on his shoulder, pecking at his face. She had screamed and fled and then fainted. They'd almost despaired of her awakening until one of the servants carried her to a large trough of water and dumped her in. She'd come up sputtering, then remembered what she saw and wished she had never awakened.

After looking at the accounts and the most recent harvest, which had been destroyed by weather-related tragedies, well, it wasn't the first time a man took the path of a coward. He'd not known Carrick well, and yet it was hard to imagine not having any faith that things might turn around. He hadn't been a gambler, although some further study might reveal that he had gotten that desperate and lost even more. It was common enough. The question was, how much to tell her? She'd suffered so much already. He found he needed more answers first. She deserved to know the whole truth.

He turned to Donovan. "You've brought all the account books?"

Donovan nodded, clearly saying, "Yes,

Your Grace."

"Leave them here and give me a day to review them. Claire, I will tell you everything I discover, but in the meantime you must be strong. Your husband must have had reason to do such a thing and we will find out what it was so you can, someday, put it to rest. Do you understand?"

She nodded and sniffed. Then she reached for the book.

I can't thank you enough, Your Grace. Will you have dinner with me tonight? I cannot bear to be so alone.

"Mr. Donovan, you are excused."

The man bristled, but Gabriel didn't care. He was watching them entirely too close for comfort. Gabriel hated to admit it, but it felt good to be needed and well, it might just be what they both needed, finding comfort in an old friend.

# CHAPTER TWENTY-TWO

"Oh, I just can't believe it!" Alex flung herself into a chair across from Montague and Baylor in the drawing room of the Dufferin Coaching Inn in Killyleagh. "You cannot believe this letter he's written me! Of all the high-handed, arrogant, brutish" — she sputtered, unable to think of another insult that fit — "duke-like thing to do!"

"Who's this duke and what's he saying to get her into such a fit?" Baylor asked Montague.

Montague leaned in with a quirked brow and half smile. "Her guardian, the one and only Duke of St. Easton."

"Sounds like an important chap."

Montague chuckled. "Only one of the richest men in the world. He's known for his vast intellect. They say he's studied everything and remembers most of it. He's done it all too. If he only had his winnings from horse racing, he'd be worth the prince regent's own ransom. He has hands into everything — mines, shipping, trading from the Orient to the Americas. I once heard that he has famous painters and musicians come to his house for private discussions and concerts. But that's not why I've always wanted to meet him."

"No? Tell us why then, it sounds like we'll meet him soon if Lady Alex is throwing such a fit as this."

Alex had quieted her tirade enough to hear Montague's description of the duke. Fear rose in slow degrees as he spoke. She thought back to her outlandish letters and clutched his recent one in her fist with a flash of horror. She'd been so impetuous . . . rash even, in her demands . . . was he really so esteemed as Montague said? So rich and powerful?

But she wanted to hear Montague's answer so she quieted her thoughts and turned, genuinely curious as to what the famed admiral would find so fascinating about the Duke of St. Easton.

"It's said he has the green eyes of a panther. The iris of his eyes, some say, are not exactly round either, but more of a slight oval like a cat's eyes." Montague laughed and slid Alex a look of speculation. "It could be all rumors and exaggerations, of course."

Alex paled further and then rallied with sudden determination. "Oh, bother. Cat's eyes? Trumped-up nonsense, that's all that is. Why, *his royal highness* says right here in this letter that you are much esteemed and he's astounded that I was able to employ you. Not that I did, but still. The man has entirely too high of an opinion of himself, if you ask me. I'll not be afraid of him."

"He mentions me?" Montague reached for the letter. "Can I see it?"

Alex stood and passed it over to him with a rolling of her eyes.

Montague chuckled after he read it. "Look here, Baylor." He made a move to hand the letter to the giant but Baylor shook his head. "Read it to me, won't you?"

Montague gave him a startled look and Alex gently asked, "Did you never learn to read, Baylor?"

He shook his head in an exaggerated way, eyes wide. "My sweet mother died giving birth to my little brother and a few years later my father left us. It was just the two of us then, he was four and I was ten, living in those mountains with a couple of sheep and some chickens. I was old enough to keep up for a time but never even thought about going to school. There was too much to do and we didn't want anybody knowing we were living there all alone together. I was afraid they might take Tommy from me, put him in a different home, or one of those awful orphanages." He rubbed his great hands together, his voice lowering in a thick Irish brogue. "A few years later, on a cold winter's day, Tommy got real sick."

"Oh, Baylor. What did you do?" Alex imagined the tall, red-headed child he must have been, trying to be so strong.

"Well, I was mighty afraid, I can tell you. I didn't know what to do for him, his fever being so high and he wouldn't take any nourishment, don't you know. So I bundled him up and put him in a wheelbarrow and pushed him all the way to Belfast to the hospital there."

He paused and looked down. Alex was afraid to ask if Tommy had made it and looked at Montague.

"That's a hard thing, Baylor, to lose the only family you have left. I know," Montague said quietly.

Baylor gave them both a broad smile. "Oh, he perked up after a few days. We ended up being taken home by one of the doctors and his wife, God bless her. She decided she wanted to keep us. I stayed there for a few months but missed the mountains in a powerful way. A sheep farmer is what I wanted to be, but Tommy, he went to school and is a doctor in Belfast now. So it all worked out for the good."

"So you went back to the farm?"

Baylor nodded. "They knew I was independent enough even though I was only about fourteen. I'd been taking care of myself all my life and they knew I would be all right, and besides, there was a pretty lass who could sing like nothing I'd ever heard living in the village in those mountains. I made excuses to travel there and hear her often."

"That's Maeve! Your wife, isn't it?" Alex leaned forward.

"We married when she was only sixteen and I was seventeen. Been happy as clams ever since."

"Did you ever go back to Belfast and see your brother?"

"Oh yes! Often I did. The doctor only let me go back to the mountains alone if I promised to come back and visit. Sometimes I would stay for a few days or weeks with them here and there. They were like family to me. I regret not learning to read though. There are times I wished I could. Especially the Holy Bible. I would like to learn to read that."

"It's not too late. I would be glad to teach you," Alex chimed in.

"You would do that for me, lass? Is it very hard? Do you think I could learn it?"

"Yes, of course you can. We'll begin tonight, right after dinner."

He looked too happy for words.

"Now, Montague, read that letter. I want to know what the duke thinks of you." Baylor motioned toward Montague to continue.

Montague read in a low voice, " 'Do you happen to have Admiral Montague with you? I must say, I am astounded by the possibility, but it gives me some measure of comfort that you had the sense to hire someone as protector and didn't attempt to do something so rash as to travel alone. I daresay I only sleep at night with the image of him standing guard outside your door, however you managed it.' Can you imagine that?" Montague asked.

"Famed duke or not, we cannot stay here and wait upon his leisure. We have to flee before he comes and leave no clue as where we are going," Alex reminded them.

"Do you know what you're saying, lass? This man has the prince regent's orders." Baylor shook his shaggy head in impending doom.

"Alexandria, you must trust him. He is

offering to hire professionals to do this job. They will have far better success finding your parents than we could." Montague leaned forward, his eyes earnest.

Alex balled her hands into fists and stared back and forth at the two of them. "Better results you say? Haven't I found their trail? *I* will find them . . . with or without you." She didn't realize it but tears, the first they'd seen of her, had sprung to her eyes and were pouring down her cheeks. "*Me!* I will save my parents. No one knows them like I do. No one believes they are alive as I do. The duke doesn't care. No one will care like I do!" She fell to her knees and buried her face in her hands.

Baylor leapt to pick her up and gently placed her in his chair. Montague poured her a drink from the water pitcher and brought it over.

She accepted the help and then looked up with a tear-stained face. "I already wrote a response and assured the duke that I would remain here. He'll be days behind if we leave now."

"Alexandria, you must stop this lying whenever you think you have the need of one. That is not trusting God at all but taking matters into your own hands," Montague said with stern kindness.

"You're right. I didn't know what else to do! If I'd replied with the truth, he would be on our doorstep this moment. Please, won't you come with me?"

They looked at each other. Baylor shrugged. "I wasn't quite ready to quit this adventure and return to my beautiful harpy yet anyway. What say you, Montague?"

Montague gave them both his best scowl. "I say unless we tie her down and hold her here she'll go without us. We've no choice really. But where to, Lady Alex? Do we know where we're going next?"

Alex sat up, wiped her running nose with Montague's offered handkerchief, and nodded. "I've not told you yet what I discovered at the Hans Sloane house. It's a clue. We're getting closer, I can feel it."

"Come then, what happened when you went to the cottage?" Baylor sat upon the only other chair in the room, a rickety looking wooden thing that creaked and moaned as he sat down. Alex's eyes widened as she watched the chair's supporting legs bow out. Montague choked back a laugh. They all breathed a great sigh when the chair seemed to settle and hold.

"First of all," Alex began, "Sir Hans lived in one of the better houses of the village. It's two storied and nicer than his neighbors.

When I knocked on the door, I asked if they were relations to Sir Hans, to which the woman said no, but she knew well of the family and invited me in for tea. We sat down and I told her that I was looking for my long-lost parents who were in Killyleagh about a year ago. She remembered them and said they had come asking questions about Hans Sloane too. She told me the same thing she told my parents, which was that Hans's father had died when he was a boy and his mother had remarried, upon which she'd abandoned poor Hans and his two brothers. When they got a little older, they'd all gone off to London to seek their fortunes. Hans, of course, made quite something of himself, becoming the king's physician and continuing his interest in antiquities."

Alex paused and took a deep breath. "I asked her if the Sloanes had left anything behind. If the attic had been checked and if there were any other stories she could remember about them. She told me no and that my parents had asked the same questions. I was about to give up and walk out her door when I noticed the thatched cottages of the nearby neighbors. I decided that I might as well give it a try so I knocked on the doors of each one and asked if anyone knew anything about Hans Sloane."

Indeed, it had been rather nerve-wracking to interview complete strangers. At one of the cottages there was an old woman who said her grandfather had played with the Sloane brothers as a child and had told many stories about them.

*"Come and sit for a spell, child, and I'll see if I can recollect a story for you." She'd smiled in a kind, motherly way.*

*"I would be so grateful." Alex seated herself in the small, dark room that held the dining table and chairs, a large fireplace with cooking utensils scattered about and a corner nook with a bench and a butter churn under a low window that let in little light. The woman made tea and asked Alex about herself.*

*Alex told the story of her parents and how she was determined to find them. Everyone who had heard the story was eager to help her and this woman, Mrs. McHenry, proved to be no different.*

*"Well now." She sat across from her and passed her a cup of tea. "Let's see what I can remember. There were three brothers but Hans was my grandfather's favorite companion. They spent much of their time down on the shores of Strangford Lough. They fished and explored the islands of the lough. My grandfather and Hans came back with all sorts*

of treasures like rocks and feathers and curiosities. While my grandfather grew out of such things, Hans never did. He kept everything he found in little jars and boxes, which became the beginning of his famous collection, you see."

"What an intelligent little boy he must have been!" Alex encouraged. "My parents were hired to find something that has gone missing from his collection. It will help me find them if I can figure out what it is they were looking for. Have you heard of anything missing from his collection?"

"No, miss, I'm sorry but I don't know anything about it except that it was given to the British Museum."

Alex sank inside. In a last effort she asked one more question. "I have reason to believe that this object may have something to do with an Italian sculptor named Augusto de Carrara. Have you ever heard of him?"

"I seem to recall something about an Italian sculptor being mentioned by my father, but I'm not sure of the name. If anything of his is in Ireland, I suspect it would be in Dublin, at the Royal Irish Academy. My father and my grandfather before him were members for many years and they talked about Sloane and his collection often among themselves. You should go and see Dublin, my dear."

"So you see," Alex said to Baylor and Montague after telling the story, "we have to go to Dublin and talk to the members of the Royal Irish Society."

"Hmm. As it happens, I have my nephew in Dublin." Montague rose and flung on his dark cloak. "Pack your things, Alexandria, and ask Mistress Tinsdale for a food basket to hold us for two days' travel. Don't mention where we are going."

As Montague left, Alex whispered to Baylor, "Perhaps we should throw the duke off course and lead him in another direction. I'll tell Mistress Tinsdale we are headed for Downpatrick to visit the famous cathedral there. It's the supposed burial place of St. Patrick himself. That should sound like something we would do in tracking down clues. Baylor, you see about horses. We won't want to risk the mail coach."

Alex nodded and hurried upstairs to pack her things, feeling a little guilty about another lie, but it was just too tempting to send his royal highness on a further goose chase.

When she opened the door to her assigned bedchamber, she gasped. The room had been ransacked. Everything lay in disarray on the floor: her clothing, toiletries, the few books she'd brought. Her heart pounded as she took a step into the room and looked into every corner. Whoever had done this was long gone, but her second-story window was open, the curtains still fluttering around the opening.

Alex crossed the room and leaned a little out the window. There was a tree close by, close enough to climb down from if one was nimble enough. She reached for the branch closest and pulled on it. It was possible that someone had left through the window, but how had they gotten in? She hadn't left the window open so she didn't think the thief could have gained entrance from there. She went back to the door and noticed the latch had been damaged. Whoever it was, and she suspected the Spaniards, it appeared they had broken in through the door and left by the window.

The sudden thought of her remaining money sent a shock of panic through her. She hurried to the open drawer of a tall bureau. It was empty. She dropped to the floor, looking for the stocking where she had been storing her money. After several moments of frantic searching, she sank back with a cry. They'd taken it! That and one of her books about Ireland. What was she to do?

She reached inside her dress pocket and

pulled out the duke's letters, which she always kept with her, and the last few coins she had. Hardly enough to get them to Dublin. She held the duke's letters close to her chest. He had her money. Well, not on his person, but in the bank. The bank in London.

The fact that Dublin was the second largest city in the United Kingdom came to her mind. Of course, the duke could get money from the Dublin bank. Couldn't he? And as the duke's ward, might she open a line of credit? She had letters proving she was his ward. She could just march into the bank and play the role of entitled aristocrat, demanding an account be opened for her. If what Montague said was true, that the duke was so powerful and wealthy, why they might do anything to please his ward, wouldn't they?

# Chapter Twenty-Three

*Stay,* her pink lips mouthed.

Gabriel stood looking down at Claire's upturned face, his gaze moving from her lips to those crystal blue eyes framed in dark lashes. She closed her eyes and lifted her chin infinitesimally higher, the invitation to kiss her unmistakable. She was beautiful. And he, at his weakest he'd ever been in his life. She had not once, over the last two days, made him feel foolish or uncomfortable about being deaf. She had looked at him with those wide, trusting eyes and taken all of his advice, reaching readily for the speaking book when necessary, writing in a wholly feminine hand, hinting at more with her eyes. Now, as he gazed down into her alabaster face and full lips, he knew she was offering him whatever he wanted from her — starting with a kiss.

It was tempting. But there was something about her easy willingness in the face of just losing her husband that cooled his ardor. She was lonely and afraid, yes, he understood her desperation. But where was her pride? It might have gone a long way on the path of making her a duchess.

Gabriel raised his hand to gently cup her jawline and rubbed his thumb across her cheek. "Claire." He was careful to make his voice soft. "You're not ready for this. You have to grieve him, and then, after a time, you will know what to do. I will see that you have that time."

He'd already explained to her the state of her finances and offered to cover the part of the debt that would at least let her keep her estate. Everything else would be sold off, but there would be enough income from her rents, if she was careful, to manage a comfortable and quiet life. She'd readily agreed to it, but now he'd offended and embarrassed her.

Her eyelids fluttered open and a look of chagrin crossed her face. She turned away from his steady gaze. "I don't want your charity, Gabriel."

"Don't you?"

She flew at him then, beating him with her paltry fists that felt more like small wings of a bird against him. He stood against it until she collapsed against his chest, clinging to him and sobbing. He couldn't hear it, any of it, but her face was all that was sorrow, her arms around him heavy with grief and then grasping his shirt front, her chest heaving against his, breathing in and out with that catch in it, that breath — *oh, God help us when we grieve* — he held her against him and bore her pain, for a moment, with his.

Maybe this was the kind of woman duty called him to marry. She was what was expected in a duchess, and fortune hunters this lovely were rare in the ton. It would be an . . . uncomplicated life with each of them knowing their place, their part to play.

All he had to do was ask. There was no doubt that she would say yes.

"Claire . . ."

She turned her lovely face toward his. . . . He could feel her breath coming fast in her chest. He could be happy with her . . . couldn't he?

"Claire. I —"

What was he doing? He didn't want the life that was expected of him; he didn't want Claire. He wanted love.

He wanted Alexandria. Her name pounded through his veins, making him inhale and step back. "Claire, I'm sorry I can't help you any longer." He took her hands and squeezed them.

"I thought . . . perhaps . . ." She lifted those gorgeous blue eyes with such questioning innocence.

Gabriel let go of her hands and took a step back. "I'm sorry. Good-bye, Claire." He watched her gather her reticule and walk from the room with her chin held high. After she closed the door, a bark of laughter escaped him. What a web she weaved! There was little doubt she would be remarried before the year was out.

After seeing Claire off, Gabriel returned to his room and sat at the desk. Exhaustion weighed him down. He cradled his head in his hands and sighed. He felt like he'd won some battle, which made little sense, but the feeling was there nonetheless. He rubbed his hands against his face and then reached across the desk for the letters. It was silly, the dark green ribbon he'd put around them to keep them together. He didn't even know why he'd done it, purchasing it at a market house in secret so Meade wouldn't know.

And the letters themselves, read so many times that he feared they might turn into tatters. It was just that . . . he felt like he knew her already. And it was time to find out if what he believed was true. It was time to finally meet his ward face to face. He unfolded her latest letter and reread it.

Dear Guardian Duke,

He chuckled at that. She always had some outlandish new form of address for him with no regard to propriety.

I do apologize for inconveniencing Your Grace in such a manner as not being present at Holy Island when you called. Had I known you were coming I would have, of course, forestalled beginning my journey, though it is of the upmost importance to me. As you will have deduced, I do not believe my parents are deceased, only waylaid by some terrible misfortune. A misfortune that I must investigate and lend what help I can.

As to the prince regent's orders that I return with you to London, I am sure I cannot. Why the prince regent of England has taken such interest in my affairs is simply beyond me. Could he be suffering from another one of his "spells," do you think? It is flattery enough that you have traveled all the way to Ireland to fetch me, but pray, help me find my parents instead. I shall welcome you by my side and know that together we shall discover the whereabouts of my mother and father.

I shall await you in Killyleagh, dear sir, with the same anticipation you have expressed and with the fervent belief that I can convince you to champion my quest.

With great affection,
Alexandria

With great affection. That was a step further than she'd ever proclaimed to feel for him. A sense of renewed strength flowed through him at the thought. There was no time to lose. He rose, packed his belongings, and then told Meade to prepare for the ride to Killyleagh. On horseback, they should be there by late afternoon.

The road to Killyleagh proved better than he thought. Even though his shoulder ached, Gabriel was glad they hadn't taken a coach and had ferried their horses over from England. He was sure Meade did not share his happiness, but his secretary was improving each time they traveled. By the time they were back in London, he would be an accomplished rider despite his abhorrence for it.

On the outskirts of Killyleagh they paused and took in the picturesque scene. Rolling hills of green dotted with brown fields, and in the distance under the warm rays of afternoon light, Killyleagh Castle. Gabriel had to admit it was grand, a castle fit for the stories in the Land of Ever Young. The town lay at the castle's feet in neat rows of cottages and shops. Beyond that was the wide stretch of blue that was Strangford Lough. Picturesque hardly described it. Striking in a way that true beauty, peace, tranquility, a piece of heaven on earth was striking.

A feeling swelled within Gabriel, a feeling of thanksgiving and awe that he hadn't felt for a very long time. With the searing pain of his "condition" had come a return of feelings, a slow awakening from the boredom, a wonder in the humbler things that he'd had in simpler times, as a boy perhaps. He was suddenly very glad to be alive and in this place. Alex's words to put his hope in God seemed possible in this moment. And this was the perfect place to first meet his ward.

They trotted down the long street toward the center of town. The messenger had come back with the address where Alexandria was staying — The Dufferin Coaching Inn — and it was easy to locate.

After seeing to the care of their horses, Gabriel gave Meade a long look and then walked up the wide steps to the Dufferin's front door. He paused, his hand on the brass latch, took a deep breath, and entered.

"Meade, find out where she is. I will go into the common room and procure us a table. I feel inclined to order a bit of a celebration for our meeting. You will bring her to me."

Meade nodded, his eyes darting around the place and then settling on Gabriel's. There was a bead of sweat on his upper lip. Ah, he was nervous to see her again. Gabriel smiled. Maybe he was afraid of being shot at again. Couldn't really blame the man, could he?

Gabriel turned to the plump innkeeper woman and ordered their best meal be brought round to his table . . . a table of three. Now that he had visited the bank, he could command establishments like a duke again.

She curtsied deep, a quiet smile on her face.

He entered the common room and took off his gloves, an awkward move with one arm still in the sling. At least he'd had one made up to match his dark coat, and it wasn't so glaringly obvious as the white strip of cloth the doctor had given him.

Patrons resided at a few tables, deep in their conversations, a few looking up at him as he entered. He ignored them, like he was trying to ignore the pounding in his veins. He sat down, setting his hat and gloves on the chair next to him. No. That was wrong. She might sit there. Right there beside him. He swallowed hard, feeling as nervous as a schoolboy on his first day at Eton. It wasn't like him and he didn't like it at all. He moved the accessories to the other side of the table, his hat covering the gloves. It looked silly but he couldn't seem to remember what to do with them.

With an exhale he sat back and turned toward the window. He could see the continued rise of the road outside, some washed-out colored buildings and then, there in the distance, the soft blue of the lough. He took a deep breath and concentrated on the soft smudge of blue that met an even bluer horizon. Did he have the speaking book with him?

Did he care?

Would *she* care? Her reaction was more important than he wanted to admit. And he couldn't for the life of him figure out why.

What was wrong with him? God help him, he'd never been so anxious in his life.

A movement from the door brought his attention around. A serving woman came in bearing a loaded tray. She set it down on the table next to him and proceeded to unload a fine silver teapot, cups that looked too delicate to touch, gold filigreed plates of delicacies containing all sorts of sweets and sauces, meats and cheeses, breads and fruits. She bowed low to him, without a word, and turned to go.

Gabriel took a sip of the sugared tea and watched the door. Surely, at any moment, they would enter.

A moment later Meade entered the room, his face gone stark, drained of all color, his hair looking like a lightning bolt had struck him. Gabriel stood as he rushed forward.

"What is it? Tell me she hasn't shot you again!"

Meade shook his head in a slow-motion move.

"What's happened, Meade? Where is she?" The words hissed through quick gasps, his stomach slowly tying into snarls of dread.

*She isn't here.*

# CHAPTER TWENTY-FOUR

"It's one of the hardest things I've ever done," Alex announced to the other inhabitants of the mail coach, a cheaper conveyance they'd been forced to use since her money was stolen, as they rolled into Dublin.

"What is that, lass?" Baylor boomed from across from her, squeezed into the corner of the seat and surrounded by bags of mail. He looked almost afraid of them, causing Montague to lean over and chuckle words into Alex's ear when they first started on the road to Dublin.

"He looks like a red-haired giant surrounded by bags of snakes, if there were snakes in Ireland." That had led to a discussion about whether or not St. Patrick had really driven all the snakes from Ireland as Baylor insisted he had.

Now, after two days of travel, they'd just crossed under the Foster Aqueduct, giving

Alex a good view of the city and the Wicklow Mountains in the distance. Church spires and glittering domes towered above the town's buildings, lending an air of fairy tales once again.

Alex answered Baylor's question. "The hardest thing I've ever done is trying to keep from pressing my nose against this window, of course." Alex laughed. "Have you ever seen anything so grand? Dublin is amazing!"

"It's the second largest city in the United Kingdom, just after London, and a good deal nicer than that place." Montague had been pointing out the landmarks as they passed them. They crossed Carlisle Bridge, where Alex had a clear view of the River Liffey and a long line of quays going right through the center of the city.

A little while later Montague pointed out the classical architecture of the Custom House with its high-pillared dome and giant statue on top. It was a massive edifice of Portland stone, sitting near the bay and surrounded by all sorts of floating craft from tall-masted ships to bobbing fishing boats. They turned down Westmoreland Street and came to the college green with Trinity College just ahead on the left. Across from the famous college was the post office and Bank of Ireland.

Alex pulled herself from the grandeur long enough to note the location of the bank. Very soon she would have to make a visit there. Upon seeing her ransacked room, Alex had sold the only jewelry of value that she owned, a strand of pearls, to Mistress Tinsdale. It had been enough to get them to Dublin and room and board for a few days. She would have to convince a dressmaker of her ability to pay through the duke; there was that letter from his own pen stating that she needed new clothes. That should do. And then she would be able to coax a substantial line of credit from the duke's accounts — it was her money she wanted, after all. But first, they had to find lodgings and she had to have a new dress made up. One did not appear as the duke's ward demanding credit in anything less than the latest fashion. It would take a little time and some convincing, but she was determined to make her plan work.

Equally important was an introduction to the Royal Irish Academy, which was said to be at 114 Grafton Street, according to the mail-coach driver. She would ask Montague to find out what he could on that front. Men would respect him, being a famed admiral and all. Baylor could escort her to the dressmakers as her guard. He'd be handy with all the packages and intimidating at her side when she called on the bank. She ticked off the order in her mind: lodgings, the dress, a visit to the bank, and then off to the academy. It would all have to be done quickly. She didn't know if the duke would find her in Dublin, but she thought, eventually, he would.

The thought of her outright lie . . . his anger . . . Alex shivered even though the coach was plenty warm inside. She didn't want to even think about what he would do to her if he ever, well, *when* he finally caught up with her. She wasn't so naïve as to think he'd give up. There were orders from the prince regent after all.

Turning her mind away from that dreaded future event, she looked back out the window at the rows of shops selling everything imaginable. She'd never been the sort to shop just for the pleasure of it, but then she'd never had any money and certainly no place to spend it on Holy Island. Her life had been about how the sheep were faring, what the fishermen had caught and harvested that summer, and whether they had enough supplies laid in to last a cold and stormy winter season. Keeping the cold out of the castle was a job unto itself. Buoying the spirits of an island folk who were hard worn sometimes, too superstitious for a sound mind and guarded to all but home and hearth — that's what Alex knew. Dublin felt a dream of a heavenly sort and she was a little afraid where it might carry her.

They pulled up at the post office and lurched to a stop. Baylor uncoiled from his seat like a big red bear, crawled out of the door, and then groaned and stretched up toward the sky. Alex could almost hear his back cracking as he twisted out the kinks. Montague adjusted his long cape and squinted into the sunlight that spilled over the city and warmed the stones to a rosy amber and brown shimmer. Alex smiled, enjoying the fact that she knew them so well now. She stretched too, her stomach growling with hunger. First thing was to find lodgings.

"Montague, the choices are overwhelming me, I'm afraid. Where shall we stay?"

He turned toward her. "Did I forget to mention it?" When Alex nodded with her eyebrows coming together, he continued. "I have a nephew who lives in Dublin. Lord John Lemon. He'll take us in and it will be safer than staying in an inn. The duke, if he figures out where we are, will look for you in paid carriages and inns. I doubt he will know of my Irish relations."

"Are you sure we can just barge in on him like this?"

Montague's eyes grew thoughtful with a glow of humor. "He's young and a bachelor, last I heard. I believe he will be delighted."

It didn't take very long to hire a coach and find Lord Lemon's address at number 31 Fitzwilliam Square. They stopped in front of a row of red-bricked town houses overlooking Fitzwilliam Street. Alex reached up to check her hair, thinking she must look frightful after two days on the road. She climbed down from the carriage and looked around. It was such a peaceful setting. A cobbled walkway in the colors of yellows, tans, and browns meandered between trees and shrubs leading to wide steps and a blue-painted front door. Montague lifted the brass knocker and rapped loudly on the door.

A maid answered, dressed in mop cap and wide apron. "May I be of help?" she asked in a pleasant voice.

Montague bowed his head at her. "I am Admiral James Montague and I'm looking for my nephew, Lord Lemon. Does he still reside here?"

"Oh, yes sir. He's here now." She looked behind Montague at Alex and then Baylor, her eyes widening upon seeing the giant, and then motioned them inside. "Please, come in and I will tell him you've come to call."

The three of them walked in, Alex impressed with the interior of the place. High ceilings with scrolling plasterwork and hanging chandeliers, domed doorways with columns, gleaming woodwork and large windows that let in plenty of light. The furnishings looked masculine and comfortable, the colors rich browns and deep blues and greens. It was homey and elegant at the same time.

Lord Lemon walked into the room, a broad smile stretched across a handsome face as he enveloped Montague in a hug. Alex thought he matched his surroundings perfectly. He was tall, blond haired, with a slight receding hairline that took nothing away from a chiseled face that had noble leanings. He was dressed in the height of fashion in a dark blue waistcoat, tan breeches, and a snowy shirt and neck cloth. His voice was very agreeable as he welcomed them.

"My dear uncle, what a pleasant surprise! I must say, I can't believe you are in Dublin. This must be some story indeed!"

"It is that," Montague agreed, turning

toward Alex. "May I present my traveling companions, Lady Alexandria Featherstone of Holy Island and Baylor of Belfast."

Lord Lemon's blue-gray eyes twinkled with interest as they settled on Alex's face. She held his gaze, a small smile on her lips. Lord Lemon took her hand and bowed over it and to her dismay, her hand went clammy with nerves. "May I hazard a guess that this lovely creature is an integral part of this story, Montague?" He didn't release her hand.

"You may." Montague's voice held a note of dry resignation.

Alex pulled her hand free. "The story is reserved for trusted friends, my lord. Shall you be a friend to us?" She was surprised by the confident note in her voice and smiled at him, enjoying the parry and riposte of the conversation.

"Ah, how could I not, my lady, when it is apparent that your beauty is only one of your many admirable talents."

"A glib tongue will only get you so far," Alex teased.

Baylor coughed and drew Lord Lemon's attention to him. "Good sir, welcome to my home. Would you like refreshments? I have one of the best cooks in Dublin, smuggled him over from France with me after the war."

"We haven't eaten since early this morning and I heard Lady Alex's stomach rumbling at the post office," Baylor informed, as Alex turned a shade pink and shot him an *I can't believe you just said that* look.

Lord Lemon only laughed and bade them to follow him into the drawing room. He spent a few minutes ordering the meal and drinks to be brought to them, then seated himself across from Alex and crossed one leg over his knee in a picture of a gentleman at ease.

"You must be wondering at my surprise to see my uncle. Ireland isn't Montague's favorite place, you know. His wife, my mother's sister, was from Ireland and she was never treated very well in England after she married him."

Alex shot a look Montague's way. Her own people on Holy Island could be a distrustful sort and had their share of prejudices. She knew the type well. "I'm sorry to hear that. Was she terribly unhappy in England?"

"She kept to herself but a better wife never lived," Montague said with heat.

"He's right. I met her once, as a boy. I still remember how kind she was."

The maid came in and poured tea and passed around a plate of little cakes. "Cook says he'll do his best to get an early dinner on, but this should tide you over in the meantime."

After she left, Lord Lemon asked for the story. Alex told it, about her parents and her search for them, the journey from Holy Island and how Montague had rescued her, and then about meeting Baylor and going to Killyleagh. The only part she left out was the part about her guardian, the duke. No need to alarm a fellow peer of the realm. When she was finished with the tale, she said, "When we arrived in Dublin, Montague mentioned that you might have room for us to stay for a few days. I need to make contact with members of the Royal Irish Academy. I need to find the next clue as to where my parents went."

"Of course, you must stay!" Lord Lemon agreed. "What a fascinating story. I should be glad to lend my assistance in any way possible, Lady Featherstone."

"Please, my *friends* call me Alex."

A delighted look flashed across his face. "And mine call me John." His voice had lowered a notch and for some reason it made her stomach feel warm.

Montague looked from one to the other

of them and let out a sigh. Baylor boomed with laughter.

Montague chuckled. "Just beware, Nephew, her guardian is the Duke of St. Easton and he is taking his post most seriously."

John's dark blond brows rose. "You don't say," he mused, looking at Alex again with a curious mix of interest and intent.

# CHAPTER TWENTY-FIVE

Gabriel stood on the shore of Strangford
Lough in Killyleagh, looked out across the
choppy water at the green-hued islands in
the distance, and tried to catch his breath.

What was he going to do with her? Of all
the scheming, manipulative, outrageous acts
— to be lied to so — to be tricked . . . He
took another deep breath and imagined giving her a well-deserved spanking. He would
have to shackle her to himself once he found
her to keep her from running off! And that
made him all the angrier. Little minx. What
*was* he going to do with her?

First, he would have to go back to the inn
and console Meade and question the
woman running the place. She had to know
something. Maybe Meade should question
her. In the temper he was in, feeling much
like the prowling panther they often compared him to, he would likely frighten her
and do more harm than good. Yes, Meade

would question the innkeeper and he would pay a call on the castle. Alexandria must have gone to the castle.

He made his way back to the inn and found Meade mopping at his brow with a handkerchief.

Gabriel clapped him on the shoulder. "Sorry Meade, I don't know what came over me. I should have expected it of her, but that last letter . . . well, I'll not be fooled again."

Meade brought out the speaking book and wrote a lengthy reply. "Mistress Tinsdale said that Lady Featherstone, Admiral Montague, and a giant Irishman named Baylor were indeed here and that they left three days ago. She didn't know where they were going, but she thought they hired a coach and gave me the address of the coaching house. Shall I go there next and see what I can find out?"

"Yes, do that." Gabriel narrowed his eyes. "Meade, do you believe Mistress Tinsdale told you the truth? Did she seem as taken with Alexandria as everyone else we've run into that has met her?"

Meade nodded slowly and wrote, "Her eyes did light up in that particular fashion when talking about your ward. She thought the threesome 'delightful' she said several times. I do believe her, though. She didn't seem to be lying or covering anything up."

"Hmmm." Gabriel reached for the speaking book. "I believe I will pay a call at the castle and see what I can discover while you look into their next direction."

"Very good, Your Grace." Meade bowed, slapped his hat down on his head, and turned to go.

Gabriel put his gloves back on and followed him to the street, turning toward the castle. If he remembered the history correctly, the Hamilton Rowans held the Killyleagh seat now and the current owner would be Archibald Hamilton Rowan, who from all accounts was a fiery character indeed. He was one of the founders of the Society of United Irishmen, a revolutionary group that wanted to end British rule over Ireland. He was a well-traveled man who had even spent some time in prison due to his political views. It was said that he escaped by climbing out a window with a bedsheet rope. Gabriel had to admit, he was looking forward to meeting the man.

In less than an hour he was seated across from him, laughing at the old stories through curls of cigar smoke. He finally turned the conversation to his ward. "So you say she was here? Looking for clues as to the whereabouts of her parents?"

Sir Archibald nodded, a small smile on his lips and wrote his reply. *I must say she convinced me that they might still be alive. Very determined, Lady Featherstone.*

"You don't know the half of it." Gabriel returned the speaking book. "I've been told that her parents were looking for a missing piece of the Sloane collection, so it makes sense that they came here, but no one seems to know what they found or where they went next. Did Lady Featherstone mention any leads?"

*No, you know more than she did, I think. I told her about Sloane and raised the questions about what could be missing from his collection. I do know one thing her parents found because I loaned it to them. It was an old journal of Sloane's that had somehow ended up in the castle's library. The Featherstones were keen to have it and I saw little reason not to loan it to them. I told Alexandria this. Another book about the history of Killyleagh was stolen by two Spaniards. I don't know what has happened to them.*

"It sounds like she found very little help here."

"I'm afraid so." Sir Archibald shrugged. "I don't think that will deter her, however. She's the stubborn sort."

Gabriel could only agree. He rose to leave and stretched out his hand toward Sir Archibald. "I thank you, sir. It was a pleasure meeting one of Ireland's heroes."

Sir Archibald laughed and shook Gabriel's hand. "Would that I were young again and still at such work."

Gabriel was just turning to leave when Sir Archibald stopped him with a hand on his shoulder. Reaching for the speaking book, he quickly wrote, *Wait! I've just remembered something. Before leaving, the Featherstones asked if Killyleagh had a dressmaker, something about needing warmer clothes. I gave them the name of Peggy O'Callaghan. My wife has had some clothing made up by her and was quite pleased with the work. She has a shop on Frederick Street.*

"Thank you, sir. I will visit her right away."

True to his word, Gabriel ducked under the low door frame of O'Callaghan Tailoring and Fine Dress within a few minutes of leaving the castle. It was an interesting place, with stacks of cloth, articles of clothing in varying degrees of completion, and a hodgepodge of items relating to sewing strewn about the room. An older woman rushed from the back room as the door closed behind him.

She took a long, considering look at Gabriel's costume and must have sensed he was a man of means as she smiled broadly and bade him to sit down and warm himself by the fire. Before Gabriel could state his business, he had a steaming cup of tea in his hand and a plate of sweets at his elbow on the table beside the chair. She seated herself and started to talk in such a fast manner that Gabriel groaned. Taking out the speaking book he explained its need, an embarrassed flush filling his cheeks, and then asked about the Featherstones.

*Oh, my yes! Such an elegant couple, they were! Goodness, and the clothes they ordered! It took everything I had and then some begging to nearby towns to get all the fabric I needed. Furs, they wanted too. Everything warm, quality materials but practical. And they wanted them all to be in browns and grays and black, though I tried to talk Lady Featherstone into some color to complement that stunning complexion of hers.*

"Did they mention why they needed such warm clothing? Did they mention where they were going next?" Gabriel held his breath as she nodded and then wrote in the speaking book.

She turned the book around. One word was written on it.

*Iceland.*

■ ■ ■ ■

The sun was setting with fiery lights making horizontal slashes across the sky as Gabriel walked back toward the inn. Iceland? What could Iceland possibly have to do with this puzzle?

He thought back to his studies of Iceland. He'd gone through a stage of studying several countries per month, usually around five. It had taken him two and a half years to learn the cultures and history of the known world. He'd visited many of the places, but never Iceland. It was still recovering from *Móðuharðindin* — "the Mist Hardships" — when Mount Laki erupted. And then there was that business of the Sermon of Fire. A tale of prayer stopping the lava flow. The devastation of the gases from the eruption destroyed grazing lands and livestock. Famine ensued and they were just now recovering, hearing of America's freedom like all the world, and pulling against their Danish harness.

How any of that tied in with Hans Sloane and his collection and a missing manuscript, such that kings were fighting over it, he had no idea. And neither did Alexandria. She had not spoken to the dressmaker, he had ascertained that. She did not know of the connection with Iceland yet. Or did she? He must never underestimate her again.

He thought of Meade and his task to find information on where she might have gone next and he stopped and looked at the cold, hard facts. He couldn't trust his ward to tell the truth. She was headstrong and determined to find her parents at whatever cost, even angering the prince regent. She might have a care for him, and he refused to believe otherwise, but she would stop at nothing to convince the people around her to help her, and she was very good at getting that help. And, more telling, she wasn't sure of him, not his allegiance to her or her cause and so she cut him off, subconsciously he was sure. She was just trying to do the impossible from a desperate heart. But nonetheless, it was true that she was a ruthless opponent when it came to matters of such great importance to her.

Gabriel stopped and laughed, a real laugh that lasted a long time. God bless her, but he loved her for it. He admired the tenacity and he understood the will behind a need like this. It wasn't as if she wanted money or fame or power or position. No, his dearest ward, his Alexandria, wanted *love*. And he was going to see that she got it.

Taking a deep breath he continued up the long hill, passing several shops that had closed for the night. A little farther down, the street turned busy in front of a place with glowing windows and people, mostly men, milling in and out. Gabriel slowed to look in, seeing a pub. The tables were crowded with citizens all staring toward the front of the room where a small stage took up one corner. A group of four musicians were playing. Without thinking what he was doing, Gabriel entered the pub.

He found an empty table in a corner and sat down. Strange how lively the scene looked and how, without sound, dead it felt. It was hard to sit there. Almost as if he were alone and invisible in the crowded room. A part of him wanted to run away from the feeling, but something told him that was the coward's way out and he had never been a coward.

Gabriel closed his eyes, stretching his hands out on the rough wood of the table, reaching for the music. A slow calm crept over him as he became aware of all the vibrations. His feet felt them hum from the floor up his legs and into his chest where if he concentrated hard enough they became a beat, a pulse. His hands, too, felt beyond rough wood planks and into the very air it seemed, catching the lighter vibrations of the pennywhistle. He swallowed and heard it, becoming so in tune with his body that each breath and muscle stretched with the music.

A sudden shot of color burst from behind his closed eyes, the colors too deep and rich for anything he'd seen on this earth. The vibrations, he noticed in the back of his mind, that part that was detached from the fear and awe and could construct a reality distinct from what seemed normal, seemed to control their movement. The colors leapt and swayed . . . he didn't shy away from them like before . . . he stayed calm and just concentrated on the vibrations going up and down his legs and arms and through his chest. A tear ran down his cheek and he realized he was crying. So deep was his concentration that he had split in two and the other half of him, the emotional half, had seen something the visceral half had not.

*He could see the music.*

A shuddering breath ran through him and he opened his eyes.

Blues and purples, yellows and greens undulated around the musicians. The violin was purple and blue, the pennywhistle yellow with streaks of red, the flute green, the dulcimer green and yellow. Together the colors moved, then apart, then together again. Gabriel studied the players, when they were most often playing, and the bursts of color around them that matched their movements.

*Dear God, if I concentrate enough, I can almost hear the song.*

A feeling of immense gratitude overwhelmed him. Of everything this new existence had taken and brought him — this was a gift.

And he must not tell anyone about it.

They would think him mad.

# CHAPTER TWENTY-SIX

One of Dublin's finest dressmakers pursed her lips and nodded to her assistant. "That color, yes, it must be. You look glorious in red, Lady Featherstone, just glorious. Wouldn't you say, Lord Lemon?"

"I *would* say," John murmured from the fireplace where he was standing, admiration lighting his eyes.

Alex tried to squelch the blush rising to her cheeks. She wasn't used to so much direct admiration, and from such a handsome and agreeable man. Turning away from him, she looked into the mirror they'd brought into the drawing room for her. It had taken two days to have three dresses made up — one day dress of soft yellow muslin and two evening gowns, as John insisted she would need both while in Dublin. They were all high waisted with cap sleeves and a fitted bodice. There were white gloves that went to her elbows, matching slippers with ribbons that tied around her ankles, and jeweled and beribboned head-bands to hold back the cascade of curls John's maid had somehow, magically, trans-formed in her hair. When she looked at the creature staring back at her in the mirror, she didn't see Alex, the girl, she saw Lady Alexandria Featherstone, the woman. It both thrilled and terrified her.

"John, which dress should I wear to the bank?" He had become indispensible in all things to do with society and propriety. He'd already introduced her to a small group of his circle of friends, and tonight they were to attend a musical event at the Rotunda where the famous Angelica Cata-lani would be singing. It was an event, Alex had been told by her new acquaintances, that could not be missed, and she had to admit she was excited about it.

"Wear the red tonight at the musical, save the other evening gown for a ball I've yet to tell you about," he winked. "A surprise for later. And for this afternoon at the bank, the yellow day dress is fine," John returned. "With that pink parasol and the darker pink slippers, you'll look as fresh and sweet as country air. And then you'll borrow my mother's diamond necklace, just to remind them who you are."

Alex laughed. He always had her laughing. "I couldn't."

"You can and you will. If my mother were still alive, she would insist upon it, you have my word. She always did like a good plot, and squeezing a small fortune from the duke without his knowledge would have been the *fait accompli* of the year."

"Oh, when you put it that way, it really is too daring. What is the worst thing that could come of it? Could they jail me as an imposter?"

"But you're not an imposter, and you have the letters with the duke's seal on them to prove it. The worst thing I can think of is that they will laugh in our faces and turn us away."

He said *us*. "You'll go with me?"

"Of course. We'll take Baylor along for effect, as you mentioned before, and I will play the role of friend and advisor." He shrugged with a lazy smile. "They may know of me and it might help — a little."

Alex took a long breath. It was a sound plan, a very good plan, and it had to work. "When shall we leave?"

"As soon as you're ready, love." He pushed away from the fireplace, took some coins from his pocket, and handed them to the modiste who had maintained a professional silence during their discussion. Alex started to protest, but John stopped her with a little warning look. She would have to tell him later that she planned to pay him back. With money. Not that he would ask for other kinds of favors; she was just being silly and letting her imagination get the better of her.

An hour later they were stepping out of John's carriage at the grand entrance to the Bank of Ireland. Alex snapped the parasol shut while John held the door open for her. Baylor loomed behind them. "Look intimidating," John whispered back toward him.

His eyes widened with a look of fear. "How do I do that?"

"Never mind." Alex patted his arm. "Just be yourself."

That didn't seem to make Baylor any less nervous.

They walked up the steps and through the big doors. Inside was a long lobby with offices on either side, marbled floors, and tall, echoing ceilings. Alex tried to slow the pounding of her heart as they made their way to one of the main desks.

A mild-looking man gazed up at them, then peered behind Alex at Baylor, his eyes widening in just the way they'd been hoping for, but then Baylor gave the man a vacant, fake-looking smile and boomed,

"How do you do, good sir! It's a fine day, isn't it?"

Alex shot a stilling glance at him and John quietly groaned. Baylor was taking his role much too seriously. He might ruin everything!

Trying to regain the banker's attention, Alex pasted a sunny smile on her face and leaned in a bit. He stood and bowed at them. "Good day. How might I be of service?"

John jumped in with his supporting role. "Good day to you, sir. This is Lady Alexandria Featherstone here visiting from England and I am Lord John Lemon, of the Kilkenny Lemons." He flicked a hand toward Baylor. "And this is our good friend Baylor of Belfast."

"I've already said how-de-do to the man. Am I supposed to say it again?" Baylor boomed, his voice echoing around the huge domed ceiling. It actually looked as if his meaty hands were trembling.

Alex gave the banker, who was staring at the three of them in confused distrust, another smile and a little exhale. "He's just a little nervous. Uhm." Oh no, this was not going well at all.

John hurried in again. "We've come on an urgent matter that has to do with the Duke of St. Easton."

The man blinked several times, glancing from John to Alexandria to Baylor and back again. "Well, ah, please be seated." He motioned toward the chairs nearby.

Baylor looked at the small chair, started to sit in it, and then changed his mind. It didn't appear as if he would be able to get his hips between the wooden arms. John said a soft word that Alex was certain she was glad she hadn't clearly heard. "Just stand behind us," he hissed.

Alex actually found herself waving at the banker to gain his attention, smiling and blinking, her head cocked to one side in the manner of a pea brain. "You see," Alex began as she folded her hands in her lap to keep them from doing anything else strange, "I am the ward of the Duke of St. Easton. He and I have been corresponding through letters for some time now and discussing the fact that he will be joining me here in Ireland. He had, some weeks ago, given me bank notes for my allowance, but I fear I was robbed in Killyleagh and am in quite a quandary."

Alex pulled forth a beaded reticule and removed the duke's letters. She passed two over to the banker. "As you can see from the seal and the contents of the letter, the duke is holding my fortune in the Bank of England. I have not been able to reach him with the news of this horrid theft, but when I do, I am sure he will send more funds. In the meantime, I would like to open a line of credit to sustain me for the duration of my stay in Dublin."

"Ah." The man opened the letters, read them, then studied the seal. His face was hard to read but Alex feared the worst and looked to John for help.

"My good man, the duke is in Ireland, and will eventually come to Dublin. I can't imagine his . . . displeasure . . . should his ward not be taken the very best care of in this matter." John shuddered. "It doesn't bear thinking of."

The man paled and nodded. "I shall have to check with my superior. Please, wait here."

He disappeared toward the back of the vast room and then through an arched doorway. Alex gave John a hopeful smile but stayed silent.

Baylor didn't have the same common sense. "That was a fine piece of work, my lord. You put the fear in him, didn't you now?"

"Shhh!" they both hissed back at him.

Alex felt instantly sorry. His face became

crestfallen and his shoulders drooped. Good heavens she would be glad when this was over.

They waited in intense silence for a full twenty minutes when the banker came back with an older gentleman. His keen gaze locked on Alexandria's, making her knees shake as she rose and gave a brief curtsey toward the man.

"Mr. Tyler has explained the situation, Lady Featherstone, and we are prepared to extend you two hundred pounds. Will that be sufficient?"

His gaze challenged hers and she got the distinct impression that he was a betting man and that two hundred pounds was all he was willing to bet on the authenticity of her tale. Alex thought of the fortune she should have every right to, the fortune left to her by her parents, and raised her chin a notch. Her gaze didn't falter for a moment; it held steady, a glint of steel coming to her eyes. "I'm afraid that won't do. I have no idea when the duke will arrive and there are . . . expenses. Five hundred pounds should tide me over with, of course, the possibility of more should the need arise." She pressed her lips into a tiny smile and waited.

"Five hundred pounds." He looked astonished but seemed to be considering it.

"Yes." She nodded once.

He took a long breath. "Very well, Lady Featherstone. You will, of course, sign for it."

"Of course."

He nodded to Mr. Tyler. "See that it's done." And he strode away, not looking very happy.

John leaned toward her ear and whispered, "Well done," as the other man hurried to fetch the papers.

"Well done!" Baylor added in an overly dramatic whisper.

Alex smiled through gritted teeth. "I'll have one hundred in bank notes and coin, if you please. The rest will be drawn upon by lines of credit with merchants and such."

"Yes, your ladyship."

Within minutes she had a reticule full of money and the three of them were back on the street, smiling in victory at each other.

"I feel the need to celebrate." John took her arm and started them in the direction of the College Green. "Let's go find a bite to eat, shall we? And then we'll do a little shopping for the musical tonight."

"John, you'll have my money spent in a single afternoon!" Alex laughed and playfully slapped his arm.

"I'm fronting the meal, love. But I'm sure

you'll want to buy some fripperies from the shops. A new fan? A colorful scarf? Irish lace? You've not experienced Dublin until you've gone along the quay and seen all the lovely Irish wares to be had."

"Oh, very well." Alex looked up at him with adoring eyes. It was so easy to get distracted from her mission when on the arm of such an elegant, entertaining gentleman.

Baylor decided that the encounter at the bank had exhausted him and he needed a nap, so they put him in a hired carriage and bid him sweet dreams while Alex and John headed for the shops along the quay. The afternoon sped by as they made their way along the streets lining the River Liffey. True to his word, John showed her every kind of shop — millinery to confectionary, furniture, linens, market houses with various kinds of seafood and vegetables, cakes and pies. There was an auction going on at one corner.

They stopped and watched the bidding on a prized painting by John Henry Campbell of Glendalough, County Wicklow. Alex stared at the soft blue mountains in the background, the lake peeping in front of them with hills of green in the foreground. It was exactly what Ireland looked like. She instantly liked it. Might someday she have a warm and inviting home where she could hang such a thing?

It was the first time she'd ever thought of it.

John leaned near her ear. "You like it don't you, Alexandria?"

She looked up at him, into his blue-gray eyes, and wrinkled her brow. "I do. Is it by a famous artist? I know little about art."

"Campbell is popular here. If you were my wife, I would buy it for you this instant."

There was a note of seriousness in his voice that gave Alexandria pause. He had always been so teasing, so glib and full of fun that this new side of him intrigued and frightened her a little. This was not the right time to be courting anyone. She had a mission and she couldn't let herself forget it.

Trying for lightness she touched his arm and teased, "And what if your wife likes five other paintings besides, and that lovely desk we saw at the last shop, and there were those sapphire earrings at the silversmith's."

John gave her a look that said he knew what she was doing and admired her ability to turn the topic toward her ends, even though he might want to hint at the possibility of something more serious between them. He joined her joke. "A weekly shopping expedition. Why, our house will be so full of things that we'll barely squeeze by each other passing down the hall."

Alex laughed and the moment passed. They continued down the quay, the river at low tide and the crowd moving up and down the street in an ever-steady flow of traffic and people. Alex felt strangely alive, stepping into this other world where there was more than a herd of sheep or the latest village gossip to think of. She found she liked it. She liked it very much. They finally decided it was time to go and dress for the dinner and the musical at the Rotunda.

Another first, Alex reflected as, hours later, she looked at herself in the mirror wearing the red evening gown. It was satin trimmed with black lace, high waisted with a square-cut neckline that made her collar bones stand out and her neck look long and stately. Or maybe it was the pulled back hair piled on top of her head, shining with pomade that smelled faintly of lavender that she'd helped Reagan, John's maid, prepare.

It had been fun mixing the ingredients, reminding her of times at home when she had gathered herbs and berries and sweeter-smelling plants to try and mix with the tallow candles and soaps. She'd even made some pretty little pots of rouge and placed them in the market shop on Holy Island. It had caused a bit of a scandal, but she'd sold them in three days and they'd asked for more. Her lip stain had sold out in two days. Over the years she'd made perfumed oils, cosmetics, soaps, and candles. It gave her something to do during the long, lonely hours when her parents were gone.

She sighed a dreamy sigh as she pulled on her gloves. She'd never looked like this though. She looked like her mother.

The thought changed her excitement into determination. This night was not just for fun, she reminded herself. John had promised to introduce her to anyone he could who was a member of the Royal Irish Academy. As wonderful as the music would prove to be, and as nice as it felt to be escorted by one of Dublin's most handsome and eligible bachelors, Alex lifted her chin in the mirror and reminded herself of her mission.

*Please God, help me find my parents.*

# CHAPTER TWENTY-SEVEN

Meade stood waiting for him in the Dufferin Coaching Inn's common room when Gabriel returned, still shaken by his discovery and turning the possibilities over and over in his mind. Might he practice this new gift? Would he someday enjoy the opera again? The thought of never hearing music again had not been worth considering — it was too painful. Now, the possibility that he might not have to felt like God had stretched a line of hope down from heaven. Perhaps God's love was perfect and he just hadn't learned to recognize all the signs of it yet.

He was still in somewhat of a daze as he sat across from his secretary. Meade took the speaking book and wrote of his findings.

*Yes, there had been a coach hired under Admiral Montague's name. It left three days ago, heading for the little town of Downpatrick, just south of Killyleagh. The roads, he was*

*told, were in terrible shape, but horses would
have a better time of it. When I asked if the
man knew why they were going there, he
shook his head and said that folks have their
own business to attend to and he doesn't pry.
I persevered with a few coins and he was
persuaded to say that he dropped them off at
Down Cathedral.*

Gabriel braced his elbows on his knees
and rubbed the bridge of his nose with a
finger. Why would she go to some little out-
of-the-way town? And to a cathedral? It
didn't make any sense. He needed to sleep
on it — too muddled, too exhausted and
exhilarated at the same time. They would
travel there for answers tomorrow.

The next morning they headed off toward
Downpatrick riding south along the shore
of Strangford Lough, through the Quoile
marshes and across the river. Worry gnawed
at his stomach as he considered this latest
direction. It was taking much longer than
he had anticipated to locate Alexandria, and
there was the army waiting back at Holy
Island. He knew they had no news; he'd
pointed them in the wrong direction after
all, and he hadn't sent them any news.

It had been weeks now and the captain
must be getting impatient. How long he

would wait was an important question. Soon, if he hadn't already, he would abandon his post and head back to London and that would not be good. Not good at all. Gabriel imagined him going to the prince regent, telling his side of the story. It was not going to advance Gabriel's case. Might even look like what it really was — a ruse.

Not that he wasn't trying to locate his willful ward and haul her back to London. Oh no, he was looking more and more forward to the moment when he had her within his grasp. But the plan to scatter the army and go off alone with only Meade? The prince regent might not be pleased with him for that. And the fact that he had thus far failed and that Alexandria was gallivanting about the United Kingdom with Spaniards on her tail? And that it appeared she was being successful in tracking down every clue her parents had left on the Emerald Isle? Well, it wouldn't do at all for the prince regent to hear all of that. He gritted his teeth with the thought. It grated, no infuriated him, that a slip of a woman had so outplayed him.

*Wait a minute.*

Gabriel reined in his horse and looked over at Meade, waiting for him to command his horse to stop.

"Meade, that coachman that you questioned."

Meade nodded, his brows coming together.

"Did he hesitate at any time when you questioned him?"

Meade shook his head.

"When he said they went to Downpatrick . . . did he say Downpatrick immediately?"

Meade nodded, brows raised.

"What about when you paid him and he said he dropped them off at the cathedral. Any difference when he said that?"

Meade cocked his head to one side in thought. *He did hesitate then. I just thought he was reluctant to answer,* Meade mouthed.

"Or, he was making it up as he went along. Meade, I'm afraid our dear Alexandria is trying to buy herself a little more time by sending us on another wild-goose chase. Wherever she has gone, it isn't Downpatrick."

"Shouldn't we go and see, just in case?"

"No. We'll go back to Killyleagh and see if we can't convince our good coachman to talk." Gabriel smiled with narrowed eyes. "Come along."

He wheeled his horse around and spurred him into a gallop, hoping Meade could keep up with the fast pace.

■ ■ ■ ■

Back in Killyleagh, Meade led the way to
the coaching house. Mr. Kelly, the coachman Meade had spoken to, was polishing a
shiny black carriage in the drive. Gabriel
went over and grasped the man by the collar, lifting him off his feet until they were
eye to eye.

Kelly gasped and kicked out, striking Gabriel on the shin. Gabriel didn't even feel it.
He pushed the man back, causing Kelly to
land on his back, sprawled on the ground.

He said something, looked like it might
have been, "What's the meaning of this,"
but he didn't try to get up.

Gabriel leaned over him. "I believe you've
been lying to my secretary," he stated in a
serious and low voice.

Kelly looked aside toward Meade, his face
going white. "Meade tells me you said
Admiral Montague and his party went to
Downpatrick, to the cathedral there. I've
decided it unlikely so I thought you should
accompany us to Downpatrick, and should
it prove to be a lie, well, I shouldn't want to
be in your position. You see, I'm the Duke
of St. Easton here on the prince regent's
business. The prince regent would not be

359

forgiving should he learn of any who are impeding my mission. Do you understand?"

Kelly started talking — fast. Blubbering actually. Gabriel couldn't keep up with it and looked over to Meade who was nodding. Meade turned toward Gabriel and mouthed the words, *She paid him to lie.*

"Where is she?" Gabriel demanded once the man's mouth stopped moving.

"I don't know, I swear." Gabriel caught that. The man was obviously terrified so he believed him. Gabriel leaned over him and glared at him. "If it comes to you, anything at all, we are staying at the Dufferin Coaching Inn. I imagine I can forgive the lie if you remember something more, something important."

He nodded, eyes wide with fear, as Gabriel backed away.

When they got back to the inn, Mistress Tinsdale ran toward them, waving a letter. "I'm so glad you've come back, Your Grace. We just found this letter in the trash bin. I confess I read it as I recognized Lady Featherstone's handwriting and thought it might be important, what with that mystery she's trying to solve with her parents and those Spanish men following her, don't you know. It's addressed to you." She thrust it into his hands as if it were on fire.

Gabriel turned toward the light of a window and smoothed it out. His heart pounded as he read.

Dear Gabriel,

Hmm. She only called him by his given name when she planned for him never to see the letter.

I despise lying to you. I loathe myself over it. Yet I cannot give up my search and you are tied with the prince regent and the prince regent has his demands. Do you not understand? I would give up my life for this search. I will do, and have done, things I'm not proud of to continue it. It's just that I didn't know I would be beset on every side and that so many would see my mission as foolish and self-indulgent and wish I'd give up all hope. I ask you to search your heart, dear duke. If you were in my position, what would you do?

I am prepared to take a great leap of faith in you and tell you where I am. I confess, my heart beats like a drum within my chest as I write, but I need you. I need you to trust me, and if you can't join me because of your duty, at least give me some time . . . a chance. I beg you, as the Duke of St. Easton — Faith for Duty — I beg you to, this time, choose faith.

Dublin.
Yours,
Alexandria

He took a sudden inhale. How had she known his family motto *Faith for duty?* They were forever at odds and he'd long ago chosen duty. It was easier, comfortable. Faith was free-falling, cliff-diving nonsense. He looked back down at her handwriting. It had changed a little, seemed terse and a little desperate. There was a tear stain amongst the inked-out lines.

She would be one to choose faith.

He knew it and he felt he knew her deeper than was imaginable from a few letters. But it was true. There was no denying it. And he loved her. He'd never even seen her and yet he loved her. He didn't know what kind of love it was . . . he'd never known anything like this before. He just knew it was so deep in his heart that it would be there forever.

And thank God she'd told him where to find her. Dublin.

■ ■ ■ ■

Dublin was a favorite city of his. Gabriel had been here before and had very much enjoyed it, the poetic sense of mood and the many faces of a creative story weaving people. It was a place of elegance and charm and fairy tales.

Gabriel and Meade trotted over the stone bridges that crossed the River Liffey on their mounts, both the men and the horses decked out in the royal blue and gold colors of the house of St. Easton. Gabriel had bought a coach and had his ducal seal painted on the sides of it, though no one rode in it. He'd hired outriders, uniformed in his family colors, four servants, one valet, two groomsmen, and a cook, just in case the hotel couldn't manage his demands. He had a plan.

It was time to be the Duke of St. Easton again.

It was time for a show of power.

They pulled up to the front of the Morrison's Hotel, a place worthy of royalty, and disembarked. He nodded to the porter, directed his bags to be brought to the prince regent's own suite and, ignoring everyone and their chattering faces, strode into the grand lobby. Meade would take care of the placing of his new staff and himself. Gabriel looked around with approval in his eyes. The place was as he remembered it. Grand, high-ceiling opulence with a thousand lights in candelabra and wall sconces. Lush furnishings in muted colors, a fountain in the indoor garden, and rooms enough to house a cavalcade. It was perfect and he was itching to get started on his plan.

He was led to a grand suite of rooms where his clothing was unpacked, pressed, and put away. He ordered food, a hot bath, and told his valet to locate Dublin's best tailor and boot maker. He needed outfitted for this mission and the clothes he'd brought on the road were not nearly up to snuff. Dash it all. When Alexandria first saw him she was going to be impressed and . . . a little terrified.

But that wasn't the spine of the plan, only one of the extremities. No, he smiled to himself, he would use every advantage he had to find her.

And this time, he was playing by his rules. This time, God help him it would not take long.

# Chapter Twenty-Eight

John led Alex to their seats in Dublin's Rotunda. Aptly named, it was an enormous round room with Corinthian pilasters and a massive, central chandelier. The crush of elegantly dressed people made the air warm but Alex didn't care. This was like nothing she'd ever attended and the crowd-watching alone was enthralling.

"Having a good time?" John handed her a set of opera glasses.

Alex nodded, glancing at his face. She couldn't help but admire how fine he looked in his formal clothing — white shirt, white high-collared waistcoat with a perfectly tied cravat. White pantaloons tucked into his boots, and a blue double-breasted coat that shone as if its threads were silken wool. His hair was brushed back in a careless-looking wave that lent him an air of artless sophistication, and his blue eyes sparkled down at her. She swallowed hard and looked away, trying to work the opera glasses.

"Here, let me show you." They sat down, Montague on her other side, while John flipped the handle around so the lenses hung correctly. Alex peered through them. "Goodness me, everything is twice its normal size!"

"Just wait," John promised, "the curtain's opening up."

She turned toward the stage and watched as the red velvet curtain parted, revealing a small stage. A few moments later Angelica Catalani came out, a beautiful, frail-looking brunette with a crown of roses entwined in her hair. As soon as she began to sing, everything and everyone faded away. Song after song Alex sat raptly, caught up in the magical spell of a world-class soprano.

During the intermission John steered her toward a hall where refreshments were being served and the attendees chatted and mingled.

"There," he leaned down and whispered into her ear, "do you see that older man, with dark red hair and ruddy cheeks?"

Alex nodded.

"That is Tad Molony. He's one of the men I told you about that is a member of the Royal Irish Academy."

Alex clasped John's upper arm with her

gloved hand and squeezed. "Do you know him?" There was a hint of desperation in her grip.

"Not so much, but I know his son a little, enough to give you an introduction, at any rate. Come along."

They worked their way to the small circle of men where Mr. Molony stood. Alex could feel her heart speed up and took a deep, calming breath before stepping into the small open space beside him. John edged in beside her and bowed to the five or six men, all a generation or two older than they were. He was nothing if not confident, Alex thought with an inner smile. They did make a good team.

The conversation came to an awkward pause as the men looked at the two of them, giving John his opportunity. "Gentlemen, we beg your pardon for interrupting your discourse on the fine qualities of Guinness. I was only hoping to introduce my young friend here to Mr. Molony. They have an interest in common."

One man chuckled. Another said something ribald under his breath, but Mr. Molony only turned to survey her and John with interest. "I must say I am flattered to be sought after by such a creature of beauty," he said in typical Irish charm. He took her gloved hand and bowed over it. "To what do I owe this pleasure?" He looked at John, intelligence and curiosity in his eyes.

John reached out to shake his hand. "I'm John Lemon. I believe I know your son, Brant Molony. We frequent the same clubs."

A look of displeasure crossed his deep brown eyes, making Alex want to kick John. You didn't remind a father of a son's indiscretions unless the father had taught it to him. She didn't know how she knew that pearl of wisdom, but it just seemed like common sense. She hurried to correct the error.

"Sir, I understand you are a member of the Royal Irish Academy?"

His gaze switched back to her face and softened. "You've an interest in scientific matters, miss?"

"Alexandria Featherstone, sir. From Holy Island in Northumberland. And yes, I have a very great interest in antiquities. I was hoping to ask you a few questions." She glanced around at the aptly listening men of their circle. "In private, that is. It is a matter of . . . some delicacy." She raised her brows at him and gave him a small smile.

"Hmm," he said, thinking about it. "There is another in our circle here then that we should perhaps include." He turned toward a thin, silver-haired man. "Mr. Sean Healy, Lady Alexandria Featherstone." He gestured with a sweep of his arm. "Healy is also a member of the Royal Irish Academy and something of an expert on antiquities, aren't you, Sean?"

Mr. Healy shrugged one shoulder. "I have a small collection."

Mr. Molony chuckled.

Another member of the circle spoke up, his Irish brogue thick and deep. "You can't leave us languishing in curiosity, Lady Featherstone. Is there nothing we can know of the tale?"

John shook his head, his chest puffing out just a bit. Alex wanted to roll her eyes. Where was his legendary charm? Maybe he saved it for ladies. She smiled at the man and said, "I'm working on a case, sir. An important antiquity has gone missing, stolen most likely, and I've been hired to find it."

So it wasn't the full truth. So it was her parents who'd been hired to find it. She couldn't help enjoying watching his eyes widen with interest.

A bell rang signaling the crowd to return to the musicale. In a move a little too desperate, Alex put her hand on Molony's arm. "Please, sir. Just a moment more of

Mr. Healy's and your time?"

He nodded and Mr. Healy moved closer, now making their circle four as the other men, some grumbling about how scientists got all the luck, made their way back to their seats.

"Come now, Lady Featherstone. What's all this about?"

"I exaggerated a bit with that last statement. It was not me who was hired to find this missing antiquity but my parents. You see . . ."

She launched into the story of her parents and the missing item from Sloane's collection. The two men stood raptly as she told it, exclaiming at times and whispering phrases to each other that made little sense to her.

"So you see, gentlemen, I am convinced that my parents are in terrible trouble. I must find them. And the only way to do that is to track this missing item from Sloane's collection. Have you heard anything about it?"

"Sloane's collection is a long way from what we are studying these days." Healy frowned.

"I do recall rumors of a theft though, about seven or eight years ago," Mr. Molony added, then he shook his head. "But I didn't pay it much mind at the time."

"There is someone else who might know more," Healy growled out the words.

"Yes, but not much good that it will do her." Molony stared back at Healy. "We shouldn't even mention it. He will never see her."

"Oh, please!" Alex leaned forward. "There must be some way. Who is it?"

"I'll see that he sees her," John put in with authority. They both ignored John.

"There is the masquerade ball. It's the only social function he attends. Might be worth a try." Molony's eyebrows rose in question.

"I've only gotten invitations to that event twice in my lifetime. How do you propose to get her in?" Healy responded.

Molony looked at John. "Lord Lemon has his connections. Do you get invited to the viceroy's annual masquerade ball?"

"Yes, I've been invited."

"Think you can get her in?" Molony flicked his hand in Alex's direction.

"Of course I can. I was planning on it. We've already had the costume made up."

"What are you talking about?" Alex asked.

"Why the masquerade ball, my dear. Remember? The special dress?"

"It's a masquerade? You didn't tell me that."

John shrugged. "I was saving it as a surprise."

"That's the only reason he attends. He doesn't like to be out in public. His face is . . . disfigured. But once a year, he dons a mask and revels in the waltz with no one the wiser."

"Who is this man?"

"His name is Jeremy Lyons. And he is an expert on Sloane. He's been obsessed with him for years. If anyone will know about this missing antiquity you're speaking of, it will be him."

Alex took a deep inhale. "Then we'll have to attend this ball." She looked up at John. "Are you sure you can do it?"

"You can count on it."

"But if he's masked, how will we know who he is?" Alex asked the group.

"Good question." John looked at Molony, who only shrugged.

"It is to all our good fortune that I have a standing invitation to this ball," the voice came from behind them, "and Lyons and I have had some dealings in the past."

They all turned to see Montague.

Molony and Healy both grew wide-eyed

and bowed. "Admiral Montague. Sir, a pleasure."

They all greeted each other while Alex tilted her head to one side and scowled at Montague. Why hadn't he told her this? Why did he make it so easy for her to forget she was traveling with a legend? Drat that man and his modest, humble, wonderful self. As if to make it up to her, he leaned down and gave her a fatherly peck on the cheek.

"We'll have to find out what his costume is though. Just to make it a bit easier. Any thoughts on that, my friends?"

"The servants," John stated emphatically. "Find out who is preparing his costume and we'll be able to get all the details."

"Sounds like a job for a young man of charm and wit." Healy laughed. "We'll leave that to you, Lord Lemon."

John looked torn between being insulted and excited. "Oh, very well," he muttered to save face, but he was smiling.

"Back to the concert then? Shall we?" Montague motioned with his arm toward the door.

Alex turned to Healy and Molony. "I can't thank you enough, sirs. When I find my parents, your names will be among the many who have helped me." Her bottom lip started to quiver so she pressed her lips together and bowed her head toward each of them and then turned, placing her hand on Montague's arm. As she left she heard a low chuckle and the words, "Now isn't she something?"

As the concert came to an end, Montague, John, and Alex made their way through the crush of people to the door. Montague stopped suddenly and shook his head. "I've left my cloak behind. Start toward the carriage and I will catch up to you."

John smiled in a delighted way, cocked his head to one side, and took Alex's arm, pulling her close to his side. "Very good, Uncle."

Montague shot him a warning look and hurried back toward the Rotunda.

The night was dark, the moon covered by clouds, as they stepped onto the walkway with various other concert goers and walked at a leisurely pace toward their carriage.

"I would say tonight was a success, wouldn't you, love?"

Alex let a laugh escape. "John, you mustn't call me that. And yes, tonight was a great success. I can't think how to thank you."

"I can think of something."

Alex tried to quicken their steps, knowing where he was leading the discussion, half afraid and half exhilarated by it, but he deliberately slowed their progress.

"How far to the carriage? It's terribly dark."

"Never fear, Lady Alex. I will protect you."

They turned down a side street and suddenly, they were alone.

"John, I'm afraid. Are we close?" Alex edged closer. "It's so dark."

"Just a little farther. Stay close." His voice sounded ill at ease too.

She kept close by his side as they walked to the carriage. The coachman would be there, probably sleeping on his perch, once they reached it. Alex comforted herself with the thought.

Suddenly John stopped, grasped her shoulders, and turned her toward him. "Alex . . . I . . ."

She looked up at him, a small shaft of moonlight peering through the clouds. "Yes?"

Would he declare himself so soon? Did she want him to? She hardly knew what to think beyond the thudding of her heart.

His head bent down toward hers. He was going to kiss her.

Unless she pulled away and did something — right now — he would kiss her.

She didn't pull away. She waited, her

breath small and short, not knowing, just not knowing what to do.

His lips were warm and dry as they touched hers. She held her breath and stood like she'd been composed of Carrara marble as they began to move against hers.

*Crack!* John shuddered and broke away from her. He'd been hit! Alex turned, too late. A man shoved her to the ground. He dove for her, but she rolled away and kicked out, hearing a grunt as her pointed slipper found its mark. She stood, ready to run, and looked toward John. He was being attacked by a second man; they looked to be in a pummeling fistfight.

Alex screamed as the shorter man caught hold of her skirt and yanked her toward him. Oh dear God, she thought as a shaft of moonlight appeared from behind the clouds, it was the Spaniards.

"What do you want?" she hissed. "I don't know anything. I'm just looking for my parents." She hoped the answer to her questions would forestall them, but it didn't. John didn't appear to be making any ground either.

Suddenly another dark shadow descended upon them. Alex screamed, wrestling against the man's arms trying to cage her. The shadow's arms came over his head and down on the Spaniard with such force that Alex was immediately freed.

She stumbled back, shaking and wide-eyed, while he whirled around, caught the taller one with a head blow, freeing John, and then in a quick circle, cape flying out, pummeled the shorter man until she heard a cracking noise and a whimper. She held her breath in awe as he slid to the ground.

Before he hit the cobblestones, she saw the wicked flash of a knife coming from behind the man saving them. She shrieked a warning. But it was too late. The other Spaniard spun too, made a deflecting move of his wrist so fast that it was hard to see what happened. She heard a guttural gasp and saw the caped man fall to the ground. No . . . no. Who was it? *Please, get up. Please, don't be hurt.* She wanted to run to his side, but the tall Spaniard turned toward her and was advancing.

John reached her and pulled her close. He was grabbing something . . . something from his back. Alex stood rigid between his encircling arm and his chest. He pulled an object around and pointed it. The moonlight spilled just enough light to see what it was. A gun.

John had had a gun all night.

At the musicale.

It didn't make any sense but she was in no position to make sense of anything. She gritted her teeth as he pulled the trigger, felt the shock of recoil go through both their bodies, and saw the Spaniard fall.

She was screaming. She knew it but she couldn't hear it. Should she be screaming? She couldn't seem to stop and think.

The Spaniard got up and limped away, dragging the other one with him. John started to go after them.

"No!" Alex pulled on his arm. "Help me!" She ran toward the cloaked man, fear vibrating through her whole being. She knew who this was. She knew this protector, and if he'd died for her she didn't know how she would ever go on.

They knelt by the still form. Alex pulled his head into her lap.

Montague! She didn't know if she said it inside or outside her head. "Wake up. Don't you die on me! Do you hear me!" *Oh, God. Save him, please. I'll do anything.*

"Lady Alexandria Featherstone!" It was an order and a bark of authority. Her spine instantly straightened. She sniffed, noticing for the first time that her face was wet with tears.

"Yes?" she asked in a very small voice.

"Quit that blubbering and act like the

woman I know you are." His voice lowered with a note of humor. "Besides, you're getting blood all over your new dress."

That brought a fresh bout of tears, but this time she was crying and laughing at the same time. "Are you all right? Where are you hurt?"

"Here, let me see." John, who was leaning over him, backed up and they saw the knife sticking from his chest. "Oh, Uncle. That doesn't look good. We have to get you to a doctor."

Alex started wailing afresh until Montague grasped her arm and pulled her toward his face. "Look at me," he demanded. "It's missed my heart, I think. And I'm breathing well despite the sharp pull on my ribs. I need you to pull it out and then stop the bleeding with something."

Alex nodded, a feeling of desperation to hold on to his calm assurance the only thing keeping her upright and coherent. "I can do it," she told them all, including herself.

"That's my girl." He turned to John. "Your neck cloth, sir. There may be a lot of blood when she pulls it out. You'll have to press hard and hold it to staunch the bleeding."

John nodded. "Yes, Uncle. I understand."

They both looked at Alex. Oh, God! Was

she really going to have to do this? She'd been on her knees, but the thought that she might need to put some weight behind the action made her stand up and lean over him. She grasped the hilt of the knife.

One . . . two . . . three. She turned her head aside, squeezed her eyes shut, and pulled as hard as she could.

Montague came off the walkway with a groan. The knife flew from her hands and clattered, bloody, into the middle of the street.

Alex broke into a fresh sob.

John pressed on the wound.

Montague grasped her hand and gasped out, "Well done, my dear. If I'd had a daughter . . . I would have . . . wanted her to be . . . just . . . like . . . you."

# CHAPTER TWENTY-NINE

Servants, porters, the hotel staff, and his valet rushed back and forth between the Duke of St. Easton's suite of rooms and the front desk where package after package was arriving. In the last week he had met with tailors, boot makers, glove and hat makers; there were all kinds of leather goods including elaborate new saddles and tack for the horses. His staff had three sets of matching livery, and Meade, an entire new wardrobe, even though he complained it unnecessary and despised the tedious sittings for the tailor.

Gabriel sat at his desk with Meade across from him as the packages arrived, were unpacked, and presented. He sent back almost as much as he kept.

"Here are the invitations that have arrived so far." Meade began opening them and handing them across the desk in the familiar routine they'd had for years. There were at least thirty invitations to all sorts of entertainments and he'd only been in town a week. The rumor mill had obviously done its job. The plan was working.

"Accept the O'Brien dinner party for tonight and Lord Donovan's ball tomorrow night. Have we heard from the viceroy yet?"

"Yes, Your Grace." Meade passed over a thick letter. "Earl Talbot has responded exactly as we hoped."

Gabriel unfolded the letter, a personal note of welcome from the Lord Lieutenant of Ireland, and the enclosed, gilt-edged invitation to the masquerade ball at Dublin Castle. He sat back with a smile. There would be any number of people who might know of the Featherstones, the missing Sloane manuscript, and possibly even know of Lady Alexandria herself. He would only have to ask the right questions and watch their responses. Meade would accompany him and direct him in how best to answer.

It wasn't a perfect system, any number of things could go wrong, but his fellow attendees would have heard all about the power and wealth of the Duke of St. Easton and would hopefully think him eccentric instead of deaf should he choose to walk away from a conversation. It was the best way to find her in such a vast city. Not that he hadn't hired investigators to scour the city too. He was leaving nothing to chance this time.

"Excellent." Gabriel gave Meade a sly look. "And is my costume ready?"

Meade snorted. "Yes, Your Grace. You will certainly strike fear into their hearts."

"Fear, you say?" Gabriel could mostly read Meade's lips, far better than anyone else's, but he still missed a word here and there.

Meade was not perturbed in the least and seemed to take pride that they could get on without the speaking book quite often. "Yes," he overly enunciated, "fear."

Gabriel laughed. "Well, that was the point of it, wasn't it? We don't want anyone too comfortable, asking too many questions."

"It is an excellent plan, if I may say so."

Another commotion at the door brought their attention around. A servant of the hotel hurried forward, bowing and hardly daring to look Gabriel in the eye. He spoke with Meade for several minutes and then backed out of the room, bowing and scraping all the way.

Meade turned toward Gabriel with his brows raised. He took up the speaking book and wrote down the message.

*We've found several men who are known to*

*have some knowledge of Sloane's collection.
They are: Sir Kiefer Donovan, Sean Healy,
Patrick Sullivan, and Jeremy Lyons. Three are
members of the Royal Irish Academy and two
are expected at the ball. You were right again,
Your Grace. The ball will be a good place to
ask questions.*

Gabriel studied the names, allowing his
mind to rove through his memories. Lyons
rang a bell, but he wasn't sure why. "Which
two are expected at the ball?"

"Healy and Lyons."

Excellent. "Find out all you can about
each of them. And find out what the two attending the ball look like, what they'll be
wearing. We won't want to miss them."

"Yes, Your Grace."

Meade hurried to do his bidding while
Gabriel closed his eyes and thought of his
quarry so close now within his grasp.

They were late. Purposefully late.

Being deaf made great crowds a challenge
that Gabriel hadn't known would ever be
problematic for him. He'd always been the
picture of confidence and control. Sought
after in any crowd and made to feel important. Now, when he walked into a crowded
room, he felt disoriented, lost, left out, and
alone. Sometimes the anxiety grew until the

dizziness haunted him, loping through his mind and making his ears ring. That was the worst. And then there was the horror of the scene he would cause if he collapsed again. He couldn't risk that here, not after all he'd gone through to convince the good people of Dublin that he was so grand as to be almost otherworldly with wealth and power.

So he and Meade arrived a full hour late. It was probably expected anyway. They would be panting to see him after hearing so many audacious rumors. The viceroy and vicereine had been ecstatic that he had accepted their invitation to the masked ball, or so he'd been told.

Dublin Castle was as he remembered it. A scrawling mass of stone buildings. He'd been in the upper courts once before, where the lord lieutenant had his apartments. But he'd rejected the offer of a tour, probably offending them at the time, but after seeing most of the palaces of the world, he hadn't been in the mood to be accommodating. He was, he discovered with some surprise, eager to see it now, especially the grand ballroom.

They passed through a gate from Cork Hill and saw the two gigantic statues of Justice and Fortitude on either side of the central colonnade. The coach with his ducal coat of arms emblazoned on the side swung up to the front and stopped. Gabriel waited for the footman to open his door and then tossed back his cape and stepped down into the drive surrounded by the courtyard.

He waited for Meade to come around, looked down at his secretary, and smiled. Meade was dressed as a crocodile, and it was all Gabriel could do not to laugh out loud every time he looked at him. "I can't believe you've worn that, Meade. You'll be tripping everyone within arm's length and you have to stay close."

Meade turned toward him, the lower half of his face plainly visible from the crocodile's wide mouth. "It's perfect, Your Grace. Only you will be able to see my mouth."

Gabriel sighed. "If I don't look like I'm mooning over you all night, it will be a miracle. Good heavens, what was I thinking to agree to this plan?"

"If I recall rightly, it was your plan, Your Grace."

"Never mind that." His mood was starting to seriously sour. "Let's pray we get through the next couple of hours." He didn't wait to hear what Meade might think of that. He had been praying. More than he'd ever prayed in his life.

They made their way up the wide flight of stairs to a grand, and thankfully empty, hall. Gabriel paused to adjust his sweeping black cape. It reached almost to his ankles in the back and swirled around him in voluminous folds whenever he turned. His black demimask was tied around his eyes, but he had made sure that he would be identifiable. He needed to be known to get the answers he wanted.

"Well?" He motioned for Meade to precede him. "Follow the noise, man, and find us the ballroom."

Meade responded like a horse being nudged. They went down a wide hall, passing a brilliant but empty presence chamber complete with the viceroy's throne. They turned a corner and Meade stopped. At the entry to the ballroom stood liveried servants in the viceroy's colors of green and gold. They saw him, spoke briefly with Meade while Gabriel pretended to ignore them, and then they beckoned them into the room. Meade turned toward him and mouthed, *the viceroy.*

He understood that the servants had been on the lookout for him and were ordered to take him directly to the viceroy when he arrived. So far, so good.

Gabriel stepped forward, feeling the rush

of battle beat through his veins as he fought with the anxiety filling him. He took a deep breath, nodded to those close to him, and started forward. As if a spotlight had been shined upon him, those he passed stopped and turned to stare. His gaze swept over the glittering crowd amassed in all manner of costumes from the exquisite to the ridiculous.

There were clowns with giant heads, dogs leading real identical dogs on a leash, medieval kings and queens, Greek gods and goddesses, sultans and belly dancers, Spanish gypsies, gaudily painted jesters, and women as sweet as dairy maids and as raunchy as the prostitutes from Covent Garden.

Their eyes seemed overly bright, their voices too loud though he could hear nothing. A sweat broke out down his back and he felt a little sick. And to think he used to enjoy these things. He used to at least be able to pretend he did. It was all he could do not to flee.

Meade tapped on his arm and directed his attention to the viceroy. He was dressed as a Turk with a high purple-and-gold turban on his head that looked ridiculous and a fake snake coiled around his back and arm.

Gabriel blinked once at the snake and then drawled out in his most condescending manner. "Good evening, Lord Talbot. You have a new friend, I see. Have you charmed the Irish into welcoming reptiles?"

The man laughed, the lines around his eyes deepening. Gabriel turned away, as if bored with the answer, but he looked into Meade's long snout to see if there was anything imperative he should say. Meade rolled his eyes and gestured that they leave. That probably meant that the viceroy was gushing over him.

He turned swiftly toward his host and gave him a bow, low enough to show respect. "Forgive me, Viceroy. I haven't been to a masquerade in years. I find myself . . . curious." He looked speculatively at a nearby beauty who was showcasing her assets.

The viceroy followed his gaze, his eyes lighting up. He thrust out his hand toward the woman and the party and said something about enjoying himself. Gabriel thanked him and stalked away toward the other side of the ballroom. Now to find Jeremy Lyons and Sean Healy and the real reason he'd come tonight.

He looked intently for the two men, one reportedly dressed as a domino, the typical costume of all black with a black mask, and the other as Benjamin Franklin, the famed American politician, scientist, and inventor.

Suddenly Gabriel slammed into someone, knocking him off balance. He looked down and discovered a woman. She fell back, bumped into another man who had his back to them, and then started to fall toward the floor.

Gabriel caught her with reflexes that knew what to do before he had a chance to think of it. He hauled her into his arms, into his chest, steadied her and righted her to stand on her own feet in a matter of seconds.

She swayed for a moment and then turned flashing blue eyes on him. His senses took in her costume in a moment — blues and greens and purples, splashes of pale yellow, more purple with red tones, all the colors blending into each other and flowing from the body of the dress into streamers of colored fabric, organza over taffeta. The colored streamers stirred and fluttered with her every movement. Most of her face was covered with a turquoise mask edged in purple lace. Her pale blue eyes, ringed in darker blue, locked with his.

"I'm so sorry." He caught that much from her pink lips. And then, as she tilted her rounded chin up she said more, but he couldn't fathom what it was. Despair and panic crashed through him. He wanted to know what she said. Who was she?

Before he had a chance to frighten her away with his confused silence, he clasped her waist with one hand and her hand with the other. "Dance with me," he thought he said. He hoped he said it aloud. If she protested he didn't know it; he didn't have the courage to look at her face.

Her body, though, followed. He felt the flow of muscle keep up with him beneath his gloved fingertips. She turned into his arms, she took a deep breath, as did he, and then he closed his eyes and concentrated on the vibrations of the music, the long-known steps of the waltz that he'd danced a thousand times and the familiar feel of a beautiful woman in his arms.

It felt good to dance again.

She was as light as moonbeams in his arms and moved with his every movement as if they were one. He opened his eyes, feeling the silence in a new way, seeing her dress come alive and flutter around them like a living thing that grasped and teased and caressed and waved . . . like the wind. She was like the wind.

Her breath was long and even, her chest going in and out in equal accord with his. There was no sound of anything, but it was as if she were a conductor and through her he could hear everything — the music, the laughing, whirling couples, the woman in his arms. She looked up then, into his eyes, and a look of startled fear filled her blue gaze.

She stopped. Stopped them in the middle of the whirling, twirling dancers. She covered her mouth with her white gloved hand, then dropped her hand, shook her head slowly back and forth, and took a step back. "It can't be," her lips read. She shook her head again and turned from him, turned and fled, silken streamers of flight in a bluish blur that quickly disappeared into the crowd.

What had he done to scare her away?

Meade rushed to rescue him before he stood very long staring after her like a lovesick fool.

The crocodile in the midst of the dancers did not go over very well. He was shot with dire looks, shrieked at by the ladies, shoved aside and cursed as one man tripped over his long tail, but none of that derailed him for even a moment. No. His stalwart secretary forged through the throng to save him.

Gabriel sighed, not knowing whether to laugh or run from him. He decided for a chuckle and strode over to the swamp monster, grasped his scaly shoulder, and hurried him off the dance floor.

"Well?" Gabriel demanded, trying to regain some sense of equilibrium. This night was not going at all as planned. "Have you found Healy or Lyons?"

Meade pointed behind him with a long yellow claw.

A small group of older gentlemen stood huddled together, looking deep in conversation. There was an obvious Ben Franklin among them and two men in domino regalia. One of them was probably Molony. Men interested in eccentricities such as ancient antiquities often gravitated toward each other at events like these.

Gabriel made his way over to them, his pet lumbering after him.

The crowd parted like the Red Sea as he came up to their inner circle. They stopped talking and turned to stare at him. He inclined his head. "Gentlemen."

He saw someone say his name and plunged forward with the plan, their faces registering a degree of curiosity and respect. "I am sorry to interrupt but I've been looking for Jeremy Lyons and Sean Healy. I have important business to discuss. Would any of you, perhaps, be the gentlemen in question?"

Ben Franklin stepped forward and bowed. "I am Sean Healy." Gabriel was almost sure he'd read that right. Meade nodded at him from behind the croc's rows of uneven teeth. "And this is" — he flung out his hand to one of the more heavily masked men — "Jeremy Lyons."

That man only stared at him, eyes too dark to see beyond the mask, but something about him sent a chill through Gabriel. This man was no fool. He would have to be told everything to gain his cooperation.

"Would you mind accompanying me to a quieter place where we could talk?"

They both nodded.

They followed Meade and Gabriel into an empty drawing room outside the ballroom that was open for guests to refresh themselves. While the three men took seats around the fireplace, Meade gathered up plates of delicacies and lumbered through the room getting them drinks and making them comfortable.

Gabriel took off his mask and, at first, did all the talking, hoping his servile crocodile would sit down and help him when it came time for them to speak.

He told them about the missing Sloane manuscript and the prince regent's orders to locate it. How he and the kings of France and Spain were determined to find it. He told of the Featherstones and their commission to find it. Then he told of his ward. He let his tone soften, talking as if she were his long-lost daughter. And then there was the prince regent's order. He must obey his prince regent — *their prince regent* now that they were the United Kingdom of Great Britain and Ireland — and bring Alexandria home to safety. Had they seen the Featherstones? Did they know anything of the missing manuscript?

The darkly masked man began talking and Gabriel turned to Meade. It was hopeless to try to read his lips so covered by the full face mask. Meade stood behind the man, looked at Gabriel, and spoke slowly and clearly.

They had heard of the missing manuscript and yes, there had been a visit from the Featherstones some months ago. The only clue they had was the rumored location of the last place Sloane's manuscript was seen in *Dimmu borgir,* the Black Castles of Iceland.

Iceland. So it was true. Alexandria's parents must have gone to Iceland. Had she followed them there already? Had he gone to all this trouble for nothing? Had he missed her?

Meade motioned for Gabriel to pay attention. The man was still speaking.

There was more. Another person had been asking about this. Tonight. Here. At the ball.

"Who?" Gabriel asked, thinking of the Spanish men who were following Alexandria.

Meade's face paled within the green cavern of his costume.

"A woman. Wearing a flowing, colorful dress in colors of blue and purple. She'd said she was dressed as the *Wind*."

# CHAPTER THIRTY

"I thought he was old!" Alex exclaimed as she walked into Montague's bedchamber the next morning. He had been in bed, recovering from his stab wound since the musicale and, as everyone in John's household knew, getting crankier with each day he was confined. Alex plopped down on the chair beside the bed. "I thought he would have a cane and a monocle and well . . . gout! I didn't dream he was so . . . he would be so . . ."

"Whatever are you talking about, Alexandria?" Montague sat further up in bed, wincing with the movement.

"The duke. He was at the ball last night. I know it."

"How do you know? Especially with everyone in costume?"

Alex squeezed her hands together in her lap. "We danced. I looked up into his eyes, his very green eyes, and then, after I suspected and turned away from him, I saw Mr. Meade in a crocodile costume heading right toward us. It was him, I'm sure of it."

"Did he know you?" Montague's voice was low and grave.

"I don't think so. I ran away. I had already talked to Jeremy Lyons and I have so much to tell you about! But after seeing the duke, I just ran away. He's here in Dublin and I don't know what he means to do."

"Describe him to me. Any number of people could have green eyes."

Heat flooded her cheeks as she remembered him. "He was tall, almost a head taller than I am, and he had . . ." she looked down, "very broad shoulders. I hardly know how to dance and yet he practically carried me around the floor as if I weighed nothing. He had black hair, worn short, and behind his demimask were very green eyes. I've never seen anything like them."

"Did he say anything to you?"

"Just 'dance with me.' " She couldn't hold Montague's gaze.

"But you don't think he knew who you were?"

"I don't think so. He asked me to dance because we ran into each other, literally, he nearly knocked me down." She didn't mention that he'd held her, for a moment, in his arms and how his nearness had made her light-headed.

"All right. Let's assume it was him and that even if he didn't recognize you, he knows you are in Dublin. Now, what did you learn from Lyons?"

The maid came in with Montague's breakfast tray so Alex waited for her to situate it and leave before speaking. "Mr. Lyons said he had spoken with my parents. I don't know how they accomplished that as he is very private and spoke in a harsh whisper I could barely hear, but somehow they managed it."

"Resourceful, your parents." Montague winked at her while he buttered his biscuit. "Reminds me of a certain young lady I know."

Alex took a pleased breath and continued. "He said they had heard of a missing manuscript from Sloane's collection."

"So it is a manuscript. Did he know what kind of manuscript?"

"No." Alex leaned forward, her eyebrows rising in excitement. "But he did know where it was last seen. And where my parents were going next."

Montague paused midbite. "Well?"

"Someplace called *Dimmu borgir:* the Black Castles of Iceland."

Montague sat back against his pillows. "You don't say."

"Have you heard of it?"

"Hmm, just barely. We sailed around the eastern shore of Iceland once. It's not what you would think from the name. At least not the time of year we were there. It's mostly known for its volcanoes. There was a huge eruption about twenty years ago. I can't imagine why a missing manuscript of such importance would end up there."

"Maybe that's why; no one would think to look there."

"Do you think that is where your parents went next? All the way to Iceland?"

"I plan to visit the Dublin Custom House today and see if I can find any records of them sailing to Iceland. And then, I plan to buy my own passage there."

"Alexandria. I'm not fit enough to travel yet, and Baylor is planning to leave for Belfast soon. It's too dangerous. I won't allow you to go alone."

Alex sat up straighter. "I have no choice. The duke is here and should he . . . have me within his grasp again, I believe he will haul me off to London. I have to leave Dublin immediately."

Montague sighed. "Maybe the duke is right. Think of it. You will be safe in his house. He has promised to hire as many investigators as you'd like to follow your leads. Think what might happen to you in an unknown land so far away, alone, with the Spaniards likely tracking you? It's not possible!"

Alex remained quiet, thinking. If she argued with him, he might do something, like try to locate the duke and tell him where she was. She couldn't let that happen. She stood, went over to his bed, and kissed his cheek. "Let me think about it. I'll see what I can find out at the Custom House and we'll talk again."

He studied her eyes and she felt a tendril of fear at the thought of deceiving him. She had to convince him to her side.

A few hours later John accompanied her to the main desk in the majestic Custom House. They told the man their names and were directed to one of the smaller desks. A man with red mutton-chop sideburns and friendly blue eyes introduced himself as Mr. McQueen.

"Please, sit down. What can I do for you, Lord Lemon, Lady Featherstone?"

Alex curtsied and sat across from him, John sat next to her. "Lady Featherstone has come from her home on Holy Island to search for her missing parents, Ian and Katherine Featherstone. We understand that they were in Dublin about a year ago."

"Sir, I have reason to believe," Alex quickly added, "that they sailed from Dublin to Iceland. Are there ships sailing to Iceland from here?"

"Oh yes. We have ships sail all over the world from Dublin," the man said with pride.

"Could you check the passenger lists during fall of last year?"

"Your parents are missing? How extraordinary!"

"Please, sir. I know it is not a typical request, but their very lives may depend on us finding them."

Mr. McQueen cleared his throat. "Well, no harm in checking the records, I suppose. You will wait here."

John reached over and squeezed her hand as the man headed toward a back room.

"My uncle is right, you know."

Alex turned suddenly toward John's face. "You heard our conversation?"

"Just the end of it. You cannot travel alone. It's too dangerous. Especially after that attack. Whatever your parents were looking for —"

"*Are* looking for."

"Yes, well, whatever it is, we know that it is very valuable. Possibly worth a fortune. It would seem there are those who will do anything to get their hands on it."

"I don't care about any of that. I just want to find my parents."

"You should care. They could capture you, torture you, even kill you should you no longer be of use to them. But if you found it first . . . think of it, Alex. Then you would have something to bargain with. Then if they are still alive, you could ransom them with it."

Alex gasped. "That's true. I hadn't thought of how I would save them once I do find them. John, you're brilliant."

He smiled and shrugged one shoulder. "I have another brilliant idea. One that even my uncle will agree to, I think."

Alex turned in her chair further toward him. "What is it?"

His smile lit up his handsome face. "I shall accompany you."

Alex dropped her gaze. Traveling alone with a man was almost worse than traveling alone. "I would welcome your company, but we couldn't possibly travel alone together. You must know that." Montague was more like a father to her and was probably thought as one as they traveled, but John was young and handsome, very handsome.

"We could if we were married." He said it so quick and low that her head shot up, not sure she'd even heard him right.

"I — I, are you proposing marriage?"

John's face flushed with color, but his blue eyes were earnest. "I beg your pardon. It's not the romantic gesture I'd planned for. I should have waited, but Alexandria, since the moment we met, I think I've been waiting to ask you to be my wife. And now, everything is happening so fast . . . you're about to sail away . . . I'm afraid I might lose you forever."

"It's just . . . such a surprise. I don't know what to say."

John took her hand and squeezed. "Think of it. If you marry, you will no longer need a guardian. The duke will no longer be able to control you."

*Or her fortune.* If she married, and she wasn't even sure how that was possible without her guardian's consent unless they eloped, but *if* she married her fortune would be hers, or rather . . . she looked into John's earnest blue eyes . . . theirs. She cared for him. She enjoyed his company — greatly. She could learn to love him, she was certain of it. But dare she trust him?

*Dear God, if I ever needed Your guidance it*

*is now. Help me know Your will for my life.*

Alex was saved answering as Mr. Mc-Queen appeared, striding toward them with a thick volume in his hands.

"Ah, here we are then." He opened the book to a wide page, turned it for them to see, and pointed his finger to a signature.

At the top of the page was the ship's name: *Achilles.* Then there were rows of names. Alex scanned them, her chest pounding. There, lines thirty-two and thirty-three, were the names: Lord Ian Featherstone and Lady Katherine Featherstone. Dated 1 December 1817.

"It's them," she whispered. She looked up at Mr. McQueen. "Where was this ship sailing to?"

He turned back a few pages and pointed to the log. The *Achilles* was sailing to New York but making a stop at Reykjavik, Iceland.

Alex looked at John and then back at Mr. McQueen. "When is the next ship leaving for Iceland?"

"I thought you might ask so I've already looked into it. There is a ship leaving for Ammassalik in Greenland two days hence. For a price, I believe the captain can be convinced to make a stop at Iceland on the way."

Alex's heart started to race inside her. She had to take this chance. It might be weeks if she waited for another opportunity. "Yes, book the passage." She looked at John's hopeful face, his eyes sparkling with love and adventure, and prayed she was doing the right thing. "Book the passage for two."

Alex stared out the coach window, watching the city blur by, dazed by everything that had happened. Her life had changed so much. She'd never dreamed she would ever be in Dublin. She'd never fathomed going to Iceland and couldn't imagine what it was going to be like. She had thought of marriage now and again as any girl coming into womanhood did. But she'd never thought of the handsome, blond stranger beside her. Her future husband always had dark hair, tall, but with a shadowy face, something that time would reveal, something she'd known she wasn't ready for.

John must have sensed her mood as he sat silent. He'd reached for her hand when they had first gotten into the carriage, but she only allowed him to hold it for a moment, and then she leaned toward the window, getting a look, a new look, at the city she might someday, when this was all over, call home. Dublin was this man's home whose carriage she shared. She didn't think he would like living in the windswept solitude of Holy Island. Would she ever live there again? Just the thought made her breath catch, trying to stop the tears.

They came to John's lovely town house, the home they would likely go back to once she found her parents, and he helped her down. She'd worn the new pink bonnet he'd picked out to go with her day dress. It shielded her face from any she chose it to, a fact that brought comfort with it when she was feeling shy and scared as she was now.

He reached down and grasped her chin in a tender hold and lifted it so she had to look at him.

She allowed it . . . stared long into his eyes.

"I love you, Alexandria."

Her lips quivered as she pressed them down into a sad smile. She couldn't say it back, not yet. She didn't know who she was at the moment. She felt swept away on a tidal wave, like the ones she'd so often watched from the shores of Holy Island, wishing when she saw them that she could ride away into an adventure, wishing her life would finally begin. Now that it had, she realized the folly of wishing away a childhood, a sudden knowledge coming to her that she'd tried too hard to be something important when she could have just enjoyed being a girl.

She was growing up. And it was hard, harder than expected.

John's lips came down and she let him brush them against hers. It felt nice, her pulse raced, but in a nice way.

A sudden sound made them spring apart. Baylor came down the steps to the town house and stood frowning down at them from his great height.

"I think it's time for her ladyship and me to go for a walk," he stated in a voice that neither of them could argue with.

John bowed to both, giving her a secret smile, and then went inside.

Alex put her hand onto Baylor's meaty arm and they started down the street of tan cobblestone. "I've tarried with you long enough, my dear. I'm missing the harpy something bad, and well, you don't seem to be needing me anymore."

Alex knew this had been coming. Baylor hadn't attended the ball, hadn't wanted to; instead he sought out Dublin's music dens and had gone back home in his heart. "I can't thank you enough, Baylor. You've been a true friend."

"That's the right of it. I expect to see you again someday with your parents in tow."

Alex looked up at him, a big smile spreading across her face. "As do I." She paused, thinking of how much she would miss him. "Promise me you'll continue your reading lessons. You've made such progress in the last weeks."

Baylor looked down at her with eyes that glowed with fondness and pride. "That I will, Lady Alex. Many thanks for your excellent teaching."

They walked in silence for a time and then Alex stopped. "Baylor, I've just had an idea."

He groaned in mock protest.

"Could you do one more thing for me before you go?"

He looked down at her face and wiggled his shaggy eyebrows. "Is it dangerous?"

Alex threw back her head and laughed. "Very dangerous. You see . . . it has to do with the Duke of St. Easton . . ."

# CHAPTER THIRTY-ONE

By the time he'd searched the ballroom for the fourth time, Gabriel was sweat soaked under his costume. Where *was* she? His head throbbed, his temple pounding in a way that told him he should get control, but he couldn't. Panic, frustration — *dear God,* love, some strange feeling that made him want to be ill — was filling him. She couldn't have slipped through his fingers once again. Impossible. She couldn't have been here, *in his arms,* and now be gone.

After a half hour of Meade and him questioning guests and even the vicereine, who was very happy to have a moment of his attention, he finally had to admit defeat. Go home. Sleep. Regroup and plan tomorrow.

They did go back to the hotel and he did climb into his bed and pull the feather coverlet up to his neck, but he didn't sleep. He could not sleep.

The next morning he dealt with his valet's frowns as he was shaved. He stared in the mirror at his reflection, seeing himself in silence, still missing the *scrape, scrape, scrape* of the razor's song against his skin. What was he doing? Why didn't he just go back to the prince regent and admit that he couldn't find her? That she was more determined than all of them . . . ?

With an irritated move of his arm, he shrugged his valet away. Gabriel took up the warm towel and buried his face in it.

There was one clue left. One more thing he thought Alexandria would do. He'd put that one thought into motion by sending Meade a note to find out if there were any ships sailing to Iceland in the next few days or weeks. He couldn't imagine that there would be.

His valet had crept away, which was good. He needed to be alone. He picked up the hand mirror and peered into it again, seeing the green eyes that to him were so normal but to others seemed strange. Is that what had scared her off?

Scowling at his reflection, he prowled about the room . . . thinking . . . and moving the restless energy from his body. Meade would be back soon with the shipping schedule. He would wait . . . as much as it was killing him. Then he would buy passage and board the ship. He imagined himself waiting for her, on the deck, seeing her board and waiting for the moment when she saw him.

Gabriel closed his eyes and remembered the feel of her in his arms, how perfectly they fit together, how their breaths matched and their bodies melded until they felt like one. He should have known the second he pulled her into his arms that it was her. *How had he not known?*

He stopped walking and leaned against the frame of the window. Perhaps he had. Some part of him had never wanted to let her go.

The door opened to reveal Meade. He knew not to knock, but he always just opened it a crack to see if he was appearing at a welcome time.

Gabriel motioned him in. "Is there a ship to Iceland?"

Meade came up to him and handed him a paper, nodding.

Gabriel looked down and read it. It was a ticket. In two days. How convenient. He let loose a shaky breath and flipped to the second page. It was a copy of her ticket, her signature. The familiarity of it slammed into him. He rubbed his fingers across his eyes, exhausted and exhilarated at the same time.

There wouldn't be far to run on the deck of a ship. Not that she would want to when he told her he was prepared to disobey the prince regent — that he was coming with her.

*God, I never ask You for much. I can't remember ever asking You for anything before all this happened. Please, help me find her.*

It was time.

Gabriel swallowed hard, adjusted his leather gloves, and mounted his horse.

He sat a moment in the early morning light, looking out over the city while his outriders mounted up and flanked him, ahead and behind. They raised the flags of the Duke of St. Easton, *Faith for Duty.* This day he would choose faith.

The sun glinted off the stone buildings as they rode through the street toward Dublin Bay. Meade rode at his side. He cast a look at his stalwart secretary and had to smile. He was dressed in his new costume, the house of St. Easton colors across his breast, his carriage erect, riding like he'd been born to it.

They smelled the sea before they saw it. A blue smudge that was grayer and moving against the horizon. Ships of all shapes and

413

sizes rocked against their moorings, their hulls yearning to follow the tide and the open sea.

Gabriel dreaded the thought of boarding the ship. To be deaf and seasick for the first weeks he would spend with her? Well, if she saw him through that, then they would get through anything together. Tears rose to his eyes as he thought of her. He commanded them away instantly.

He took a deep breath of the sea air, saw the white gulls take flight from the shore, and accepted the silence of the horses' hooves, the silence of the birds, the silence of the waves.

His horse moved beneath him and he directed it without thinking, realizing that he had grown more attuned to touch and sight. His mind felt sharp and alive as they approached the quay.

Suddenly a great cart rolled from a side street in front of them. Gabriel and his men hauled back on the reins, pulling their horses back from the danger. The men stopped behind him, their horses huffing and blowing, looking to him for direction.

A giant, red-headed man got out of the seat of the cart and moved in a slow, lumbering way toward them. His mighty arms waved them back.

"What is the meaning of this?" Meade surged forward on his horse, causing Gabriel to smile. This adventure had made a man out of him, to be sure.

Arms waved and their lips talked fast as they conversed. His men waited as the giant blocked the street for more minutes than Gabriel wanted to think about. Then, in a sudden move, the giant looked up at him, locked eyes with him . . . his eyes full of meaning, full of knowledge.

Everything stopped inside of him.

Another ruse! It was a stalling tactic!

"Come on!" Gabriel tried to turn his horse around in the narrow space. He dug his heels into his mount, causing Meade's horse to rear up and buck, which made the horses attached to the cart startle and stamp.

One of the horses in their cavalcade took off down the side street, the servant unable to control him. Meade's horse took it as a lead and bounded away after him. In a few minutes they all began to stampede down the narrow street, the whole lot of them plunging forward, knocking down carts and plowing through shopkeepers' goods out on the street for sale. They raced down the cobblestones away from the quay and the waiting ships.

Gabriel was left alone with the giant. His heart pounded like the horse beneath him, both their breaths blowing from their nostrils, both of them straining toward the sea, the ship . . . Alexandria . . .

"Let me through!" he shouted, pinning the man with a raging glare. The giant slowly moved his cart across the street. Gabriel kicked his horse into action. Once on the crowded docks he threw himself from the horse and ran toward the shipping office. He ran to the ticket desk and showed his ticket for passage to Iceland.

"I'm sorry, sir. Boarding is past for that voyage." The man motioned his hand toward a great white ship. "As you can see, she's already set sail."

Gabriel turned toward the ship. It was massive, its hull rising at least twenty feet in the air. He couldn't see. Confused panic filled him. It couldn't be. He couldn't have missed it.

He ran. Feeling the beating of his heart. Seeing the shadow of his form running beside him across the shore, everything too sharp and unreal. He came up to the edge and saw that the ship, her ship, had broken free of the coastal tide and was about to escape on the waves of the Atlantic.

"Wait!" His voice felt hoarse and desperate.

He stopped at the edge, where the shore dropped off into pure blue sea, and scanned the deck, the passengers standing at the rail, waving good-bye to loved ones.

He was breathing too heavy, he knew it, but she was on that ship, she had to be. His gaze swept up and down the deck of the ship, so close and yet unreachable. A sudden movement, an arm of a woman clamping down on the hood of her cloak, caught his eye. He turned toward the leeward side of the ship and everything within him stopped.

The ship was still close enough that he could see her face — unmasked, unguarded, unfathomable. She turned toward him. It was as if she knew he was staring at her, caught, completely undone, beside himself with barely concealed anticipation.

She looked right at him, her gaze locking, startled, and then registering the same shock — the fear and the familiar sense of finding your other half. She was all that was beauty to him. She lowered her arm and the wind blew back her hood, revealing dark hair surrounding a perfectly sweet and yet familiar face. She was all that was his everything. His chest shook with tiny trem-

417

ors that made him blink heavily, but he did not let go of her gaze.

Her hand rose to her mouth and then down to her throat and then down further, where her fist curled and pressed into her chest.

His arm reached out, involuntarily, asking her to come back.

Her arm reached out . . . and then she lowered it.

*No!* Everything in him cried out.

She looked down.

"Come back!" *God, why won't she trust me?*

She was turning away! *God, make her look back at me!*

She did pause, but not to turn back to him. Gabriel's breath whooshed out of him as another man, a handsome blond man dressed like a gentleman, came up and put his arm around her waist, walking her away from the railing, from him. His stomach quivered as if he'd just been smote by a weapon he'd not known existed.

And in that moment he knew one thing: She was his family. *His. Family.* And whatever it took, whatever he would have to do in the next weeks or months or years . . . he would do it. Deaf and haunted and broken man that he was, he didn't care. He would not give up. Not ever.

She belonged to him . . . *forever.*

Dear Reader,

A devastated duke.

A girl of lonely exile.

Both have a path to follow, a heart's desire to find, and choices that could change their lives forever.

Do you ever wonder if you are on that perfect path for your life? Are you "following your passion" and "finding your gift?" These popular catch phrases make us stop and ponder our lives and the direction we are going. While there is nothing wrong with that, we must keep in mind Matthew 6:33: "But seek ye first the kingdom of God, and his righteousness; and all these things shall be added unto you" (KJV). This entire chapter in Matthew is amazing! It contains the Lord's Prayer, instructions about our treasure (our gifts and calling), our money, our needs, and the worries over those needs, and then it ends with an exhortation to trust and seek God for *everything.* A true blueprint-for-life kind of chapter.

But let's be honest. To really live in that place every day with all the storms and trials, the challenges and distractions? Well, it's only possible with God's help. And my characters, these wonderful characters who I love as if they were real people, are no different.

My hero — the brilliant Duke of St. Easton — wants his affliction healed and taken away. And he wants love on his terms. He wants his control back even though he was miserable when he had it.

My heroine — sweet, determined Alexandria — wants what she can't have. And she'll stop at nothing when it comes to taking care of her own heart.

Their journey is like ours — that push and pull against God — the desire to find freedom and purpose on earth but in our timing and our way because His way is too hard or scary or just doesn't make sense.

Dear Reader, join me on this journey with Gabriel and Alexandria as they struggle to come to the end of themselves. I pray we might, too, lift up our lives as a sacrifice, and in that place, come face to face with the living God.

In Him,
Jamie Carie

# DISCUSSION QUESTIONS

1. The unthinkable happens to the Duke of
St. Easton in the opening scene. It is so
devastating that he goes through the stages
of grief when dealing with it — denial,
bargaining with God, anger, confusion,
depression, and a numb kind of accep-
tance. Have you or anyone close to you
had something like this happen? What
happened and how did you/they cope?
Can you mark the emotional transitions?
What is the state of affairs now and what
can you do about it?

2. Alexandria Featherstone has the heart of
an adventuress and the imagination of a
storyteller. What about you? I know life
can get in the way of an adventurous
spirit. There are any number of responsibilities — parents, marriage and children,
lack of finances, lack of courage, lack of
faith. Life gets in the way. Do you feel like
you are living your grand adventure? If

not, why? Can you change that?

3. Alex has an extended family system that helps to support her. When I was growing up, my father was the pastor for a small congregation. Those people became sort of an extended family. What about you? Do you feel a part of a community? And if so, how does it play out? If not, do you wish for this? Are you willing to deal with all the challenges that come with living in close community or are you more comfortable going it alone? Discuss.

4. What role do you automatically take when in a group of close family/friends? (i.e., peacemaker, counselor, mother, teacher, friend with judgments, etc.) What could you work on to be a better friend/family member?

5. Gabriel looks to music to fill something missing within him. The "fix" only lasts a little while, but even though he is so wealthy and intelligent, it is all he has found that gives him life. What in your life gives you a "fix"? Gossip? A substance of choice? Controlling the people around you? Shopping? Eating? Fill in the blank. How can we stop and trust God for our every need?

6. Gabriel becomes attached to Alexandria in a way he never knew possible for him

— through letters. How did love find you (whether God's love or man's)? If it hasn't happened yet, how do you imagine it happening? Are you open to the possibility of something you never considered? Think of all the ways love could show itself to you and from you. Make a list of how you could love others in a new way.

7. Have you ever struck out on a new adventure without enough money or resources, just by faith? (Think of the disciples leaving everything to follow Jesus!) What happened? Do you want to do it again? What's holding you back?

8. Alex longs to be a successful investigator and she has some talent for it, but the people she loves most, her parents, have discouraged her. Has this happened to you? If you could do or be anything, and you knew you wouldn't fail at it, what would you do/be?

9. Gabriel and Alex both allow outside influences to side track their mission. How easily distracted are you from God's calling on your life? What does the trap look like? Is it a matter of not recognizing it or it is too appealing to deny? What can you do about it?

10. A little like Mr. Magoo or Forest Gump, Alex stumbles through life with everything

falling into place for her. She has a natural way with people that makes her likable and gains their friendship and loyalty. For most of us this isn't the case. Do you know someone like this, someone with the "golden touch"? How do you feel about this? Why does it seem like God blesses some and not others despite what they do?

11. Gabriel comes to depend on his friend and secretary, Meade, more and more as he deals with his affliction. His pride takes a blow in the process. What about you? Are you a caregiver or think you someday might be? What if something happened and you needed care? What might happen and how would you feel about that? Do you talk about these issues with family/ friends?

12. Gabriel goes from a powerful, wise, and knowing duke in charge of his life to a broken, wretched soul on the chase for the love of his life. But he is more alive than he's ever been. Sometimes the hard times are the best. What is one of the hard times in your life when you felt the most alive? What happened and where are you now?

13. Meade is the strength in flesh that Gabriel needs during this time of testing and Montague is Alexandria's champion. Has

God sent you "angels in flesh" to help overcome the tough times in life? What happened and who are they? Have you been that to another?

14. This one is for fun. This series is called the Forgotten Castles series as I love discovering hidden treasures. Have you traveled abroad? Visited any castles? Where is your dream vacation?